The Maxwells at No. 9

A novel

Cai Barran

First published in Great Britain in 2020 by Sentinel Projects.

Copyright © Cai Barran 2020.

cai.barran@sentinelprojects.com

Cover designed by Lorna Stewart - enquiries@celtiques.uk

ISBN: 9798636776086 (Paperback)

ISBN: 0952442353 (Kindle)

Sentinel Projects

http://sentinelprojects.com/Maxwells.htm

Coordinator at Sentinel Projects: barry.sentinel@gmail.com

Author's Note

This is a work of fiction. What is told here does not reflect the military or other experiences of the author, nor his country of origin.

Actions of the protagonist are seriously questionable, not least from a child protection perspective. It was long ago and far away, and the world was different then. Judge if you wish.

"A dystopia isn't so bad – as long as you are in charge."

Table of Contents

Chapter One

Roman

The bedside phone rang after 11 pm, so I assumed that it was work. I answered it in my professional voice. Debbie stirred into wakefulness on the far side of the bed. It wasn't work. It was Alvin, the teenage leader of the camp that Roman, my older son, was attending. He was calling from a public pay phone. That will give you an idea about how long ago this was.

"Is Roman okay?" I asked.

"He's homesick," the teenager told me. "He's just crying all the time and he wants to go home."

"Roman's homesick," I told Debbie, and she reached out for the handset. "Can I speak to him?' I asked Alvin, before surrendering the handset.

Roman came on, but he couldn't speak, just sobbing and struggling to breathe.

"I'll come," I told him. "Here's your mom. I love you," and I handed it to Debbie who started her loving mummy talk. Roman was nine. He's been on camps before, but that was with Cubs. This was his first camp with `the big boys'.

I pulled on my outdoor clothes, and out of Debbie's sight, I opened the safe in my wardrobe and took out my security pack, clipped it to my belt, and pocketed my pager. I walked to the boys' room, seeing six year old T-Roy lying spread-

eagled on his nest on the floor, and although knowing he was a sound sleeper, I cautiously opened the top of the cupboard and pulled out the two-man tent and a sleeping bag. On my way out, I stooped to kiss his forehead, and without waking he made a little murmur of acknowledgement. His Superman duvet had migrated down his chest, and although he was warm enough, I pulled it up to under his chin.

"Sleep well my beautiful boy!"

"I'll see if I can settle him down if I stay the night with him there..." I told her, as I said goodbye.

Without covering the mouthpiece, Debbie said to me; "I want you to bring him home!"

I wish she hadn't done that. Now Roman knew what the bottom line was, it would be less likely that I could persuade him to stay on, if I stayed overnight with him, and thinks might look brighter for him in the morning. This would save him from the defeat of coming home early.

Debbie had Alvin back on the phone, to tell her the number, so that she could phone back and keep talking to him after they had run out of coins. I waved to Debbie from the doorway, which she acknowledged without looking away from the receiver, and I heard her tell Roman; "Daddy's just leaving now..."

*

Even though it was Friday night, the roads were quiet, especially as I was heading out of the suburbs and towards the country. I knew where they were, as I had been one of the parents who had helped to transport the boys out to their campsite, and I knew where the phone booth was, some distance from their campsite.

I was saddened that it hadn't worked out for Roman. He had wanted to be more grown-up than I thought he was ready for, but he had begged and pleaded, and we had decided to let him go. And while I would not argue with Debbie about parenthood, giving her the lead, I had hoped that I might help to salvage the situation if we could get him through the first night there. But this was unlikely with him having heard Debbie's instruction to me.

I had become mates again with T-Roy, reconciled by the time he had drifted off to sleep, although he had milked it, and I had spent more than an hour reading him bedtime stories of his choice, in compensation. I had refused his expectation that he could come along as well when I had helped to transport the boys out to their campsite that afternoon. I thought that it was important for Roman to take the step of going camping with the big boys on his own, and not to have his more charismatic younger brother travel out with us, and distract from his adventure. There was no way that I would have been able to explain this to T-Roy – and how personally he took it of being left out of what was obviously an adventure, and how he would have made a case for him being allowed to stay and join in with the camp. But he had forgiven me – though reserving the right to raise

6

it again in the future. It wasn't as though I needed any excuse to indulge my son, reading to him with him cuddled up next to me was one of the many delights of fatherhood.

Oh yes; my `beautiful boy'-phrase. I could say it to them in my head, or if they were asleep, and I love the alliteration. But not while they were awake. At a surprisingly young age, Roman had told me off; "I'm not beautiful," he rebuked. "I'm handsome!"

Within half an hour, I was at the phone booth, correctly expecting that Debbie would have kept him on the phone, saying things that mothers do to reassure their children. Roman was in the booth, the handpiece to his head, so he was the last to see me. Alvin was standing behind him and put his hand up in greeting in my headlights. I could see another boy, who I knew to be James, standing behind him. I parked up and walked over. Alvin started to say something, but I was too concerned about Roman to listen to him. When he saw me, Roman had the dilemma of whether to release his line to his mummy, or embrace me, until I was close enough for him to do both.

Debbie knew that I had arrived by what she had overheard, but I confirmed this to her and I hung up the phone. I think Debbie had managed to calm him down somewhat, but now that I was there, he showed more distress again, grasping me tightly as I lifted him up to chest height, sobbing into my shoulder, and doing a strange little motion which he had done since he was little, of wiggling in a way that seemed to

be boring into my chest. I embraced him, and nuzzled his neck briefly careful not to scrape him with my chin stubble.

I gave him time to calm down, aware of Alvin and James looking slightly awkward in front of me but I smiled reassuringly. When Roman had relaxed his grip a little, I told the boys that I would give them a lift back to the campsite. Both of them got into the back seat, and Roman accepted me setting him down in the front passenger seat.

Soon we were back at their campsite, in a corner of a friendly farmer's field next to a forest, dark in the night. The other boys stood in front of their tent, illuminated by the headlights as we drove up, and I parked. Alvin and James got out, but Roman didn't move.

I knew how this would end, and with Roman having heard Debbie's instruction to me, but I felt that I needed to try anyway.

"Shall I stay here tonight? You can sleep with me, and then we can see how things are in the morning?" This wasn't what Roman wanted to hear at all, and he started sobbing again.

"I want Mummy," he moaned despairingly.

I decided not to even start suggesting that I could put up the little tent, and he could sleep in it with me for the night or, assuming the boys would not dare to object, I could sleep next to him in their main tent.

"I want Mummy," he repeated through sobs.

"Okay, I'll take you home. But we need to do this properly. We need to get your kit and say goodbye to the boys." I got out and went around to his door and picked him up so that he was up against my chest, and again he buried his face in my shoulder.

I carried him over to the tent, with Alvin dutifully at my side. "Will you go and get your things?" I asked Roman.

Alvin intervened. "I'll get them for him," he offered, and went into the tent, and all of the other boys followed, and I could see torches shining inside, and soon they emerged with his rucksack and sleeping bag, which they brought to the car.

The boys had assembled in front of me, while I still had Roman hugging and holding my chest, with his back to them.

"I would appreciate it if you guys would keep it to yourselves how upset Roman got," I requested. There was a murmur of assent.

"He's young, and I think I might have pushed him too far, before he was old enough to come camping with you guys." Here I am making it quite clear that I am in command of the situation, that it was my responsibility and my fault — if there is fault to be allocated. "I'm sorry that this has spoiled your evening, and I'm sure you had fun things planned... which Roman would have enjoyed as well."

I murmured to Roman the suggestion that he shake hands 'good bye' with the boys, but he started sobbing again, so I

9

didn't push it. "Thank you," I said to Alvin, and the others, and moving to hold Roman up with my left hand, I moved amongst the boys, shaking hands with them and thanking them by name. It's important to show them that I know their names.

Those little shits! I actually apologised to them on Roman's behalf. I wanted him to shake hands with them. If I had known then what I learned later that would have been very different – possibly a short sharp shock – but I didn't know then!

"Enjoy the rest of your camp," I wished them, before turning to take Roman back to the car and settle him in. I wrapped his sleeping bag around him, even though it wasn't a cold night, and then strapped him in with a seatbelt.

The boys were illuminated in the car headlights, and they waved in a subdued fashion, as I turn the car around, and we headed for home.

"I'm sorry, Daddy!" Roman sobbed.

"Don't worry," I told the sobbing Roman. "We'll get you home, to your mum and our nice warm bed, and things will get better."

"Are you cross with me?" I stopped the car – fortunately we were still on the farm roads. I pulled him over to me and hugged him firmly, and he moulded into me, as best he could with us both being seat-belted in, and the gear stick in the way.

"No, Roman! Not at all! I haven't succeeded at everything I've tried. You tried, and that's all we ask of you."

"We don't want you growing up too soon!" I added.

It would probably take us half an hour to get home, and I hoped he would go to sleep. Even as his father, I knew that he really needed his mother's love at this moment, and try as I might, I wasn't enough.

"I'm sorry," he said after a while. "I'm sorry you had to come and fetch me ..." and seemed to start to feel upset again.

"Don't worry. It's not a problem. We'll get you back home."

"We do like having you at home ..." I added. "Even T-Roy!"

"T-Roy is always asking. 'What do you think Roman (I'm the only one who calls him by his proper name, but I fight on in the face of all adversity ...) will be doing now?'"

I persisted, knowing that I was laying it on thick. "T-Roy says he misses you even more than he would miss 'a big fat bowl of ice cream ...'" Okay, this is a family catch phrase, which I'll explain later.

This got a snigger from Roman. Good! "No he didn't!" Roman admonished between his tears.

Supposedly I'm good at my job, but my nine-year-old son can catch me out lying.

"Are you lying to me, Maxwell?" - I whispered to him as a prompt. (Another family catch phrase, adopted from my work colleagues long ago. The boys were allowed to refer to me by our surname, as long as they were quoting ...)

He understood. "Are you lying to me, Maxwell?" he asked softly, still having some difficulty in controlling his breathing. (The joke within the joke was that I work in Truth. Truth is my business. And I have my George Orwell T-shirt!)

He was trying, bravely, to play a little game that we had, as part of our family culture. I got the idea that he felt obligated, so I didn't develop this as I might. I kept talking to him in what I hoped was a fairly dreamy voice, hoping that he might drift off. He was never the sound sleeper that his younger brother was, but his breathing steadied.

We arrived home. I parked the car in front of the garage door, aware that Debbie had switched the lights on, and was walking towards us. "Do you want to walk, or do you want me to carry you?" I asked him.

"Carry me..." He murmured. He was very tired, emotionally it had been a very long day for him, and I thought it was sweet how childlike he became. I detached him from the seatbelt, and still wrapped in his sleeping bag, I carried him to the front door, where Debbie awaited us, and she embraced him. I put him down so that they could do this properly, and then I picked him up again and followed her through to the bathroom, where she had started to run a bath when she heard the car pull up.

12

I'm sure that Roman was exhausted, emotionally at least, and he was content to be infantilised for now. I held him up while Debbie undressed him, and slipping my own shirt off, I gently cradled him up to lower him into the bath. Debbie poured in some aromatherapy potions, and lit some candles, and sat beside the bath at his head, reaching over to stroke his head and shoulders, as he lay there, feeling calm and safe.

I loved watching her be a mum to our boys. She had so wanted them, and had undergone so much emotional suffering to conceive them - and now she valued them so much. We were so blessed to have the most beautiful boys in the world. I had been reluctant to bring anyone into the world having seen what a bad place the world can be - but I hadn't been through anything like Debbie had been through, and I compromised because I love her, but knowing I would do everything I could to my death to protect them. And now that they are here, I couldn't be without them.

Debbie was a paediatric nurse, and I believe an excellent one with a great reputation. I was surprised, though, with the science underlying this, that she also had beliefs in aromatherapy. We had discussed this early on, and I had teased her with my cynicism. We had reached an agreement which I was content to honour; I don't suggest that she is a witch and she doesn't suggest that I am a hitman. I'm not, but I can understand why people might sometimes make that mistake.

I had to agree that she created a wonderful ambience there for Roman, the warmth and the pleasant sensations on his skin of the essential oils, the perfume, and the magic of the candlelight after I switched off the main light. He was being stroked and massaged, safely back in the domain of his mother whom he worshipped.

I tore myself away, fetched his belongings from the car, put the car in the garage, and then I locked my security pack back into the safe in my wardrobe, which was best discreetly done without reminding Debbie about it. It wasn't secret from her, but she preferred not to know. I moved Romans kit into the kitchen, and we would sort through it the next morning – or with the passage of time, later this day! I sneaked into the boys' bedroom, where T-Roy was fast asleep, oblivious to everything, and fetched a pair of undies from Romans chest of drawers and put them in my pocket.

Then I moved back to the bathroom and rested on the floor with my back to the wall just enjoying watching Debbie mothering the dreamy Roman. She decided that the time was right to take him to bed – no question that it would be to our bed straight away – and she murmured to him; "Don't wake up!" as, with my hands in his armpits, I stood him up initially in the bath so that she could dry him, and then I lifted him out to stand him on the bathmat while she dried his feet. I don't think he was asleep, but he was not far off.... I carried him back to our bedroom, and laid him on the inside of where Debbie slept. That was his normal sleeping position, although usually after going to bed in the boys' room, he would slink in and spend the night cuddled up

beside Debbie. Debbie and I knew he was a defensive barrier between us, which she liked so that I would not roll over and bump into her in my sleep.

I put his undies on one leg up to his knee, so that they were in place for him to pull them up if he wished to. Debbie joined me, having drained the bath and blown out the candles, and we both got into our different sides of the bed.

Our family was all back together again, and slept soundly, all under one roof.

*

I seldom dream, or if I do, I don't tend to remember them. I remembered this one though, although it was more of a memory than a dream. It was some 18 years ago, when I was doing my time as a paratrooper, before Debbie and I got together. It was coming back from our second operational mission, a blooding, where supposedly as `military advisers', we had conducted a raid on a force hostile to one of our nominal allies in the developing world. We had parachuted in, and subdued – and I'm using that as a euphemism – all resistance, before being collected by helicopters and flown back to our forward operating base. We had retrieved our parachutes, which is usually an indication of the extent to which a threat has been neutralised. We boarded the helicopters, which we always did in a hurry, and they took off and we headed for home, me in the open doorway, opposite the door gunner, who sat behind the co pilot, him having a little drop down flap to sit on at the back of the

15

pilot seat. Kevin sat beside me, with Leon opposite him; the three of us having been together since our childhoods together at Ferndale Hall. These were the days when Leon was at his leanest, before he bulked up with weightlifting and bodybuilding making him what he is today. We were in the last helicopter to leave, aware of the implied bravery of being the last out. There were several other soldiers also on board, but as we had filled up the preceding helicopters before us, we had more space than usual. Without the seats, we sat on our bagged parachutes, smelling of sweat and cordite, and aware of the adrenaline gradually working its way out of our blood streams leaving a sense of euphoria.

Suddenly I heard the sound of metallic pinging as bullets hit the helicopter. A bullet hole appeared in the floor in front of my foot, and another in the fuselage behind my head, and the door-gunner swore, yelled and grabbed his leg, red blood showing between his fingers. Immediately the adrenaline went up to full blast again. The noise of the engine roared louder as the pilot threw the helicopter around the sky in evasive action. I rapidly looked around; Kevin sat wide-eyed next to me. Leon looked behind him between the pilots' seats, and then looked back at me, and gave a `thumbs up' that neither pilot had been hit, and there was no apparent damage in the cockpit, but we were already moving to attend to the wounded door-gunner, pulling him down onto the floor between us. The pilot calmed down with the evasive action, as there were no further shots after the initial burst. Must have just been some lucky shots fired up from some hostile on the ground.

Leon had cut away the fabric of the gunner's trousers to expose the wound as I set to work with my medical pack, stanching the bleeding, and Leon injected him with morphine. Leon reached his bloodstained fingers through to the pilots to indicate that we had wounded on board. They would radio ahead so that he could be more properly attended to by specialists.

Job done, I sat back, only to find that Kevin had slumped over to where I had been sitting. I spun around to find him face down on my parachute bag, a sinister red stain spreading. Leon noticed that at the same time as I did, and was beside me as we carefully pulled him up right against the bulkhead. He was the first dead person I had seen close-up. There wasn't any question about him being dead. His face was misshapen in a way that was a sin against nature. The skin of his face was unbroken, but blood flowed out of his nose and mouth and his open eyes, still wide were sightless. Below us, his blood had soaked onto our parachutes – the bullet that had killed him had entered him from below, shot up through his body, and stopped when it had taken the top of his head off and into his helmet. We knew that there was nothing we could do for him.

All that we could do was to offer him dignity in death, keeping him upright sandwiched between me and the soldier on the other side of him, and to help with this we put a cord around his chest and secured it to the bulkhead. I didn't want to look at him; I had seen enough. We had grown up together, along with Leon, and now we were sitting side-by-side, him dead with the blood oozing out of

17

him far slower than his life had left him. Memories flashed through my mind of the good times and the not so good that we had shared together. I looked up into Leon's eyes, who had locked onto mine, neither of us wanting to look into the distorted dead face of our friend. The distortions to Kevin's face and head were an abomination.

Beside Leon, though surely still in pain, the door gunner had quietened down, his wound padded and his leg bandaged, and the morphine taking effect, but he was silenced by reverence to the dead Kevin.

I had lost all sense of time to these thoughts as I became aware of us arriving at the Forward Operating Base and touching down, and the medics moving in to help the door-gunner hop over to the ambulance, and with as much dignity as they could offer, to move Kevin's body onto a stretcher. One of them lifted Kevin's helmet off his head before pulling the sheet over his face, and I wished I hadn't seen that. Certainly, the medic, or the medical assistant or whoever he was, was shocked at what happened to Kevin's head without the structure given to it by the helmet, and he stood rooted to the spot. I took Kevin's helmet from him, and on the stretcher, Kevin was taken into the ambulance.

Everyone, apart from the departed medics, watched me holding his helmet, and no one moved. I took it with me back to our tent, and with respect I cleaned out the parts of his head that had remained in it. It stayed with me, as something more profound than a memento, and stays on my filing cabinet in the study.

And no, the boys are not allowed to play with it. And no, I am not going to explain it to them, and it's probably best if I don't tell them much about the man who would have been their Uncle Kevin, who would probably have loved them even more than Uncle Leon.

Then I was awake. Vivid memories fresh in my mind, and tears in my eyes which I had controlled at the time. I reached over to touch Roman's arm and moved my hand down to his. He made a dreamy enquiring noise. "Please let me hold your hand," I asked, and he clasped my hand.

*

"What's he doing here?' demanded T-Roy, the 'naked-ninja', halted abruptly mid challenging karate move, which he always went through before climbing into bed on my side. Young T-Roy's reaction to Roman's early return belied what I had told Roman in the car on the way home.

T-Roy did climb into bed beside me, but he sat up, looking over me, demanding answers. Wide-awake and interested, it was difficult to get him to leave it alone. "Did you get homesick, Romey?" T-Roy asked, with feigned sympathy, but knowing him, there would be some delight at his older brother showing weakness, which with his shatterproof confidence, he could declare that he would never suffer!

"Just leave him alone," I tried to silence, if not appease T-Roy. "Just snuggle in, and be peaceful." This would be impossible for T-Roy at any time, let alone when there was a mystery to be solved.

Roman was tired and sad in the morning. Debbie was happy to comfort him and have him cuddled in to her, seeking assurance. , T-Roy was fascinated by this change of plan, and he wouldn't let it go. He wouldn't let me distract him, despite my best efforts. He wanted to know, and Roman really didn't want to answer him, feigning sleep. I got up and took T-Roy along to shower with me, with him continuing to grill me with questions, promising to keep secrets, which I knew he had a total inability to do.

Having expected that Roman would be away camping until late on Sunday afternoon, we didn't have anything particular planned as a family, so we had many options. I thought it would be best if we could do something that would actively involve Roman, try to keep him busy, and possibly to distract T-Roy. While T-Roy was getting dressed in his room, which I knew he would do as fast as he could so as not to miss out on anything that might be discussed about Romans mysterious presence, I suggested to Debbie that I take the boys into the gym at the barracks – which was usually a special treat for them, but, being privileged to the suggestion whilst being so close to his mum, Roman said that he didn't want to, and that he wanted to stay with his mum. I was puzzled, because he had so enjoyed the Cub Camp, and had been so enthusiastic – nagging – about going camping with Alvin and the boys, but we all knew that he was closer to Debbie, and I trusted her judgement with the boys' emotional needs.

"You can take T-Roy," Debbie suggested. And T-Roy jumped at the chance when it was suggested to him, although I

could see the calculation going on in his mind that he would be missing out on the mystery that had occurred. We made a morning of it, with me taking his Speedos along, knowing that he wouldn't use them – little nudist that he is! As was usual for daytime, we had the swimming pool to ourselves. T-Roy loved having me to himself, but I was aware, that like me, he was also wondering what was happening with Roman back at home.

I phoned Debbie in the late morning for her guidance as to whether we should return for lunch, or whether she and Roman needed some more time alone together, and she suggested the latter, so I took T-Roy along to the army canteen with me, which was an ultra-special treat for him – the novelty, rather than the quality of the food; him being the only child in the dining hall populated mostly by young soldiers, some in uniform and those who knew who I was offering the necessary salutations.

When we returned home in the early afternoon, T-Roy was faster to check up on Roman than I was, my having been delayed by putting the car in the garage. I don't want to say that Debbie was indulging in him, but he had spent the day so far in our bed, with Debbie treating him as though he was ill, something that she would not normally have done. T-Roy started an interrogation of him, asking him directly if he was homesick, and Debbie gently shepherded him out of the room.

"Could you keep T-Roy busy for us," Debbie asked me quietly. "Maybe take him to the park?"

"Is Roman okay?" I asked.

"I just need some more time with him…"

So T-Roy, becoming more suspicious of the amount of one-to-one time he was getting with me, was content to have me go along to the park with him. I jogged with him tagging along on his bicycle which, much as I love my son, spoiled my run as he seemed unable to just keep riding beside me at my pace, but needed to go slightly ahead and then cross over in front of me so that I had to slow down and take avoiding action to avoid crashing into him. This ended when we got to the park, and although there were other children around who he knew, he prioritised spending time with me, but shared me with his friends, so I found myself spinning a fairly heavily laden merry-go-round. We spent a couple of hours there, but our thoughts kept returning to Roman at home, and unusually for T-Roy, he was content to return with me when I felt we had spent enough time there.

Again, T-Roy went straight in to check up on Roman. We knew that it wasn't brotherly love; it was just curiosity and him being tantalised about secrets and mysteries. I don't want to think this of my beloved younger son, but he might have had some element of pleasure that his older brother might have failed at some challenge, that of course, T-Roy, with his abounding confidence, would be sure he would have succeeded in. They didn't often show sibling rivalry.

"Romey is just not feeling well," Debbie tried to placate T-Roy, but this gave him a different line of enquiry.

"Have you got a runny tummy, Romey?" was the most obvious question that T-Roy could ask, with some slight one-upmanship to humiliate his older brother.

To my surprise, Roman told him; `yes' and after a pause he added; "I am not in the mood to talk or play." That was quite a big concession for Roman. Why did I not believe him?

"T-Roy, please could you ride your bike around the block for me? I'll time you!" Debbie suggested. T-Roy knew full well that he was being removed from the place where secrets were disclosed, and was very reluctant to leave. Generally, Debbie was less of a soft touch to him than I was. "There's a bowl of ice cream in it for you when you get back."

"A big fat bowl…" I embellished.

Reluctantly, T-Roy dragged himself away. Debbie indicated with her eyes for me to follow her out into the back garden as we couldn't guarantee that T-Roy wasn't going to be somewhere carefully placed where he could overhear what we said.

At a suitable distance from the house, Debbie stopped, and I could see that she knew what the mystery was. "Those little shits!" she said – unusual for her to use such language! "They rubbed Deep Heat into his balls."

"He's very upset!" She said, striding after me as I walked back to our bedroom to embrace and comfort my son. Not that I doubted in the slightest that Debbie had comforted

him and reassured him all day so far, but I needed to do that as well.

I knew that things like that happened, from my own childhood, but I had just assumed that it had died the death and it hadn't occurred to me that it might still happen – or that it would be done to Roman!

Roman must have heard me arrive and was expecting me, but he flinched when I walked into the room. It was just a brief flinch, but I saw it and it horrified me. Debbie was right behind me, as I sat down on the bed and reached out to embrace him. He hesitated briefly before he cuddled into me and we hugged.

"I am so very sorry," I told him. I kissed his neck.

"Please don't ever be frightened of me, my wonderful son!" I whispered to him softly, but loud enough for Debbie to hear. "I am so sorry that happened to you. I am so sorry that I wasn't there to protect you..."

Roman was crying. "You're not angry?" He asked with faltering breaths.

"Not with you! Not at all!" I assured him. "I am very very angry with the boys that did that to you."

"I wasn't supposed to tell," Roman sobbed. "They made me promise not to tell!"

"It's very important that you told your mum," I explained, hugging him even closer to me. "A promise made under

pressure like that doesn't count. I am very proud of you for your bravery for not being bullied into keeping quiet, and for letting us know."

Then Debbie surprised me. I had never seen her in a situation like this before, but I was very proud of her very slick delivery of a cover story for Roman, which I was more than happy to fully endorse. "You didn't tell tales at all, Romey." She told him – us! "When I was sorting through your rucksack and putting stuff in the washing, I smelled Deep Heat from your underpants. I asked you about it, and there wasn't anything that you would have been able to say apart from the truth. That's not telling tales! That's answering a direct question, and none of them would have been able to come up with an answer to explain." That was as good a narrative as any, and I was happy to repeat and help develop that into something that Roman believed.

At this stage, T-Roy was back, knowing that he was owed the promised ice cream, but more interested to try to work out what had happened while he had been sidelined. He found Roman cuddled into me, Roman still looking slightly tearful, and Debbie distracted him away to the kitchen for his reward.

"Don't you want some ice cream, Roman?" I asked, but he said he didn't.

"I'm so sorry I didn't realise what they might do to you," I whispered to him, knowing that T-Roy was out of earshot.

"It's my job, as your father, to protect you, and I have let you down!" At this, he hugged me tighter.

"They are going to be very sorry for what they did," I promised him.

"What are you going to do?" he asked.

"I don't know – yet! What do you want me to do?"

"I don't know." He was still hugging me, but it seemed stale – and becoming uncomfortable.

"It's best for T-Roy not to know what happened," I said to him, and he murmured in agreement." It's best for you to let him think you were homesick and maybe that you've got an upset tummy, so that he thinks he understands. You know how he can't keep secrets and I don't think you want people to know – do you?"

"No!"

"But you, your mummy and I know that you weren't homesick. You weren't homesick on Cub Camp and you would have been absolutely fine if they hadn't done this to you. You are a very brave boy for wanting to go with them, braver than I was." And I decided not to qualify that further; braver at his age? `Brave' – a compliment that will bring pride to a young boy who doesn't need to be bothered with the philosophy.

He seemed to be cheering up a little bit now. "But you were a parachute," and I loved it that he got it slightly wrong.

26

"That's different. That's not really brave. You were braver than I am. And your mum is braver than I am." Probably best not to develop that further now as it would not be for many years, if ever that he should learn about how brave his mum was – to bring him into the world!

"I don't want to push you," I said bringing us back to the here and now. "But it will be good if, as soon as you can, you get up and get dressed and we can do family things together."

*

After about half an hour, and with some gentle encouragement from his mum, he did join us, and accepted the bowl of ice cream which he was due – and T-Roy had the decency not to suggest that he should only get it if he too cycled around the block. And so we spent family time together in a more dedicated way than normal, with all of us lying on the lounge floor playing board games, and then Roman and I cooked our family meal of his favourite foods, and although he still had his suspicions, this blunted T-Roy's enquiries.

I had helped with transporting Alvin and the boys and their equipment out to the campsite, and I knew that he had arranged for others to collect them when they were due to finish camping on the Sunday afternoon. I would contact him once he was home, and I would give him an hour or two to settle back in, but I rather expected that he would know that I would call.

I phoned Alvin when I thought the time was right, and after some awkward and strained pleasantries, I got down to business. "I have something important to discuss with you, but I think it can be sorted out. You okay for me to continue?"

"Okay," a very small voice replied.

"Something happened to Roman on the camp and I am not happy about it. Do you know what I'm talking about?"

He didn't say anything, but I could hear that he was still holding the phone.

"If I didn't think we could sort this out, I would be speaking to your parents – or worse."

There was a pause, and then a gulp, and then "I think so!"

"Okay, you have options. You have the option of telling your parents, and see what they say, and then in a couple of days I'll check with them that they know what I am talking about."

Again, there was silence, but I could tell that he was there.

"Or we can talk, you, me and Roman, and see if we can sort this out..."

"What will you do ...?"

"We have a discussion and see if we come up with a plan that you feel is fair ..."

There was a pause, and then that little stressed voice again; "I'm sorry. I'll tell Romey I'm sorry."

"That's not enough."

Again, that agonised silence.

"I suggest that we meet and discuss options – just discuss options, and it is important that you agree to any decisions we make. You can stop and leave at any time. But then you would have to tell your parents, and I will check."

The silence, so I checked; "Are you there?"

"Yes," said that very small voice.

"Just to let you know that Debbie knows, and she is in the room with me here. You can speak to her if you want to. She will be in the house, but not in the room if you are willing to meet with Roman and me. Do you want to speak to her?"

"No," came that stressed voice again.

"Do you want to have a day or two to decide whether you want to meet with Roman and me, or would you rather just tell your parents?"

"I don't know."

"I would have to tell your parents that I'm not happy about the way that you treated Roman on the camp, but I would say to them that because I respect that you are fifteen" (I knew he was fourteen) "that I would prefer to sort this out between us if they could live with that."

"If you want you could bring someone along with you, but then they will find out what you … what happened."

"I don't know what to do," he confessed.

"Have a think about it and get back to me. I'll be seeing your parents at the church picnic next weekend anyway, so if I haven't heard back from you by then, I can ask your Dad if you have told him."

"My dad would kill me."

"I don't think so, but he won't be pleased." I knew who Alvin's father was; a mild-mannered and inoffensive man, very proud of the young leadership role that Alvin was moving into. I would hate to be in his position to learn that my son had been involved in such semi-sexual bullying of such a young child, and to be told this by someone like me, in a passive aggressive manner, demanding that he punish Alvin to my satisfaction, and report back to me about this. A silent prayer to my boys; 'Please don't ever put me in this position.'

"But do not misunderstand me. You need to be punished so Roman knows that there has been justice. It's important

that we agree what punishment is suitable, and that you accept that."

"What punishment?"

"That would depend on our discussion. But not without your agreement and permission."

"Can't I just tell Romey that I'm very sorry and we won't do it again?"

"That's not good enough!"

"I don't know what to do!" he confided after a heavy silence.

"I think maybe you want to have the discussion with Roman and me. It's not an ambush. Debbie will be in the house when you are here. You will be free to leave at any time."

Again the "I don't know what to do!"

So I suggested that he have a think and get back to me, but if he decided to throw himself upon my mercy, he needed to give me some notice so that we could arrange for T-Roy to be elsewhere. T-Roy would be fascinated at us being visited by Alvin, with the status that Alvin enjoyed amongst the younger children. And T-Roy would work out that he had been deliberately excluded – that seemed to be happening a lot lately – so I would need to make it a treat that he would value. Spending quality time with Uncle Leon was called for.

For a brief moment, I thought of the alternative of T-Roy staying with us, and Leon having the meeting with Alvin and

31

Roman, but that would be far too cruel! Leon excelled at intimidation – part of his work role – and though he might not harm a hair on Alvin's head, I know that Leon could easily do lasting psychological damage to the teenager.

I could have shared with him a true anecdote from my own schooldays; 'Come back on Monday to get caned. Have a nice weekend!' but that might influence him, and it was important that he make the choice.

*

In a not entirely convincing manner, he indicated that he would think it over and get back to me, and I understood he was having difficulty putting his thoughts – and fears – into words. I realised that he was shocked to find that Roman had told us, and he could be in very serious trouble.

It was later that evening that I heard from Alvin. He had probably thought of nothing else, but he was a bit calmer. "If I accept your punishment could you please not tell my parents?"

"I can't have a serious discussion with you as a fifteen-year-old without them at least knowing that we are meeting."

"Can I tell them?"

"No, sorry, it has to come from me."

"Please ...?"

"It's not negotiable. I don't plan to tell them what I know, but I can tell them that I want to discuss with you how to manage situations like where Roman decided he wanted to come home early." I know I am being hypocritical here, and I would certainly want to know if another grown man was having a conversation of the kind I was intending with my fourteen year old son, but if my prayers are answered, that won't happen.

"You won't tell them what... happened?"

"I don't plan to. If they ask, I can suggest that they ask you."

"Did you hear what I said about how you can leave at any time if you wish to?"

"Yes," Alvin confirmed.

*

Leon willingly stepped up to the mark and agreed to look after T-Roy, to keep him out of the way while I had my discussion with Alvin. T-Roy was very conflicted, and aware that he was being distracted, although he wasn't quite sure from what, but the idea of spending time with Leon was an attractive one, especially on his own with Leon, without his older brother being along as well!

Alvin arrived slightly early, on his bike and with a small rucksack which puzzled me slightly. I walked with him down the side of the house to stow his bike conveniently, and the tension was palpable. "I'm not going to hurt you!" I told him,

wanting to reassure him at least slightly, as it would do no good at all to intimidate him into being a gibbering wreck!

Debbie was there to greet us as we came in at the back door of the house, with Roman standing in front of her with her arms protectively downwards and her hands on his chest. She was civil, but cold as she greeted Alvin.

"I'm going to be here all the time," she told him. "But I'm not involved in your discussion with Jason."

I suppose I was quite amused that she called me Jason, adding formality to the encounter, and Alvin probably had to think for a moment before realising she was referring to me by my formal name.

She offered him a hot drink or a soft drink, still with the chill to her, but he declined. A wise move! While the four of us were still in the kitchen, I outlined how I proposed to have our conversation. I would first show him around the living area of the house, where Debbie would be, and Roman would be with her for part of the time, where we would have our conversation, which was in the study despite it being dominated rather by the massage table, with my filing cabinets up against the wall, and I showed him where the bathroom was and told him that I would be happy to get a drink if at any stage he felt that he wanted one. He nodded in acknowledgement, but he wasn't in the mindset to ask any questions at that stage.

Further setting the agenda, I explained that he and I would have a conversation on our own at first, while Roman was

34

with Debbie, and then Roman would join us for a discussion of what happened, and we would `take things from there'.

I wouldn't say that I had put a lot of thought into the environment, but I wanted it clinical and businesslike, as opposed to a sitting in the greater comfort of the living room. I hadn't deliberately put them there, but Kevin's paratrooper helmet was visible in its usual place on the filing cabinet, and – too far away for him to be able to see – a group photo of us kitted up with parachutes standing posing in front of the aircraft that we were soon to jump from. I had pushed the massage table over to the side of the room, against the filing cabinets, but I liked it to be there. I believe that one of the strategies of the Spanish Inquisition was before an interrogation, they would introduce their victim to the implements of torture, possibly in the hope that the man would decide at that stage to tell them everything they wanted to hear, thereby making actually starting the torture unnecessary.

I stroked Roman's head as he turned to follow Debbie to the lounge, and I heard the television go on – was it louder than it would have been normally? Being slightly warmer to Alvin than Debbie had been, I showed him into the study and showed him where to sit, which he did after a hasty look around the contents of the room. I know what he saw.

"I say again; I am not going to hurt you! You can leave at any time if you wish to, but there will be consequences which we will talk about. I will not stop you! If you need to go to

the bathroom, that's fine. If you need a drink, I will get you one."

"If you decide that you want to have your parents involved in what I have to say, or anyone else, that's fine." And I checked with him the amount of time that we had available, and I wasn't surprised that at his age he said that he didn't have to be home by any particular time.

"Okay," I began. "I am going to be kind to you by not dragging all that I want to know out of you, but I'm going to suggest things, and you can correct me where I go wrong. Are you happy with that?" Happy was probably one of the most inappropriate words I could have chosen to describe the atmosphere.

He started to reply, but croaked, his mouth having dried up. "I'll get you some water. You stay here. I won't be a moment." I left him there, to examine the torture chamber and came back with a glass of water with some ice cubes clinking at the top, and one for me as well.

"Okay! Roman went camping with you, and he became very unhappy the first night such that you weren't able to comfort him, and you called me. I had thought that if I reassured him, and possibly spent the night there, then he might be fine the next day, but as we know he was too upset for that. So, I brought him home."

"Next morning, Debbie is sorting through his kit and she notices a strange smell coming from his underpants. She asked Roman about that and he burst into tears. Okay, I

36

know – Roman knows better than to try to keep secrets from Debbie, and so he told her what had happened."

"I don't know whether you think this makes Roman a tattletale?" I looked inquiringly at Alvin, who shook his head. Not that he really had any alternatives. "There aren't really any explanations that a nine-year-old could come up with to explain that."

Okay, I wasn't being truthful here. Somehow, the boys had managed to cover their tracks, and there were no underpants smelling of Deep Heat. But, if Alvin noticed this, he wasn't going to contradict me, and this made a good narrative.

There might not have been that actual physical evidence, but Roman had been camping with Cubs several times before, which he had enjoyed, and he had never been homesick – well not to the extent that anyone noticed, and he had come back tired, dirty, but buzzing with excitement. A far cry from how he was when I had fetched him!

Hopefully I had moved the narrative away from it being possible for Roman to be branded as a tattletale, so I moved on.

"I understand that amongst you and the others, you suddenly held him down, and somebody rubbed Deep Heat into his balls. Am I right?"

After a difficult pause, Alvin did the inevitable and confirmed this. "I'm disappointed in you. I trusted you to look after my son..."

"It wasn't me that did it..."

"You were in charge." I snapped back. "It was you that I entrusted to look after him. You could have stopped it from happening!"

Alvin silently assented to this.

"You and the others have hurt and humiliated Roman. You are going to be punished, but we are going to see if we can agree how we can get this sorted."

Now, from looking downwards and avoiding eye contact, he looked up into my eyes with the question.

"One possibility is that I meet with your parents, tell them what happened and ask them what they think would be a suitable punishment for you, and if I am satisfied, then I could leave it at that. But I presume that you would rather that your parents didn't know?"

Again, a nod from Alvin, his eyes fixed on the floor again.

"If I was not satisfied with the punishment your parents proposed, I could report this to the police. I don't know if you realise it, but what the six of you did was a sexual assault against a nine-year-old child."

"You're fifteen years old, so they wouldn't..."

"Fourteen. I'm fourteen," Alvin corrected me in a small voice.

I knew that, of course. I was boosting him slightly, complementing him that I thought he was older, but it was a trivial point.

"As a fourteen-year-old, you wouldn't be treated like an adult, but you would be interviewed by police officers, and social workers, and they would interview your parents as well, as well as people around you, who would even know what you had done, or else would probably be more worried if they didn't know what it was about, but that they were being asked questions about your sexual behaviour, and their imaginations would go into overtime. The same would happen to the other boys. Rumours spread. I don't think that this would be something you would want?"

"No!" Alvin confirmed in a very small voice.

Then there was a silence which I allowed to extend until it became uncomfortable. Alvin lifted his eyes up to meet mine.

"What I propose to do now is to fetch Roman, and with him here I want you to give me a detailed description of exactly what happened. Roman will be able to confirm this, or to let me know if you have left anything out."

"It is most important that you take full responsibility, realise what you – and I'm saying you because you were in charge, I trusted you, and you could have prevented it!"

"You won't mind if I take notes while you tell me what happened?"

This was completely unnecessary, as I would remember all the details. Despite me being used to extracting and sorting details, our whole conversation was being recorded. Old habits die hard!

Writing it down added to the formality, and it would be known to the other boys that I had a contemporaneous note of Alvin's statement, which – I envisaged – I could allow them to make similar statements themselves should they wish to.

At the end of the evening, I locked the tapes safely away in my filing cabinet.

*

Does it sound as though I am being too hard on a fourteen-year-old? I have repeatedly assured him that I will not hurt him though he is properly not entirely convinced. But this is a boy who allowed my son to be held down, hurt and humiliated. I have never been a big fan of physical intimidation. Let their imagination do the work for you!

"What punishment?" In that parched voice that made me indicate his untouched glass of water from which he took a gulp!

"I'm not sure yet. It is important that it is something that you consider to be fair. It does me no good, and it does Roman no good, if you feel that you have been treated

40

unfairly and are resentful to Roman. He does look up to you, and he persuaded us that he was old enough to go camping with you, and from what we know about you, we thought he would be fine!" Let's give that knife a little twist, shall we?

"So I'm thinking, if you – you as the person in control, regardless as to whether you actually did it or not – rubbed Deep Heat into his balls, how about you present yourself to him so that he can do the same back to you?"

"Roman do it to me?" Alvin sounded incredulous.

"I would take an educated guess, and suggest that I think it has happened to you before? He paused. "Yes..."

"But not by someone so much younger than me!"

I stayed silent for a little while for him to think.

"Couldn't you just cane me? Even in front of Roman? I think that would be fair." This was still a time that, although it was going out of fashion, corporal punishment was still occasionally used at school, and was probably more legendary than actually happened.

"That would be an easy way out for you," I said to him with a wry smile. "No, that's not an option!"

I allowed another pause. "I think that Roman was very embarrassed and humiliated by what you guys did, that as well as the pain."

"Even if I caned your bare arse with Roman watching, I don't think that would match what you guys did to him." Let's just put nudity – for Alvin – on the table for discussion.

Some more thinking time for Alvin! "Couldn't you – do it?" What? He doesn't want to use the word `balls' to an adult?

"No! As I've told you, what you did is legally a sexual assault, and I, as a 35-year-old man am not going to sexually assault a 14 year-old-boy."

Some more thinking time. "No, it has to be Roman. But it would just be you and Roman – no other people holding you down. And you would have to accept and allow Roman to do it to you."

"But you'll be there?"

"It's important that you agree – and genuinely agree that this would be fair, and you allow Roman to do it back to you. And you accept it so that you don't intimidate Roman or plan to get back at him later. I don't think you would do that, as I don't think you are that sort of person. Which is why we trusted you to look after Roman."

"You can have some time to think about it. You don't need to decide now. You can see if you can come up with any better solution that I would consider fair."

"So, shall I go and fetch Roman, and then you go through a detailed account of what happened? "

"What will you do to the others?"

"We haven't decided what we're going to do to you yet. As I say, you were in charge, it was you I trusted, and it was you who let us down."

Another pause. "Do I have any other choices?"

"Can you suggest any?"

His silence answered that!

I stood up, but then remembered to ask; "I'm just assuming that this was an initiation or something? It wasn't a punishment for anything that Roman had done wrong?"

"It was just initiation. He hadn't done anything wrong. Everybody likes him!"

"I'll ask you that again in front of him. I think it's important that he hears that."

*

Roman was cuddled up next to Debbie on the sofa when I went to fetch him. Both turned to look at me with big eyes, immediately losing interest in whatever was on the television.

"How's it going?" Debbie asked, and I would tease her later about how impossible such a question was for me to answer, especially as she had told me she wanted me to deal with it, but she didn't want to know the details.

"We are making progress," I told her, which was a suitably meaningless answer to an impossible question.

43

Roman walked towards me, but seemed rather subdued, moving slowly and looking downwards. I knelt down to hug him. "You've done nothing wrong!" I told him. "It was my fault for letting you go, and for trusting them!"

Roman hugged me back, and then followed me back to the study. There were only two chairs, and the imposing massage bench, but I sat him on my knee and cuddled him into me, with a protective arm over his shoulder and to his thigh. The body language experts would say that this was a protective barrier between him and Alvin. There are many protective barriers in our household.

Roman was a little resistant to this at first, which I could understand as I suppose my efforts to comfort him might have made him concerned at looking babyish in front of Alvin. I took this head on. "Do you mind if I comfort my son?" I asked him, not adding `while I torture you in front of him?'

Roman then adjusted to lean against me, cuddling in, watching Alvin intently.

"Now I want you to tell me exactly what happened," I told Alvin. "I'm relying on you to be honest and not to hold anything back, so that Roman doesn't have to correct you."

Alvin assented.

*

Roman stirred. "Can I go and get myself a chair?" He asked. He didn't want to be seen as a little boy in front of Alvin. I

could understand that. He went and returned with one of the dining room chairs and sat on it, rather awkwardly watching Alvin without looking at him directly.

I recapped for Roman that I held Alvin responsible, even though Alvin might not have done the worst part to Roman, but he was in charge and should have prevented it from happening. I asked Alvin again whether it was initiation rather than punishment, and Alvin said the right thing, but we had to briefly explain to Roman about initiation, and I could see that it didn't really make sense to him. Hurting people because they are new?

"It happened to me as well," Alvin mentioned, possibly trying to normalise it for Roman. Did he realise it was in his interests to try to get sympathy from Roman? Was he thinking of the possibility of Roman doing to him what he had allowed to happen? Probably!

Let me counter that straight away! "Were you Roman's age – nine – when that happened?"

That shut him up! "No," he admitted. "I was older."

And so we got into the narrative. After their evening meal they had gone for a swim in the river. It seemed that Alvin had decided not to withhold any detail, so he gathered his courage and told me they had all gone skinny-dipping. He seemed to expect me to disapprove, but this was misplaced.

"I have no problem with that," I told him. "I expect that Roman would have been okay with that. I would have a

problem if he hadn't wanted to, and you guys had stripped him."

"No, they didn't do that," Roman confirmed. "You told me that it was okay if it happened." And he was right I had told him that and some other things about what was allowed when he was away from parental influence.

I turned to Roman; "Tell Alvin some of the other things that I said to you about what was acceptable while you were camping with the big boys."

Roman looked at me, not knowing quite what I meant, or whether I did actually want him to disclose.

"About smoking?" I prompted him.

"Oh, yes. You said to me that if the boys smoked, then..."

"We didn't smoke," Alvin chipped in.

"I'm not accusing. I just want to let you know that I briefed Roman about some secrets being allowed..."

"You said that I was not allowed to smoke, but that I should not tell on them if they did..."

"Yes, that's right. And swearing?"

"You said that they might swear and tell bad jokes, and I wasn't to use any swear words or repeat any rude jokes that I heard myself."

"Good boy!" So, hopefully demonstrating to Alvin that Roman had been primed not to tell tales, I continued to Alvin. "So skinny-dipping is fine as far as I'm concerned. I think Roman would be fine with it... Okay, then what happened?" I had my pen poised over my notepad, waiting expectantly.

"So, as we got back to the tent, one of the guys said that we should do it to Roman."

"Who said?"

"Must I say?"

"Oh yes!"

"Has Roman not told you?"

"Debbie and I haven't asked him for any details. I want the details from you!" Alvin hesitated, conflicted, and I expect that he was now finding himself forced to tell tales. But that was not my problem, and part of his punishment was to make a full disclosure. And I wanted it to come from him, to clear Roman of telling stories...

"Okay, it was Tom's idea."

I knew who Tom was, and knowing that one of the boys must have suggested it, I would have guessed that it would have been Tom.

Alvin realised that he needed to describe what had happened, and so he did, about James having protested that

Roman was too young to do it to, and I suggested that James – who had surprised me – had given good advice which Alvin would have done well to have followed. They had held him down, Alvin at one shoulder, Dan at the other with Ben keeping James at bay while Tom sat on Romans legs and pulled his pants down, and pushed his legs apart. Roman had been protesting, crying, and pleading `no' and James had been trying to get in the way, and push Tom off.

By now I had reached out to Roman again and gathered him onto my lap where he cuddled into me, with me but in my left arm around him defensively.

"And then Tom put the Deep Heat on him."

Okay, that was probably the climax of the narrative, and Alvin paused. There was still tension, even though Alvin had said what I had expected. From experience, I knew that there was something more that he did not want to say.

"Tell me more…"

"What?"

"Did you do anything else to him?"

"Like what?"

It's not a good idea to introduce ideas into a narrative, but I reminded myself that he was a fourteen-year-old-boy, and not a possible threat to the State!

"Like putting any under his foreskin, or up his bum?"

Roman jerked back to look up at my face when I said this, and Alvin looked shocked.

"No," Alvin recovered. "Just on his balls!"

Not having a foreskin myself, I am not an expert on such matters, but having heard of the greater sensitivity of an intact penis, I expected that the burning to both skin surfaces would be very painful, much more so than the defence that scar tissue would offer. The ability to remove a burning substance from a rectum, without the fortuitous need for a bowel movement, didn't bear thinking about.

Had I given them new ideas? This is plainly something that they hadn't thought of. It might be a new idea, but package with my deal was that they would not ever do this to anyone ever again, so I think I had that covered.

Still I considered that there was evasiveness. "I think there's something you're not telling me!"

"Like what?"

"What Tom said…" Roman prompted.

Alvin stiffened. So, this was where to dig further. I looked at Alvin with my eyebrows raised, pen poised again, as it had been for a little while now.

Alvin's awkwardness was not easing. "Do I have to tell?"

"Look, my willingness to sort this out between us depends on you being fully honest with me. If I find later that you

49

have not told me everything, the deal is off, and we might start again..."

With a deep breath, Alvin took the plunge. "Tom said he couldn't find his balls."

Roman was cuddled into me again now, more so than before. "Anything else?"

Another intake of breath. "Then he said, `maybe he hasn't got any'."

Roman started to cry into my shoulder. "James told him not to say such things," Roman said through sobs.

"And then?"

"Then we let him go."

"Do you mind if I confirm this with Roman?" As if Alvin was in any position to object? I asked Roman and he confirmed this.

"So then what happened?"

"I've told you everything that happened..."

"Okay, so you've got off him. And is he still crying?"

Alvin's eyes dropped to the floor again. "Yes," he admitted.

"Okay, so you've got off him, and he still lying there, and he's crying, and he feels that his balls are on fire... "

"Well... Then James got to him, and was trying to comfort him, and James helped him pull his pants back up, and put his arm around him, and started to take him outside to help him wash himself... "

"And what did you do?"

"I went along with James to help." I allowed Alvin some further silence. "I realised I'd made a mistake! I wished I hadn't let it happen."

"So, James is trying to comfort Roman, and helping him to wash himself... What then?"

"Well he wouldn't stop crying, and he said he wanted his mom – his dad – his mum and dad..."

"It would have been his mum he wanted. I know that. That's okay."

"And James – and I had helped him wash it off as best we could, but he wouldn't stop crying. The other boys came along and were trying to comfort him and telling him that it was over, and that it wouldn't happen again, and that it had happened to all of us, and it was just something that happened to boys the first time they came along on the camp. But he wouldn't stop crying. So, we told him we were sorry, and we asked him not to tell on us..."

"Which he didn't – until his mum found his underpants with Deep Heat in them and asked him to explain." Let's make sure that stays part of the narrative!

51

"So, whatever we did, we couldn't get him to stop crying, or saying that he wanted his mom, and he wanted to go home."

"Eventually I realised there was nothing more we could do, and that's when we took him to the phone, and we called you." There is a lot of power in silence, so I let there be silence for a while.

"Is that everything?" I paused. "As I say, us sorting things out between us depends on you having not left anything out."

"That is everything. You can ask Roman." I looked down to Roman, who looked up to me and nodded.

"So, what are you thinking now?"

"I'm really wishing I hadn't allowed it to happen."

There was a natural in there, but the matter wasn't resolved. Punishment was deserved.

"Okay, I've told you what I think would be a suitable punishment. But it's important to me that you agree that I am being fair with you." There was a pause, Roman still on my lap, but less tightly cuddled into me. "Do you want some time to think about it?"

"I don't know."

"Do you want me to make a suggestion?"

"As I said, you were in charge, you could have stopped it, I had trusted you to look after Roman, and I think you

deserve punishment. I will speak to the other boys, and the deal will be that they won't be specifically punished, and I won't tell their parents or the police, but that is on the understanding that none of you do this to anyone else in the future, and you keep it a secret about our discussion and about you guys humiliating Roman. If I hear that any of you have done it to anyone else, or that I hear of you telling stories of what you did to Roman, or if I pick up any suggestion that any of you are bullying Roman, or saying that he tell tales, then the deal is off, and I will decide what to do."

"Yes."

"There's the church picnic coming up on this Sunday," I contemplated. "I expect most of the boys will be there anyway, but you could advise any that aren't planning to be there to make sure that they are, so that I can have my chat with all of them together. So, I think you need to make a decision about whether you accept my punishment, and to allow time for it to happen before then." He nodded, but was still clearly conflicted.

*

"Does Roman know what the punishment is?" He asked.

"No, not yet." Roman looked up to me inquiringly but I left it for a while. "I don't mean to rush you, and you can have the rest of the week to decide, but I think that the best deal for you is to accept the punishment. If you do, it can be over and done with by the time you leave here this evening."

"How?"

"It can happen in this room. When I'm content that you suffered enough, you can shower and wash. You can get dressed and go home but that's your choice."

"What are you going to do to punish him?" Roman asked.

Okay, I know that I was labouring the point, but it was important that both he and Alvin understood. "I know it was Tom that actually did it to you, but Alvin was in charge and should have stopped it. Therefore, I feel it is suitable for you to do to Alvin what Tom did to you."

Roman was shocked. Still sitting on my knee, he pulled back from me to look into my face. "You mean you want me to rub Deep Heat into Alvin's balls?"

Now I realise that I hadn't taken into account that the beautifully fair aspect of Old Testament justice; and eye for an eye, might not appeal to Roman. That despite assurances that Alvin would accept this and passively allow it to happen, and undertake that there would be no consequences for Roman, Roman might not actually wish to touch the teenager's testicles.

It would be best not to have this discussion in front of Alvin, and now at this point I realised that Roman would never want to do this. That it would be wrong of me to try and make him do it – that could make the situation even worse for Roman.

54

"Would you excuse us for a minute please," I said to Alvin, this pseudo-politeness being something I used at work as well, fully knowing that there is no way the person I asked this from would ever object. And Alvin did not do so.

I took Roman through to the kitchen, and cuddled him on my lap, knowing that we were out of earshot from Alvin, me having shut the door as we left, leaving him to brood in the torture chamber. "They did it to you, so I think its fair you do it back to him," I tried to explain, but I knew that I wouldn't convince him.

He had started crying again, but was cuddled in seeking comfort from me. "I don't want to do it," he sobbed. "I just want it to stop!"

Debbie appeared in the doorway behind him. She looked to me with eyebrows raised in enquiry. I showed her the flat of my palm, indicating that everything was okay, but there was an inevitability about how things would go now. She stayed in the doorway, and I realised, with our son in tears and seeking comfort, there is no way she would go back to the lounge and leave me to proceed.

I gestured to her to come and join us at the table, and now I found that I felt embarrassed if she had learned what I had asked – had assumed – that our son might be willing to do. Roman turned as he heard Debbie moving into the kitchen, and immediately transferred over to her lap, and buried his face into her seeking comfort. She stroked his back to soothe and calm him further.

"Are you sure?" I asked him, knowing full well that he was absolutely sure.

"I just want it to all stop!" He sobbed!

"Do you want him to get away with it?" I asked, but I knew I had lost.

"I just want it to all stop!" He said again. And I accepted that at this stage.

"That's fine, my wonderful son!" I said, trying to soothe him, and I reached over to ruffle his hair. "I'll just go and finish things off with Alvin, and you can stay with your mum."

"Don't hurt him," Roman asked. Where did that come from? Unless he thought that I was now going to do to Alvin what I had wanted him to do. Roman would not be aware of the assurances that I had given to Alvin that I wasn't going to hurt him.

"I won't hurt him. I promise you that!"

Debbie led Roman back to the sofa in the sitting room, and cuddled and reassured him, and they were still like that when Alvin and I joined them later.

But Alvin didn't yet know that nothing was going to happen to punish him physically, and I was going to milk it a bit more before finally letting him know this.

He looked up when I opened the door and entered alone. "Have you had any thoughts?" I asked him.

"Yes. I really wish I hadn't let it happen. I'm sorry."

"And...?" He was tired, and I knew that I had put him through it psychologically, so I prompted him. "Do you want time to think about it, or do you want to get it over and done with?"

"Is Roman going to do it?"

"Yes," I lied. "He's not keen, but I explained it to him."

"And if I accept it happens now, is that the end of it?" All these people wanting things to end!

"Yes, for you. But you'll be there on Sunday and you'll make sure that all the boys are there for me to have my little chat with all of you, and after that, it's over, as long as you all keep to your side, and you don't take it out on Roman, or try to make out that he told tales – because you know that you have told me all of the details – and that you never do this or anything similar to little kids again. And I'll add in that I want you to keep it secret what I – what I have ordered Roman to do to you."

"So, what must I say if they asked me what punishment you did?"

"I'm quite happy for you to let them know that I have vowed you to secrecy and that if you break this, the deal is off, and we start again..."

"I accept that," he decided, and then after a breath, he took the plunge and said; "Let's do it now and get it over with!"

57

Mission accomplished, in a rather compromised way. He had decided to submit himself to my punishment which to me was more important than the punishment itself. But some final details before the big reveal!

"But before I fetch Roman, do you accept and agree that you won't take any revenge against him for doing what I've told him to do? You can hate me as much as you like, but don't take it out on him."

"I won't do that. Romey is a lovely kid. Everybody likes him."

I held back on the obvious observation that `if you like him so much why did you hurt him?'

"Okay, so what happens now is you strip off, and you wrap that towel around your waist, and you sit on this massage table. When I bring Roman in, we will just discuss again and agree that you are willing to accept the punishment, that you open your legs to give him access to your balls and you will not obstruct him in any way. When he has finished, he will come and fetch me, and you put the towel around your waist again so that you are covered when I come back in. I'll let you suffer until I think it's enough, and then I'll take you to the shower and leave you to clean up and dress. Then you meet up with us in the lounge. Do you understand?"

He nodded. "Will you cooperate?"

He nodded, and then made one desperate bid to salvage miniscule dignity; "Couldn't you do it instead of Roman, even if Roman watches?"

"No, I've explained to you. I am not going to sexually assault you. With Roman, as a small boy, doing it to you adds to the humiliation. And what Tom said about his balls seems to have been as humiliating to him as the pain was."

"Okay," Alvin said, with a hangdog expression on his face, and I moved to the door as he stood up and started unbuttoning his shirt.

He noticed that although I had my hand on the door handle, I was not opening the door. He looked up inquiringly.

I told him to leave his shirt and to sit back down, and I returned to my seat. "You are very lucky! Roman is a much nicer person than I am!" I left a brief pause. "Roman doesn't want to do it to you, and I'm not going to make him."

"So, are you going to do it?"

"No, I've told you why. So, because Roman decided that he doesn't want me to punish you, I'm not going to. That isn't what I expected, but I respect Romans' wishes. You can get dressed properly, and then you are free to go. We still have that meeting with you and the others on Sunday though. And I would like you to apologise to Roman, in front of his mother, before you go."

The relief in Alvin was palpable.

As he buttoned his shirt back up, I clarified; "I still want you to keep secret the punishment that I suggested to you, and I want you to let it be known amongst the others that you were punished. I think I have given you a fairly hard time

59

during our discussion, but if Roman hadn't decided he didn't want to, that is what would have happened to you. Are you happy to let them think that you were punished?"

Alvin agreed. There was still one more thing that puzzled me, and with my hand on the door handle, I asked; "There's something I'm still puzzled by. Do you know what work I do?"

"You used to be in the army, but you are not anymore. Are you something in the government?"

"And knowing that I used to be in the army, that didn't make you a little bit cautious about doing that to my son?"

"We didn't think he would tell – that you would find out. It's happened to all of us, and we didn't tell."

"But you won't do it to anyone else. Roman is the last one, and he won't be involved in doing it to anyone else. Do you understand?"

He agreed. With that I led him back to the living room, where Debbie and Roman were cuddled up on the sofa. Both of them stood up immediately and walked over to us, Debbie looking at Alvin with concern, and asking him if he was okay. Suddenly she is playing good cop to my bad cop? I had beaten Alvin psychologically, and it had been difficult for him, but that had been less than he deserved, in my humble opinion, for what he had allowed to happen to Roman, and for not protecting him.

Was it because Debbie is female, showed concern, and asked if he was okay? Maybe with him being a hormonal teenager, her question pressed the button, and he burst into tears. Despite what he had allowed to happen to her son, Debbie's maternal instincts kicked in, and she embraced him, as he cried into her chest, and Roman too started crying again – the stress in the room seemed pervasive, and he hugged into Debbie's side, and – I was surprised – put his other arm around Alvin's waist, hugging both of them from the side.

Over Alvin's shoulder, Debbie looked at me, and her expression asked; "What have you done to him?"

"Nothing," I indicated back with raising my shoulders and opening my palms to her. Then I pointed my index fingers of both hands at the side of my head to indicate that it was all in his head. Debbie glared at me then, and I realised that I was in a paradox that I found myself in with her occasionally, where she required me to sort something out, without involving her, but to be disapproved of for the way in which I dealt with the matter, despite her refusal to be involved.

So there I was, wanting to have punished a teenager for what he had allowed to be done to my son, and not only has he not been punished apart from what I had done to him psychologically, but he is now being nurtured and protected by my beloved wife, while my son who was offended against, is sharing in the comfort of his tormentor.

61

Okay, it will all be resolved, and there will be a positive outcome, but at the moment, I am the bad guy. I can phone Leon and ask him to bring back my little buddy, T-Roy, but my little buddy will be treacherously buzzing of the fantastic time that he has had with Uncle Leon, and for a little while he will let me know that he has a new best friend forever.

Welcome to my life!

*

I don't know if I got the timing right. I didn't want to tell Roman too soon, and I didn't want the fact that I told him that it had been done to me to diminish from the sense that he had of it being wrong – of him having been wronged. Humiliated. Hurt.

It was after Alvin had gone, and before Leon arrived back with T-Roy that I gestured for Roman to come and cuddle in with me, which he did, Debbie still being with us on the couch. "That happened to me as well," I told him, which made him jerk his head back to look into my eyes. "When I was a boy, but I was older than you are."

"Did you tell?"

"You didn't tell!" I told him emphatically! "Your mum found Deep Heat in your undies. She asked you and you had no choice but to explain. Okay?" Repeat the official story often enough and hopefully he will believe it.

"Did you tell?"

"There wasn't anyone for me to tell." And I wish I hadn't said that – or in that way – because it made me sound as though I was playing the 'poor pityful orphan that nobody cared about', when that wasn't how my childhood had been. I probably could have told my House Mother, or House Father, but I didn't. I understood the secrecy, the silent conspiracy of not telling, which allowed the practice to continue over the years – though I had been surprised to find that it was still happening. Why had I thought it had ended, just because it was all so long ago for me? "But it's a bad thing to do to anyone, and I have never done it or been involved in doing it to anyone."

He wanted to know, so I told him the details. It hadn't happened in the home, but on an activity with other boys, from ordinary families, together, away, and without close adult supervision. It was the same old tired initiation idea, an opportunity for the bigger boys to demonstrate their dominance over the younger boys, as if their size and status was not enough. Was it dominance, or was it curiosity about other children's privates, which they couldn't satisfy by furtive glances? An initiation to supposedly belong to some club or society, which would have held no appeal to us anyway, let alone the supposed price of admission.

There had been three of us new boys, and with the power of their size and numbers, we had been told what would happen to us. There was nowhere to run and hide, no escape from what we had found our fate would be.

We were seized from behind and held in a standing full Nelson – a substantially bigger boy standing behind me, his arms hooked under my armpits, his hands, fingers laced, at the back of my head pushing my head forward. We were facing inwards in a semicircle, while the torturer – almost executioner – `did' the first boy; pulling down and off his trousers and undies, while henchmen held his ankles apart, and with one hand holding the boys penis out of the way, the other gathered the testicles into the scrotum and rubbed Deep Heat into them.

I was the second, the middle one. I heard and saw the anguish of the first, but didn't have to wait as long as the last. "What's wrong with your cock?" asked the thug rubbing my scrotum with his Deep Heat coated fingers.

I dreaded this. "It's called `circumcised'," I told him – and them. None of them seem to know about it, and I found myself yet again having to explain, although these were in the harshest of circumstances. "The skin was cut off by a doctor when I was a baby."

"Why?" Thinking back, I remember there was a change in attitude then, from the dominance to curiosity.

"I don't know. It happened before I came to Ferndale. My House Parents don't know."

"What's Ferndale?" Asked my torturer, his fingers moved my penis from side to side, as they saw the scar going completely around the shaft. The others crowded closer to look.

"Ferndale Hall!" One of the local boys told him. "It's the orphanage." They were curious, and they paid more attention to me in this way than the other two boys who were intact. Adding insult to injury!

After that, we were released, and allowed to go and wash – the boy who had gone first having suffered the most. There was a James -like figure who came and apologised and tried to comfort, but unlike Roman's James, this boy hadn't attempted to make any intervention at the time, either physically or verbally.

Roman listened on my lap and allowed me to cuddle and comfort him.

"Men!" Debbie stated disapprovingly.

"Boys!" I corrected her.

"Males!"

"I think it was worse for you, Roman," I told him. "I was older when it happened to me, I think about twelve. And there were two other boys there that it happened to as well, so I wasn't on my own like you were." No need to tell him that one of the other boys, who was 'done' first, was Leon and that the third was Kevin.

*

And so, it came to pass, that things were set in place for me to meet and have my conversation with the other boys who had been involved. Alvin reported back to me that all of

them would attend, and that they knew that together they had to come for me to speak to them. I had choreographed it, of course. One can't leave things like this to chance, although something unexpected might always happen. Alvin was briefed to tell the boys that I wanted to speak to them together, in view of but out of earshot, of their parents and others attending the picnic, and that my discussion was ostensibly to discuss with them how to assist a child who became homesick on camp. That was to be the cover story. Alvin was to assure them that I had held him responsible, and that I had dealt with him, and if I was satisfied with the discussion, and what they had to say for themselves, the matter would be over, but not forgotten.

There was a tall willow tree on its own, some distance away from where the people were setting up their barbecues, and I indicated that this would be where we would meet, and the sign for them to join us would be when Roman and I walked over to the tree and stopped there.

Of course, T-Roy was a challenge, as I didn't want him to know what was happening, and certainly not for him to be present. He hated being excluded from anything, little busybody that he was, and although Leon would have been willing to attend long enough to keep T-Roy occupied, I knew that Leon did not feel comfortable in such situations, and that his presence was likely to draw yet more attention from those who would be aware of me meeting with the boys. I had a pep talk with T-Roy, saying that I needed him to be obedient and to stay away while I discussed with the boys things about the camp that I had had to fetch Roman

66

back from early. T-Roy didn't buy it, and I had to be firm and just tell him that this was the way that it was going to be. I outlined to him a line between two objects and told him that he had to stay that side of the line, until I signalled to him that he could come to me.

*

Once I had seen that all the required boys had arrived, which involved eye contact at some distance, I set off with Roman to the tree, and they trooped after us; Alvin, Tom, Dan, Ben and James. I stood and invited them to sit on the ground in front of me. At first Roman stood beside me, but I was aware of an 'us and them' optic, so in his ear gently asked him if he would sit next to Alvin, who, having been dealt with and knowing that there was no further threat to him providing that the deal was kept to, was possibly more relaxed than the others. I asked Alvin to look after him, without labouring the irony with this request, and Roman was content to settle down on the ground next to him.

What I had not expected, was that there was one more boy than I had expected. I knew him to be Luke, and as far as I knew he had not been on the camp, let alone involved in what happened – what they did to Roman.

"What are you doing here, Luke?" I asked him – using his name to show that I knew exactly who he was, just as I made a point of addressing the other boys by their names. There was no anonymity offered to them.

67

"I'm part of the group," Luke replied respectfully. "I wasn't on the camp this time, but I normally would be."

"Do you know what this is about? I mean – really about? More than the idea of Roman being homesick?"

"Yes, I think so."

"I told him," Alvin admitted. "I told him before you told me not to tell anyone and to keep it secret."

"Do you want me to go?" Luke asked.

"I think you can stay, if you already know. You weren't there so you aren't responsible for – what was done to Roman, but if you're part of the group, and you know about it, then I include you in the deal I am offering your friends."

I outlined what I had told Alvin previously starting by restating the narrative that Roman had not told tales, and that Debbie had found his underpants smelling of Deep Heat and of course this was not something that any mother, or parent, would ignore, and faced with such direct questions, Roman had had no choice but to admit what had happened.

I noticed that Alvin was nodding along to this, which I was pleased with, as they might have remembered that they had covered their tracks better than I was giving them credit for, and there was a pair of underpants missing from the kit that Roman had brought home with him, so presumably one of them had had the sense to hide the evidence. A possible recruit for my Directorate in the future?

68

Then there was the point that I had required Alvin to make a detailed statement to me on exactly what had happened, and who had done what – again to reinforce the narrative that Roman was not a tattletale. Alvin confirmed this, adding; "and he wrote it all down!" Good boy!

When I repeated what I had told Alvin that an offence had been committed, and that the punishment was deserved, that I held him responsible, and he had been punished, and providing that I witnessed them offering a sincere apology to Roman, undertaking never to do that or similar to anyone else in the future and not to divulge our discussion, that would be the end of it. Breaches in this agreement would lead to the agreement being invalid, and probably my first step would be to tell their parents what they had done and demand that the parents punished them in a way I considered satisfactory, or I could take things further – repeating that it was a sexual assault, and that the police would have to investigate.

"So that is my offer to you. I am satisfied that Alvin has told me the truth about what you did to Roman, so I don't feel I need to go through that with you. If any of you feels that you want to meet with me to tell me your side of events, I will be happy to give you a chance to do that."

From their seated positions, they were looking up to me, but none of them responded – which did not surprise me in the slightest. I asked each of them by name specifically if they were content that Alvin had told me the truth and although reluctant, I pushed them until I got a yes from each of them.

69

Despite allowing for the unexpected, it had thrown me a little how Luke had come along, not involved, and so not at risk of punishment, but in the know, and therefore needing to be bound by the secrecy I was imposing on the others.

"What was the punishment that Alvin got?" He asked innocently.

I had to feed the legend here, and not admit that apart from me threatening and intimidating a fourteen-year-old, Alvin hadn't actually been punished because I not foreseen Roman's unwillingness to execute the punishment I felt was appropriate with the good old-fashioned `an eye for an eye'!

I looked at Alvin, who met my gaze. "We have agreed that we will keep that confidential between us," I told Luke. "But if anyone of you really wants to know, I will make you the offer of the same thing happening to you… Then you wouldn't have to listen to my speech…" (Which you've already heard by now.) And then Alvin surprised me, but reminded me again that he was a teenage schoolboy, with some banter with his mates, now that the situation was heading towards resolution. Possibly too much bravado …

"But I'll tell you something," he said to his mates. "If I had to choose between getting caned six on my bare arse, I would choose that over… what happened."

I'm not sure that I wanted him to develop this much further, in case their imaginations run riot. "Don't over dramatise it, Alvin!" I intervened; "but would you agree that I was fair with you? Did you agree to what I did?"

70

"Yes, it was fair. Yes, I agreed."

And I warned him off. "I think you'd better stop there, Alvin. Don't make them too curious...."

Again, with the bravery of not being under threat of punishment, Luke asked again; "Can I ask you something, Uncle Max, without making you angry?"

"How am I going to know that until I know what your question is?"

"I'm sorry it happened to Roman, but it's happened to all of us. It's something that happens."

"But it stops now!" I said firmly, shutting down his question, which was essentially about traditions. "Roman is the last person that it was done to, and he will not want to do it to anybody else." (I can say that with some authority!) "None of you are to do this to anyone else in the future. And I expect you to stop this from happening to anybody else, even if it's not you that does it. Do we understand each other?"

There was a murmur of ascent. We were getting close to my choreographed finale, but I had one specific little knife to twist and turn.

"How big are your balls, Tom?"

"Huh?" He grunted at me before a sidelong glare at Alvin demanding without saying it; 'Why did you tell him that?'

71

"Are they the same size now as they were when you were nine-years-old?" I pushed Tom, who had dropped his gaze to the grass in front of him, with him pulling out a tuft or two with his fingers.

"Yes, his balls are still the same size as when he was nine!" Alvin joked, his punishment over, he was more relaxed. All of the boys, except for Tom and Roman, burst out into laughter, possibly excessively at some relief from the tension that I had created. If looks could have killed, the glare that Tom shot at Alvin at that moment would have vaporised him. It was still too raw in Romans mind for him to have found it funny, despite the humiliation of Tom. Tom moved his gaze back to the grass in front of him which he continued to torture.

"Just know, Tom, that I have the image in my mind of you, more than any of the others doing what you did to Roman, and saying what you said. I will not forget it."

I let that settle in with the silence, long enough to make my point. Then I repeated the deal, and again asked each boy by name if they agreed to my deal, would consider it binding on them, and accepted the consequences if they broke it, me specifying that if one broke it, I would be telling the parents of all what had happened.

Luke complicated matters, because there was nothing that I could charge him with to his parents, but from what I knew of him, he was a decent lad. If he had been on the camp, I would like to think that he would have joined with James

and talked the others out of doing what they did. He did not hesitate to agree to be bound by the agreement as well. I left Tom until last, and then clarified that although I knew what role he had played, and would not forget, I would do nothing further to him if he complied, and he agreed.

Then there was the cover story to agree, because my meeting with the boys would have been noticed, and questions would be asked. "If anybody asks what we have been talking about, I have been discussing with you how to help somebody who is homesick on camp." There was a murmur of agreement. "This isn't really fair on Roman, as he's been on Cub Camp, and he didn't get homesick at all."

"So, if someone hears that this is what we have been talking about and they ask `so what did Max suggest?' What are you going to say?" Blank faces looked up at me. "That I told you that you should try to keep him busy, actively involved in things, encouraging him to do things helpful to the camp even if – and don't let him know this – they are unnecessary. Keep praising him and telling him he's doing a good job and being helpful. Don't let him be on his own." I paused for that to sink in. "Agree?"

Again, there was a murmur of agreement.

My frustrated inner-choreographer kicked in again, to bring the meeting to a conclusion. "To end this, I want each of you to come and stand in front of Roman, apologise to him, and say that you understand he had no choice but to tell when his mom asked him, and to promise that you won't be doing

73

anything like this to anyone again. But only do this if you mean it. Then you shake hands with Roman. Then, if you agree with our deal you shake on it with me, and then you are free to go."

"Tom, I know what I've said to you here, but if you can do this, and you keep your part of the bargain, it ends now." He had stopped torturing the grass, but was still avoiding eye contact.

I told Roman to come and stand next to me, and, Alvin first, I got him to repeat after me an oath of the wording I had outlined, he shook hands with Roman, and then shook hands with me and stood aside to allow the next boy. I prompted Tom, who did what was required of him, and when he was shaking my hand, he looked up to me and I could see there were tears in his eyes. Maybe there are other things going on in his head. Luke was the last, and he surprised me by taking the initiative and telling Roman; "I'm very sorry about what happened to you. We like you, and I hope you come camping again." Then he shook Roman's hand and moved over to shake mine.

This completed, the boys started to head back to the barbecue area, but I called James back to me, assuring him that it was `nothing bad.'

"I understand that you tried to protect Roman, and you tried to stop them..."

I had been surprised to hear this of James, as my impression of him was that he was a bit of a wimp, and, if anything,

likely to be slightly bullied by the other boys. So, for him to have stood up to them, to try to protect a vulnerable child, was that much more commendable.

"I tried, but I couldn't," James answered, apologetically.

"You tried, and I am very impressed with that. Most of them are bigger than you, and you did your best to protect my son. I owe you, and if I can ever be helpful to you, just let me know. I don't know what this might be, but please remember it."

"Thank you!"

"I know that we are being watched, but this publicly, I would like to shake your hand. Is that okay with you?"

"That's fine," James replied, and I shook his hand, adding my other hand over his wrist as a magnification of the handshake. When it ended, I patted his shoulder as he turned to follow his friends back to the barbecue area.

Roman had returned to the barbecue area with Alvin and the others, de-emphasising the 'us and them' that had taken place. With James trotting off after them, I could then see my most favourite little martyr in the entire world, T-Roy straining at the invisible boundary that I had imposed upon him, a study in dejected solitude, having fended off all attempts by his little friends to engage him in their games as he stood scowling his displeasure – awaiting my signal that would release his restrictions.

I patted the top of my head in the `come to me' signal, and `releasing the dogs of war' does not do justice to the speed with which he bounded over. "MyDaddy!" He yelled as he ran, and leapt up into my arms, and enjoyed me rolling him around my torso for a little bit before, with my hands in his armpits, I plonked him down sitting on my shoulders. He had forgiven me already, and we were best mates again. That, along with all the other roles I served to him, as a sparring partner, climbing frame, activity centre... The list goes on. Even what he called me; `MyDaddy' was the name he had developed and stuck with, part of it denoted that I was his property. I could live with that!

"MyDaddy," he asked, his voice going up as part of a question. "Was that about them putting heat in Romey's willy?"

Oh fuck!

If T-Roy knows about it, it's going to be common knowledge. T-Roy loved secrets, but his ability to keep them – what's a good way to say is `non-existent'? And he knows!

He was sitting on my shoulders, so I couldn't see his face, but I feign disinterest to try to minimise the game that he would play of I know something that you don't and you won't be able to get it out of me, and also so he wouldn't exaggerate.

"No, that isn't what happened. Sam put Deep Heat in his bellybutton!"

"Oh no," I was corrected by the world authority on everything sitting above me on my shoulders. "It was Tom, and he put Heat in Romey's willy."

"How can you put anything in someone's willy?" I asked, feigning not knowing anything on the subject. I did know that T-Roy was most interested in his penis, and paid little attention to his scrotum, apart from an exaggerated pull away from my hand, sometimes when I washed him there.

"On the outside, at the bottom of his willy..." Of course he's going to try and say the word `willy' as much as he possibly can. "Where his willy joins onto his body. And on his balls."

Okay, so he's confirming what I believed happened, and I really didn't want to think about them forcing any Deep Heat into his urethra. I don't think they were sophisticated enough to think of anything like that, and certainly Alvin seem stunned at the idea of variations on the Deep Heat on testicles, which was a known practice.

"I don't want you to tell anyone about this," I told him, and I lifted him off my shoulders to be at eye level in front of me while I told him this. "If anyone ever says they want to do anything like that to you, you tell them that you will tell me straight away, okay?"

"I'm not supposed to tell tales," T-Roy told me, triumphantly at being able to quote law to me, although I don't think that this was anything that I had ever tried to impress on either of my boys, wanting open communication.

"No one is allowed to do anything to you that you don't feel is right, and no one is allowed to hurt you. When you are big enough to look after yourself, then that's fine, but until then if anyone is bigger and stronger than you, or if there's more than one person who wants to do something to hurt you, you tell them immediately that you will tell me."

"And what will you do? Will you go and beat them up?"

"Hopefully by you just telling them, they'll decide that they had better leave you alone."

"But if they don't, and I have to tell you, … would you shoot them?"

In time I might tell him about my time as a combat soldier, but not for a while. I didn't want the conversation of 'Did you kill people?' I didn't want him to know that. I preferred to leave that vague, despite his interest.

"And I don't want you to ever do that to anyone," I told him.

"Why not?"

"Because it hurts people, and it's very rude, and its bullying…"

"I know it hurts…"

"How do you know?" I asked, but it was obvious where he was going.

"I tried it on myself. When I was in the bath. It hurt, so I washed it off!"

78

"Who told you about this?" But I knew, that he would have nagged, persuaded, and cajoled Roman into sharing the secret of why he had come back from camp early, and to get some peace and quiet from T-Roy, Roman would probably have told T-Roy how secret it was, and that he was not to tell anyone. And T-Roy would have 'crossed his heart and hoped to die' and wouldn't even have had his fingers crossed to invalidate this as he assured Roman that he would keep the secret.

T-Roy knows, so we have to assume that everyone will now know. But the boys don't need to know that I know, and I know the source of the information so it might be good to keep them on their toes, as, if it is discussed, as I'm sure it will be amongst T-Roy's age group, who would have a big boy's story to tantalise older brothers with their secret knowledge. Let the boys I had just agreed a contract with start to sweat when they find that it is common knowledge, that it might reach me, and I might very well do as I threatened; negate our deal and demand satisfactory punishment from their parents.

Back up on my shoulders, T-Roy sensed that there was still more he could milk from this conversation. "If not willies, am I allowed to put Deep Heat in somebody's tummy button?"

"Why would you want to do that?" That shut him up while he tried to think of some answer, as we reached the picnic area.

It occurred to me how different it would have been if Alvin and the boys had done to T-Roy what they had done to Roman —at the same age. Little show off that he is, if he had managed not to tell them before his pants were pulled down, he would delight in telling them that his daddy didn't have skin covering the acorn at the end of his willy, and that it had been cut off when he was a baby. Circumcision wasn't common, and the boys might be a bit puzzled about this – wondering whether I might have been of Jewish heritage, despite them knowing we went to a Protestant church. T-Roy would have been enjoying all of the attention being directed at his willy, and if Tom had said to T-Roy what he had said about Roman, T-Roy would have been more than willing to have found his testicles to show Tom. T-Roy would have enjoyed all the attention, until suddenly the pain hit him, and then he would have been surprised and emotionally hurt that they would wish to cause him pain. The boys have very different personalities with, only mild traces of Debbie and my personalities in them.

*

That's the end of this story really. As far as I know – and from the information I got – or didn't get from the grapevine, none of those boys did anything like that to another younger child. It seemed that somehow, despite what they might actually have known, I never got wind of anything about any of them accusing Roman of having told tales, or having informed on him, and they seem to be as friendly with him as they had been, prior to them inviting him to go camping with them. I did ask Roman from time to

time, in general terms, whether there had been any consequences, and the way that he didn't seem to know what I was talking about indicated to me that there weren't any, rather than him becoming tense, and denying that.

Roman went on another Cub Camp after that, which he was fine with, but he didn't want to go up to Scouts when he was the right age. And although Alvin and the boys kept inviting him to go camping with them again – to give them a second chance, possibly – he never did.

Chapter Two

T-Roy

This chapter belongs to T-Roy

— (signed) T-Roy Russell Maxwell

You knew when T-Roy had arrived! The phrase `the doors burst open' is the description that would best describe T-Roy's entry into our bedroom most mornings, except that the door would not be shut. He would suddenly appear, as he leapt into the room, the naked ninja, standing at the foot of where I lay, making rapid pseudo-martial arts poses, of being about to strike. He was stark naked as he did this, and I did my best to conceal my amusement at the way his willy jiggled around as he made his ferocious high kicks and punches into the air. Thinking back on to it later, it probably was a variation of a Maori *haka*, but we didn't know much about such things.

He knew that he was not allowed to make any sounds, which might disturb Debbie, but couldn't quite manage to do it silently, so his ferocious moves would be accompanied by half stifled little war-cries, which sounded more like a kitten mewing than the bloodcurdling shouts and screams he wished them to be. I would play along, silently, showing him a cartoonlike war face, and we would stare each other down, until – there was always a mutually agreed point, at which time I would raise my hands up in surrender, and open the bedclothes beside me for him – his mission

accomplished – to slip in and cuddle up beside me. He was 'Mr Giggly Wiggly' and he could not keep still, and it was for this reason that his place was on the far side of me, to reduce the disruption to Debbie who really liked to sleep in. It was good that we had bought the biggest bed we could find!

T-Roy's place in our bed was on my side and between me and the edge of the bed. He grudgingly accepted this, as he would dearly have loved to have been between us, as Roman was. But on the rare occasions when we gave him another chance, his temptation was too great for him to bear, and subconsciously at first, his hand would migrate to his willy and he would start fiddling, which Debbie would be aware of despite Roman being between her and T-Roy, so his position was relegated to the far side of me, with me tolerating his relentless fiddling, and cuddling him into me. For discussions, he would generally be sitting up, and looking over me to join in the conversation with Roman and Debbie, so he didn't really miss out.

When we awoke, Roman would always be between us, cuddled up on Debbie's side, having slunk in during the night. To some extent, Debbie encouraged this, to have him as something of a human shield between her and me, and it will sound harsh, but she explained that it would mean that I didn't bump into her directly, if I stirred in my sleep. I knew there was more to this, but it was important to her, and at some stage Roman would no longer wish to slip into bed with us. T-Roy was incapable of slinking.

Roman was a lighter sleeper than I was, and although he was not tired during the day, his eyes always seemed to be open, and he watched what was happening around him. This did not strike me as vigilance, but rather of curiosity and interest. He liked to watch.

When he slept, T-Roy slept more soundly even than Debbie, and was inclined to lie on his back and snore in the nest of the mattress and blankets and other soft furnishings he had gathered in the room. Debbie called his sleeping arrangements `his nest'! When T-Roy was awake, he was awake, and he wanted to be up and active. I would tell him that that it was not `fighty fighty time' and he would have to be still if he got in, and he would snuggle into bed beside me. But even if it was not `fighty fighty' time, any hope of quietly, drowsily staying in bed ended with T-Roy's arrival, as he would squirm, and engage me in conversation.

*

I have two sons, and I didn't grow up with brothers, and growing up in Ferndale Hall was, I suspect, a different experience from how my childhood would have been if I had grown up in a conventional family, with parents and maybe a brother and sister or more. Debbie had no siblings, and her extensive knowledge about children is mostly from her nurse training, and experience as a paediatric nurse, and while she studied exhaustively, there is probably a very academic aspect to her knowledge about children, which is not necessarily a bad thing.

I got to name both boys. Roman and Troy - suitably martial names. Debbie could just about live with that. She would have got to name them if they had been girls. But Roman lent itself to being shortened to 'Rome' or more usually 'Romey', and at a surprisingly young age, Troy rebranded himself as 'T-Roy,' because he liked the sound of it better. (Just go with the flow, Max. Don't make an issue about it. He'll grow out of it. We live in hope.) Roman is the eternal dreamer, while T-Roy is a physical dynamo.

I was intrigued by the differences in personality between T-Roy and Roman, and what evidence this presented for the 'Nature-Nurture debate', even accepting their two-year age difference. Roman, when he was little, and tottering around, would take great delight in going and fetching things and bringing them to present to Debbie, who had to accept them graciously, even though she often had no use for the various leaves and pebbles et cetera that he brought to her so proudly. When we went on holiday to the beach, Roman would investigate the rock pools, and collect all sorts of shiny minor treasures which he found fascinating, and he would take these back to Debbie, partly as gifts to her, and partly for her to store for him to consider later.

T-Roy was turbocharged, in contrast, and would delight in chasing the seagulls, until they decided to leave him as the king of the beach, after which he would chase the waves as they retreated, and flee from them when they chased him up the beach.

Similarly, at the park, Roman would be content on the swings, and would seem to go into a state of bliss, while T-Roy would start with the swings, then go to the seesaw, where he would need my attention to help him go up and down, then he would be all over the jungle gym climbing frame, then the roundabout, before returning to the swings, which Roman had never left. Roman would be willing to ride on the roundabout as well but seemed content to spend most of the time on the swings. At home, from when he was old enough to start to take an interest, I would engage Roman in board games of drafts, in preparation for chess as soon as he was old enough, and he would be happy to help me with cooking tasks in the kitchen. T-Roy was a Snakes and Ladders enthusiast, and really enjoyed Lego, making fantastic crafts of various descriptions, which would then involve noisily flying them around and creating stories leading to their eventual violent destruction, and either being rebuilt into something different, or a different activity would be sought. I had to be very careful with T-Roy in the kitchen, and Debbie and I agreed that she would spend time with him while I was cooking with Roman, as he had a fascination with knives, and their possible use as weapons, which I wished to discourage. Both had bicycles, which again Roman enjoyed the aesthetics of riding, whereas T-Roy would be ramping over things, attempting to do stunts and I had to do much more repair work and adjustment work on T-Roy's bikes than I ever had to on Roman's.

I had been as active as I could as a dad from the start, being surprised just how much interaction and what utter delight

even young babies could be, and just how happy having them gazing up into my eyes made me. I would like the world to be a better place for Debbie than she knows it to be, and where I could, I would do the nappy changes, which were practical, and I concluded that most of the men who protested about it where making a mountain out of a mole hill.

Roman was our first, and he loved to be touched, would seem to be catatonic with bliss while I changed him, and powdered him, and as a boy he loved being stroked and massaged, which would always send him into quiet ecstasy.

T-Roy was different from the start, and would see being on a changing mat as being an invitation to play, reaching up to engage with me with both his hands and his feet; a very active baby. It hardly took him any time at all, since he worked out that he could direct his hands and arms, for him to discover his willy, and that's where his hands would head when he found himself naked on the changing mat.

T-Roy would be easily distracted by me tickling his tummy, walking my hand up his chest and tapping his nose or any of the other little things that one can do that absolutely delights a baby, who will squeal and giggle again, and again! But, during any downtime, his hand would gravitate down to his willy.

I am aware, despite not having grown up in a conventional family, that little boys with the hands down the front of their pants were seen as 'dirty' and, somehow, 'immoral',

but how could one judge a toddler in that way. Certainly, I was aware that this was something that T-Roy did excessively, and we had Roman to compare him with, who would touch his, but nowhere near the amount of time that T-Roy did. It could have been an issue for Debbie, due to factors which I will allude to later, but I was glad that she shared my view that he did it because he liked it, and did not indicate anything wrong with him, either physically or psychologically. We did pay attention when bathing him as to whether there might be some infection, but never noticed anything, and just as a precaution when he was about four, Debbie arranged for him to meet with one of her consultant paediatrician colleagues, who agreed that there was nothing physically wrong, and when the lady asked him the obvious why do you do it, his reply indicated that because it felt nice – no, more than that, it was `better than a big fat bowl of ice cream!' And that's saying something! `A big fat bowl of ice-cream' - became a family legend, not just a quotable quote between Debbie and me in our intimate moments.

Several generations before, such behaviour would have so outraged parental morals that physical steps would have been taken to prevent it, including possible circumcision, but Debbie and I without debate would not have entertained any suggestion of this; Debbie was fully against any unnecessary pain for our beloved child, as was I. Despite having been circumcised myself, I was very clear that I wanted my boys to remain intact, and we would do everything we could to relegate that to being the last

possible step, if either of them had medical problems, which they didn't.

We knew that judgements could be made, and comments made, and possibly that he might get a reputation of being `dirty' or a 'pervert' – surely not as a preschool child, but we knew there could be social consequences for him which we would wish to prevent happening. So we did the best that we could to contain it, to let him know that he could do it at home, or with his granny – having told her our philosophy and policy, which she accepted – keeping any reservation she might have had to herself.

I believe he tried hard to keep his hands away from it in public, but when he was in his bath, his penis would get his full attention. He would make it stand up or lie down. Roman didn't like bathing with T-Roy because of his play, and the way that when they were both naked, his interest would extend to Roman. Sometimes T-Roy would be trying to persuade Roman to bath with him, and a precondition that Roman would attempt to get from him was `no touching me!' I don't think that T-Roy ever managed to keep to his side of the bargain. As long as he wasn't being touched, and it was just amongst family, Roman quite liked being able to be superior to the childish behaviour of his little brother, or so he maintained, but I think he was very discreet in his interest.

T-Roy heard the part about `don't let anyone touch you there unless you allow that' differently from the way most people would assume that their child would interpret it;

with an emphasis on the `don't' whereas he focussed on the `my choice'. We were aware that he was quite likely to be liberal in who he allowed. We need to think of a different strategy!

*

Debbie was tolerant of my preference to sleep naked, and when I had offered to wear shorts, her bravery kicked in and she decided that she needed to fight her demons and didn't want her issues to inhibit me. When the boys were out of nappies, the boys could sleep naked, although we agreed that they would have pyjamas available to them, and that they would be required to put them on as part of the bedtime routine. Roman, being so tactile, and the way that he loved the feelings of the sheets on his skin meant that he usually shed his pyjamas, but, as always, it would become a game for T-Roy, who would playfully pull on his pyjama bottoms, way too high, but would then immediately pull them down and off, and jump stark naked into his bed with a cheeky Cheshire cat grin on his face. I probably have to acknowledge some responsibility for the role model I served to them.

We bought a four-bedroom suburban house, Debbie and I commandeering the master bedroom, with the boys having bunks in the second-largest room, with the third-largest room being Debbie's and my shared study, with the massage bench, my filing cabinets and our bookshelves for the books we didn't want in the lounge, and the smallest bedroom was nominally for Roman, with him being the

elder, and when he wanted a room to himself, although we would probably juggle things around when we reach that stage. At present, Roman preferred to continue to share with T-Roy, the top bunk being his, where he could watch what his younger brother got up to, as T-Roy was always very busy. We had a spare bedroom, which was nominally Roman's.

On weekends and holidays, if we were not in a hurry to get up, the boys would join us in our bed, but it wasn't restricted to those days, it happened every night, and we liked it as it was. Roman would saunter or slink in, quietly and gracefully and snuggle in beside Debbie, sometime during the night, after having spent an hour or two in his own bed. I would be aware of him joining us, even though he had to climb over Debbie to get between us, but he cuddled up to Debbie. Debbie was a fairly heavy sleeper, but when she felt him curled in beside her, she would stroke his arm, as if he was a cat, and he would go into a trancelike state. We never made love in our bed, so there was no risk of him walking in to find us in a compromising position. There was no need for man and wife privacy in our bed. None of what lovemaking we did happened there, and it was a place for relaxation and conversation - and sleep! Debbie slept in white shorts and a white T-shirt and the boys knew I slept naked.

*

I know that many – if they knew – would consider me to be wrong to tolerate this behaviour from T-Roy, and that by

With a discussion, of this type or another, Debbie knew that her dozing time was over. Certainly T-Roy could be annoying, but he had the most disarming smile and knew how to turn on the charm so few people managed to stay annoyed with him for long.

"Do you want the lecture?" I asked. It was a lecture that they had both heard before about us needing food, the miracle of the body digesting food into energy, and the waste products which were normal and natural, and that defecating was a necessary part of one's life, though not pleasant and to be done in privacy. I would map out on one of their tummies the approximate location of the different organs on their chests and tummies, which they pushed down the bedclothes to reveal and make available. I gave T-Roy the brief chance to lie between his brother and me for this demonstration. Debbie watched with amusement, delighting in correcting me every inch of the way on the internal anatomy, from her acknowledged greater expertise with being a paediatric nurse, and with me touching tummies, there was a teasing ticklish action.

T-Roy loved it of course, because of the `how does the liquid come out' would take him straight back to his favourite subject. He was enjoying it deliciously. I outlined, just above his groin, where his bladder would be, and he had an erection.

"What's this then?" I asked him, brushing my hand over the bulge it made in the blanket.

"That's his penis," Debbie informed me. Ah, she was joining in. "It's like yours, only ... (mischievous exchange of glances between us) ... His is smaller!" There were fits of giggles from both boys.

Sometimes she would surprise me by spontaneously joining in, but at other times, feigning outrage, she would tell me; "You're just as bad as they are!" which would get protestations from Roman who was subtle and discreet generally in his crudity, whereas subtlety and discretion were not part of T-Roy's repertoire.

No matter how provocatively crude T-Roy tried to be, Roman could always trump him. I am sure that outside of Debbie's earshot, Roman would remind T-Roy that he, Roman, had weed in my mouth. It had been when he was a baby and I had been changing his nappy. Apparently Debbie, and her mom, knew that little baby boys, if their bladder hadn't emptied into the nappy that was being replaced, felt pressure building up, they would get an erection, which would then direct a flow of wee upwards, and right into the face of anyone naïvely changing their nappy. So when it was that my beautiful innocent older baby son wee'd upwards, I had my mouth open as I was talking to Debbie, and the inevitable happened. Debbie was very amused, and the story became part of our family heritage. There was an aspect of Debbie's humour that, although she was clear how important it was for me to be her protector, it amused her to see me taken by surprise in situations that I had no knowledge of, especially, when she had been warned. I accepted this – eventually – and I saw the joke. T-Roy

94

thought it was profoundly unfair, because I learned from this, and so whenever his willy stood up when I was changing him, I placed something absorbent over it. It was amongst his repertoire of conversations to have with me, usually subtly out of earshot of Debbie of how he felt he had been deprived because Roman had weed in my mouth, and he never had the chance. And he never would, despite how sweetly he might ask – and he knew it!

*

T-Roy had a party piece, and this related to circumcision, a subject he found endlessly fascinating. He knew that I was circumcised, and that he was not.

Probably my favourite anecdote on the subject was, before he realised the provocative and attention seeking element to exploring his privates, while massaging his foreskin, he declared proudly; "I love my willy! And I've got another one inside!"

Usually there would be an interest in my body, either him sort of exploring my body downwards, or else he would just ask straight out; "Can I see your willy?" He would never say `it'; he relished saying `willy', or `penis' when we were being serious.

I would allow it, as long as I wasn't erect. Even if it was, that wouldn't be too much of a problem, as the boys accepted the explanation that willies stood up if they were happy, but if they didn't, it didn't necessarily mean they were sad. They knew not to show them to others or make their willies

happy deliberately when they were in company, which wasn't an issue for Roman, but we had to keep a watch on T-Roy.

Today he was following one of the variations on a well-worn path. "Where's the skin over your acorn, MyDaddy?" He asked, and I told him – as he well knew, that it had been taken away in an operation when I was a baby.

"Did it hurt?" Roman asked.

"I can't remember. It happened before I could remember anything."

"It would have hurt," Debbie informed him. "In hospital I've seen the operation being done, and I've nursed little boys afterwards. It's very sore for a couple of days."

Sometimes Roman would make the point that he didn't want the conversation to take place. Was this because he felt awkward - or was he just asserting himself - so I would suggest that he clamped his hands over his ears, which generally satisfied him, and having made his point about not being interested, he certainly seemed to be following every word.

"What's the word for it?"

"`Circumcised.'"

"`Cir cum cised ...'" he savoured the word. "Why didn't you do it to Romey?"

"Have you asked Roman if it's okay for us to talk about him?"

"Its okay, Romey, isn't it?"

Roman did what we knew he would do, he clamped his hands over his ears, implying that he couldn't hear, but we knew he would be listening. It's a good system. Debbie knew what was coming, and just wanted to keep out of it, trying to grasp a few more moments of sleep, but she and I knew this was doomed to failure. Often, she just tolerated the banter I had with T-Roy, but on some occasions, she signalled to me that she wasn't in the mood, and I would shut it down.

So, I started to tell the well travelled story, which, probably like a favourite bedtime story, T-Roy enjoyed hearing, even though he could probably say it word for word along with me. "I asked Roman if he wanted to be circumcised when he was a baby, and he said `weeeh weeeh' " - my impression of two baby cries, "so I checked and asked him if he wanted his foreskin left alone and he said `weeeh', so I knew he wanted it left alone."

"So, when you were a baby, I asked you " - me hastily clamping my hand over T-Roy's mouth - gagging his words. Or the impression he would make of the impression I had attributed to the baby Roman. Which he knew I would do because we have had exactly the same conversation several times before – "and you said;` '"T-Roy loved this, tugging

ineffectually at my hand, shouting into my hand, with his eyes sparkling as he enjoyed the game.

"See! You didn't want it either."

I let T-Roy go. He bubbled with pleasure. "Why don't you ask me now?" he giggled.

"Okay," I said. "T-Roy, do you ..." and now I do a `Roman' and clamp my hands over my ears. " ... want to be circumcised?"

"Yes, yes, yes," T-Roy shouts, trying to tug my hands away from his ears. I have to break my gesture to put a finger over my lips to remind T-Roy to quieten down, as Debbie was still being tolerant at this stage. He waited for me to return my hands to my ears. I turned to Roman beside me, his hands now as tightly over his ears as mine were to mine. "Can you hear anything?" I ask Roman, who vigorously shakes his head `no', with probably as big a grin as T-Roy has.

"No, neither can I!" I confirm conspiratorially.

"I want it!" T-Roy tugged my arm to convey his urgency.

"Want what?" I knew that T-Roy struggled to remember the word.

I was aware of Roman behind me, hands still clamped on his ears - no one is fooled, but it has some symbolic value - exaggeratedly mouthing `cir - cum - cised' to T-Roy. The hands-on-his-ears is to signify `I want no part in this', but his

98

mouth betrays this. Roman, you are a hypocrite. Just like your father!

T-Roy was trying to make it out, and then had a guess – "Cir cun strised" ... and then he remembered and said it right. Triumphantly!

There were different variations on this game. I was amused at how he struggled to remember the word.

"What's the magic word?" I asked him.

"I said it," T-Roy replied, but he had lost the word again.

"The magic word," I repeated, and then I had to help him. "It starts with P... "

"Penis?" He offered.

"No, if you want something you have to say `please'!"

I continued the inevitable – please can I have it – please can you have what – please can I have and again he lost the word, but his oh so helpful older brother prompted him again, and he got it.

"Oh, all right then!" I said feigning reassignment in my voice. "You go and fetch a towel, so we don't get blood all over the sheets, and I'll go and fetch my knife." (Mention of my knife would attract the attention of both boys, as they were fascinated by it, and wanted to touch it.)

Now T-Roy and I had entered a game of chicken. Who was going to blink first? We both knew it would be me.

T-Roy, the little nudist was almost out of the bedroom to fetch the towel.

"No," said Debbie suddenly. This brought T-Roy to full stop!

This surprised us, as she was used to just listening to the permutations of these conservations between T-Roy and me, which she tolerated patiently as the price to pay for having three boys -including me. Normally she just feigned disinterest less demonstrably than Roman, as she steadily stroked Roman's arm or back, while his eyes glazed over and he almost purred. Had I pushed things too far - was she finally exercising her role as the responsible adult in our family?

"If you are going to do it, do it in the bathroom, not in my bed," says Debbie. "I don't want the screaming to spoil the tranquillity for Romey and me."

"I won't scream," I promised, which earned me a theatrical glare from Debbie.

I called T-Roy back to me. "Calm down now, T-Roy," I ask him. "I know I have been teasing you, and we've had fun, but please calm down now. Come and cuddle in." He didn't immediately, but voicing a superficial protest, I pulled him over and snuggled him in beside me as I enveloped him in the sheet.

I had once asked him why he wanted it, and his immediate reply was; "I want to be like you!" What father would not have his heart melted by a son making such a statement.

100

Let's see if I would ever hear him say that when he was a teenager!

He was calm again, beside me, and inevitably his hand was down there and fiddling. We'd had the conversation before, and I had explained to him that it was my definite choice that he and Roman remain intact, and that Debbie was in agreement. If he really wanted it done – which I'm sure wasn't a serious consideration for him – he could pay for it himself, which would certainly be after he turned sixteen.

"The only reason it will happen to you, if I have any say, would be for medical reasons," I told him.

"Like what?"

"Like if you kept getting infections or if it hurt you. But that won't happen if you keep it clean."

"I could stop cleaning it."

And in best Pantomime tradition I would love to have had a chorus of "Oh no, you couldn't ...!" but I was on my own in this.

"You know I love you..."- really when this whole conversation is a two-way tease-a-thon! – "... but I don't think you would be able to leave it alone for a couple of days without cleaning it. You love the pleasure it gives you way too much to be able to leave it alone!" And I cuddled him in tightly.

There was more of a possibility him wearing it out, than of him being able to leave it alone long enough for infection to set in.

*

Fairly often, sadly, T-Roy got it wrong when he tried to have teasing games with Debbie. There was one where he gauged her mood correctly, and I remembered it fondly.

"Why haven't you got a willy, Mummy?" He piped up one day, when he wanted to stir up some excitement.

We all knew that he knew the answer; the difference between men and women, males and females, and – at a level we hoped was appropriate for his age – how women are equipped to have babies. We knew he was showing off and being provocative. This time, Debbie played along;

"I have," she told him. "I am the boss of three!"

This stopped T-Roy dead in his tracks. He looked puzzled but knew that teasing was brewing.

"Your father's your brother's and yours!" Debbie explained.

"She is the boss of mine," I confirm to T-Roy.

"... and you, Romey?"

"Mine and Mummy's ..." Ever the diplomat, Roman!

"Well mine's mine!" Fighting talk, little boy!

Debbie got up, probably to go to the bathroom, and she paused at my foot of the bed, and dramatically glared at T-Roy. T-Roy giggled, and cuddled into me for protection. "Why are you hiding behind me? You know I'll just hand you over to your Mummy!" T-Roy was just giggling furiously, loving every minute of it.

I grabbed hold of him, pinning his elbows to his torso, and lifted him up out of the bed clothes, presenting his privates to Debbie. T-Roy struggled in token gesture, and squealed theatrically.

"Shouldn't you be protecting your son?" Debbie chided me.

"He doesn't need it. He's fine. Aren't you, Roman?"

"The other one!"

"Oh, T-Roy!? Do you need protecting?"

"No ... YES!", he said as I held his wrists to his sides, restrained, I presented him naked, groin first, to his mother for her to do as she pleased.

She played along, more than usual, and reached out to take his penis in one hand, and immitating scissors with her fingers, dramatised snipping it off.

"Now it's definitely mine," she declared dramatically. "And I'll keep it in my pocket!"

Job done, I released T-Roy, he bounded back over me, and snuggled in on the side away from his mum. Giggling, he

103

was enjoying it. So then he remembered that he should be protesting a great injustice done to him, so he cuddled up beside me, making little bursts of a noise that I can best describe as `chuntering', and jabbing me with hands held claw like, to register his disapproval, or sense of being aggrieved.

So here we have a little boy, pretending to seek protection from his father who moments earlier had presented him restrained to have his mother pretend to cut off his penis. And he seeks refuge with his father? Put that in your pipe and smoke it, Herr Doktor Sigmund Freud!

"We could raise you as a little girl," I said in a stage whisper. I was rewarded with more chuntering, and another stab.

"Roman will have a little sister!" Another chunter and stab.

"We can grow your hair, and put plaits in it…" Another chunter and stab. "Or a ponytail?" Another chunter and stab.

Debbie had left the room now. I decided to stop teasing him, but I ended with a flourish; "I'll still love you, even if you don't have a willy," I told T-Roy.

"It will grow back!"

*

When the boys were little, Debbie decided that the family word for `glans' would be `acorn' - which resulted in many sniggers when the topic of oak trees or anything related

came up! Somehow this developed a momentum between the boys, so that I knew that it would be a rich topic for childish entertainment, when the need arose. If there was a risk of them getting bored and irritable on car journeys; "What do you get in oak trees?" I would ask Roman.

It was a well-rehearsed drill, but it worked every time. What psychologists would call a conditioned response? Normally there is nothing particularly funny about concept of an oak tree – except in our family.

It would be addressed to Roman, but it would invariably be T-Roy who would call out `acorns' and they would both be giggling.

"I was thinking of squirrels." I would chide them mildly. "And in particular a Squirrel called George."

Then it would be a match on to suggest squirrels with different names – always avoiding any reference to `acorns' which just stoked up the giggles. We contemplated squirrels called `Tom', `Squirrel Squirrel', `Fred the Squirrel', `Roman the Squirrel', `T-Roy the Squirrel', `Roman a different other squirrel', not to be confused with the squirrel already mentioned.

Debbie would generally listen with a slight smile, and then do her bit to represent females, suggesting `Cecily the Squirrel' and some others. The boys weren't generally interested in girls at all - `apart from Mummy, of course!' I knew not to push too far with the mindless chat which the boys loved, of just producing lists of silliness, which had the

boys giggling, but Debbie could tire of it, and asked me to desist which I would. As always, I would try to get the balance right to amuse the boys as much as I could while stopping short of annoying her.

`Roman Warren Squirrel', `T-Roy Russell Squirrel', `Jason Wonder-dad Squirrel', `Debbie Amazing-Mummy Squirrel' ...Quibble with that, boys - if you dare!

They would giggle until they were `beside themselves' (what does that even mean?) and then keep going until they were crying. I tried to rein it in before they wet themselves – but it was probably touch and go on a number of occasions.

There was a word which I introduced to our family vocabulary, as although we weren't an American English family, I like the word `buns' in preference to `buttocks', with the image, like emerging on a baking tray of rounded mounds, with the cuteness of the girl in the 1960s Coppertone sun cream advert, taken by surprise by the puppy pulling down the back of her bikini bottoms. Debbie accepted this important word, so it was a word that we used with the boys, although they would prefer – when they dared – to use naughty words, which they knew they would be corrected for.

*

I felt for Debbie, how she might have liked at least one daughter that she could do girly things with, that they could do dressing Barbie dolls and `my little pony' and make up etc - not that Debbie was a `girly girl' at all. She would probably

have so liked to have a `sugar and spice and all things nice' daughter, and she ended up with T-Roy and me being `snips and snails and puppy-dogs' tails' - boys, with Roman occasionally descending to our depths.

I know that's a superficial and playful thing for me to say. I think she was relieved that both our children were boys. She would have liked T-Roy to be more receptive to her, as his attachment to me was overwhelming, and although we know that bad things can happen to boys, from something she said from time to time, I think she would have been very anxious if we had had a daughter or two, especially when a daughter started to want to date boys, and stray from the guidelines we had as a family.

*

The boys knew that they had a grandmother, but had never met her, and Debbie would be very vague about her when the boys expressed interest in her. They knew that there had been a stepfather figure for Debbie, the infamous `Bobby' which they were so used to hearing her say with contemptuous tones Debbie had told them that he was `not a nice person' and that, no, they would never meet him and, no, she didn't want to tell them about him. There were parts of the family history which they did not need to know of, yet, such that `Bobby' had been Debbie's stepfather and that her real father had died when she was very young. They also didn't need to know – at this stage – that Debbie had been married before, to Graham, who was also `not a nice person', but not in the league of unpleasantness of `Bobby'.

Alice was always polite and deferential to me, and even at grandmother age, showed signs of having been bullied all her life. The boys loved her dearly, in a manner befitting a gentle and kind grandmother, but sadly she often looked nervous if I ever questioned something she had done or said to the boys, as though she expected to be told off – or the ultimate sanction of having her time with the boys limited, let alone ended completely. Debbie mentioned that Alice had tremendous feelings of guilt for not having been a better mother to her, and not having protected her from `Bobby' and I knew that this was not something I should attempt to explore – my alliance was with Debbie, and I would take her side automatically. Debbie wrestled with whether her mother hadn't known about `Bobby', and if this was the case, how Alice could have been unaware, or worse, if she had had suspicions but had not done anything about them. Certainly when Alice had suddenly separated from Bobby, she hated him with the same vengeance that Debbie did.

Despite her discomfort with me, there were times that Alice dropped hints that she was pleased that Debbie had got together with me, that the relationship we have is what she wished for Debbie, but when Debbie had got together with Graham, probably for reasons of leaving home and `Bobby' behind, Debbie had gone with the wrong man, for the wrong reasons, and from his selfishness, he had probably added to the damage that `Bobby' had already done. But it was during her breakup with Graham, and the harassment she was getting from him, that at our chance encounter, she asked

me for help and protection, which developed into more than either of us had expected and led to us being where we are today.

*

The boys knew that I had grown up in Ferndale Hall, a State children's home, and that I didn't have a mummy or daddy.

We were watching the film `Oliver' on television when the penny dropped for Roman. "You grew up in a children's home!" he remembered, seeing through all the jollity and adventures and the deprivations illustrated by `Food Glorious Food'! Probably with as much compassion from Roman as I had ever seen for me, he moved closer to me and started to stroke me, reassuringly. He looked so sad! I tried to reassure him, as I had told them when they had asked before, that the home I had grown up in was nothing like what was shown in the musical; that we were well looked after and cared for, nurtured and encouraged – and any special interests were encouraged and funded - and this didn't seem to be limited. Sure, we were children of the state, but very definitely seen as resources to be invested in, to be optimised to take on crucial roles in society, or - should I say - the State. We were the future of the State, and raised to be so! We certainly were fed well. It seemed to take a while for Roman to feel reassured, but he stayed very near to me, probably still wanting to comfort me.

Predictably, T-Roy had a whole different approach. His plan was that he would rescue me, which consisted of swinging

down on a large rope, Tarzan style, picking me up and further swinging on to a dramatic escape.

"So where would you take me then?" I asked.

"I would bring you here," he decided. "And I would ask mummy if you could stay here. And I would look after you!" Have I mentioned that T-Roy sometimes sees me as a pet, rather than as his father?

"And if I said you could only keep him, if you kept your room tidy?" Debbie was quick to question even though we agreed to be tolerant of them having a messy bedroom, as long as there was no food or actual dirt flying around.

T-Roy started to agree to this, and I interrupted before Debbie could convert this into a negotiation. "Where would I sleep?"

"You could sleep with me," T-Roy had worked it out. "At night you could sleep with me in my nest, and in the morning we could come through to mummy and MyDaddy."

"And where would I be?" I asked, already suspecting a slight flaw in his fantasy. "We would have to get a bigger bed," T-Roy reasoned. "You would sleep next to me on the outside, I would sleep next to MyDaddy, then it would be Romey and then mummy.

"You've got daddy in there twice!" Roman added triumphantly at having caught his younger brother out.

"No, I haven't!" T-Roy was adamant. "On the edge of the bed is MyDaddy as a little boy, and on the other side is MyDaddy as a big man!" I embraced T-Roy then, touched by his compassion – following his imagined adventure, and Debbie hushed Roman from arguing how T-Roy couldn't have me as two separate people at different ages, despite what some of the children's films he had seen would suggest.

*

Please bear with me for a slight detour, which does lead us back to the narrative. There was considerable resentment and unspoken antagonism towards the state, as it was then, and the military and security forces, from the middle-class environment in which Ferndale Hall was located, and in which we grew up. This was the society that I was born into, so I knew no different, although I notice that during my lifetime things have eased off considerably.

The philosophy of Ferndale Hall was that we should be raised with middle-class values and aspirations, as it was in this environment that we could expect to serve. Little curiosities creep in, which over the years, as I look back, I have wondered how much was carefully thought through and how much happened by accident. Although we, like all of our peer group, knew that we would do two years compulsory military service, we also knew that it was likely we would stay on longer, possibly for our professional lives, or branch into other aspects of State service. It was expected that we would become officers and gentlemen.

111

Against this background it is surprising that we were encouraged to be Boy Scouts, rather than army cadets, and I have a number of theories about this, although this might not have been part of any master plan. As always, we were encouraged, and supported.

As a Boy Scout patrol leader aged fourteen, (Alvin's age!) leading my first patrol camp, I had to arrange transport for the boys and our equipment. For children growing up in conventional families, this would have been something that fathers would provide or arrange through friends, but in the absence of this, I raised this with my guardian at my weekly meeting with him. Each of us had our own guardian, separate from but who coordinated with our House Parents. He assured me that he would make arrangements, which I was confident he would.

On the morning of our departure out to camp, I and the others were gathered at the Scout Hall, with our equipment ready to pack, waiting for the vehicle to arrive. Not waiting, really, in the sense that the appointed time had not arrived, but in the habit of a lifetime I was there in good time allowing margins for error. Parents had gathered around, waiting to wave young Scout sons off on camp, and younger brothers and sisters chased each other around with excitement. The Scout Master was there, but he wouldn't be attending the camp, leaving me as the leader, although he would come out and visit, and would be contactable by phone if necessary. Knowing as he did that I came from Ferndale Hall, as did Leon and Kevin, he had checked with me that I had arranged the transport, which was a task that

could be expected of a patrol leader, but I gathered that behind my back he had contacted my guardian, who had confirmed that the necessary arrangements had been made; that I was being given the resources that a child from a conventional family could expect.

My guardian arrived, as he had said he would, but in an ordinary saloon car not nearly big enough to transport the numbers and equipment. He saw the dismay on my face, as I had been very specific about what was required. "Don't worry," he assured me. "Everything is under control."

The attention of the crowd turned to focus on the road, and the squealing children quietened. Coming towards us was a large white armoured personnel carrier, the wheel kind rather than on tracks. I remember my feelings at the time being a contradictory combination of mortified embarrassment combined with pride. The APC, in clean white paint and no decals, stopped at the gate outside the Scout Hall, and a smartly uniformed corporal climbed down from the passenger seat.

He seemed to know who to approach, as he came across to my guardian beside me, him also being smart in his civilian clothing, possibly betraying his military status. Also, my guardian would have been in his mid-twenties then, too young to have been my father, or the father of any of the Scouts, and too old – generally – to have been an older brother. I suspect, looking back, that he had the appearance of a military man pretending to be a civilian. "Mr Maxwell?" The Corporal asked my guardian. My guardian reached out

his hand and placed it on my shoulders, identifying me to the corporal.

There were multiple levels of games being played here, some of which were as compliments to me. Again, within a monolithic bureaucracy, there can be many individual people who – almost against human nature – reach out and make little positive contributions to people who might benefit from them. The corporal braced to me in respect, and - remember that I was fourteen-years-old at the time – I didn't know the greetings and salutations being played here. Beside me my guardian braced in return.

The corporal spoke to me deferentially, stating the glaringly obvious of who he was, his purpose for being there and his willingness to take direction.

It was obvious that the kit had to be loaded, the Scouts loaded, brothers and sisters extracted from the excitement of exploring the insides of the vehicle, with its bullet-proof windows, rows of minimalist seating facing each other, roof hatches, and the view to the Spartan driver's compartment. The corporal barked for the driver to join them, and together with the dads and the bigger Scouts, the equipment was soon loaded, and the corporal and the driver stood smartly to one side – beside my guardian – as I made my little speech to the parents, confirming our venue and return time.

I hadn't had any dealings with the formal military before, meaning those in uniform, although I was aware that many

people that I came across, at Ferndale and associated with it, although inevitably in civilian clothing, held positions of rank and influence in the military. The corporal was a novelty to me, and my first exposure to how someone could play the military game regarding etiquette and discipline, while being able to switch into being positive and playful with people to whom this did not apply, and especially to children. I also realise that this was not a basic training type corporal. He overheard one of the children talking excitedly about being in a `tank'.

"This is not a tank," he said to them with theatrical indignation. "This is my battle taxi!"

`Battle taxi!' The children loved it and repeated it gleefully to each other. He had spoken to them. They were in awe. The corporal found himself with the undivided attention and admiration of the children gathered around him and could not but rise to the occasion. "A tank goes clunk clunk clunk, squeak squeak squeak," he told them. "My battle taxi goes…" And he gave an impression of a deep throated roar. His audience giggled with delight, and gleefully repeated to each other what they had just heard. For a brief moment, if he was the Pied Piper, and had he struck up a tune with his flute, they would have followed him to the mountain. But if they – and I'm talking of the younger brothers and sisters here – had heard him say `all aboard', they would have clambered aboard his battle taxi, and enjoyed the ride!

"Will you be travelling upfront, Mr Maxwell?" the corporal asked me. I did not perceive any sarcasm in this, and since

115

then I have wondered whether he was genuine in respecting a young child who was a patrol leader at that time, working his way through a structured system, as the corporal was doing with his own career.

Beside me, my guardian murmured; "Don't separate yourself from your Scouts!"

"I'll ride with my Scouts," I told him.

My guardian went through a brief repeat with me of information he had given me previously – his contact telephone number, and an alternative if he wasn't available should I have any needs that the ordinary Scout leaders were not suitable for. He reminded me that he would be present to collect us again, praised me, wished me well, patted my shoulder, and shook my hand. He never hugged me, even when I was younger – maybe he wasn't allowed to!

As I stepped up into the troop cabin, I looked up, and into a pair of eyes which had a look of strong dislike and contempt, or so I thought at the time. This was from 'Bobby' – who I knew was the stepfather of Debbie, the Ice Princess in my class. "(Sorry, Debbie, my wonderful wife, but that's how I saw you in those days. It was only later that I had any understanding of what was going on!). There was no reason for him to be there, as I know that he only had one child, and I knew of no link between him and anyone present there. He and Debbie and Debbie's mom tended to be a

fairly isolated family, Debbie and me being academic rivals in our class, jostling for top place in most subjects.

The corporal was too young to have had children of his own, but he understood what would appeal to young boys. When we came to the end of the formal roads, he got the driver to stop, and coming to the hold, opened the hatches in the roof to enable the boys to take turns in standing on the seats with heads poked through the hatches, rotating through so that each boy got a chance. Another cherry on the top of the many coverings of this particular treat!

There are many things in my life that remain mysteries to me, and with my vocation being in gathering information, joining dots, and solving mysteries, this niggles me. , I can't let it go, and there have been times when I have pondered what the background to the battle taxi being made available to us was. Generally, as I do with my boys, I don't want to glorify the military so that, apart from their military service, it won't have been me pushing them into it if they choose military careers, and Debbie supports me fully with this. Ferndale Hall, and the wider State behind them, didn't generally want us to be seen as soldiers, and servants of the state in waiting – though this might have been blown on this occasion!

Had there been some administrative indiscretion, in the sense that my guardian had raised the need for transport with one of the transport depots, and had specified a non-camouflaged, non-armed vehicle, thinking that a 16 ton truck would have been provided, only for the dispatching

NCO to have misunderstood? Had it been something more benign, and an NCO, understanding the context, knowing the boost in status it would give to a future leader to be provided with such a prestigious vehicle, when it would still be present in most peoples' minds that children from perceived `orphanages' were deprived and undervalued? Or could it have been a common ops involvement, with knowledge of the area from which the Scouts came being middle class, and from people often antagonistic to the military to provide a demonstration of generosity, that all of the young children would be greatly impressed at being able to play around however briefly in the battle taxi, and the funny and interesting corporal that had been friendly to them? `Through your children, we will get to you!'

Or there might be other explanations that I haven't thought of?

*

There were set piece discussions which the boys enjoyed, especially when they knew that some mystery was being hinted at, and which if they persisted long enough, they might discover the key to – even though they might not have the ability to comprehend this.

They knew that Debbie's job was a children's nurse, though fortunately they were very healthy, and so had not required nursing input. Debbie told them that her job involved giving children injections in their bottoms, which delighted the

boys – as any mention of bottoms or willies seem to at that age.

They were aware of the jobs of the parents of some of the children at school. There seem to be teachers and nurses, one doctor, accountants, electricians and plumbers, and a police officer and so they got around to asking about my job.

It would probably have made sense to have fobbed them off with some vague career line, but it had become a sort of game between Debbie and me to drop hints without revealing that I was in the military, fairly high in the military, but that I very seldom wore a uniform. They knew that I had been a soldier when I was younger, and were familiar with Kevin's paratrooper helmet in the study, but at present, although they knew that Kevin had been a school friend of Debbie and mine, they did not need to know that that helmet had been on his head when he died. Or that I myself had respectfully cleaned parts of his head out of it.

They had grown up with regularly attending barbecues with the staff of my unit at the barracks – which wasn't my usual place of work – and were used to the procedures of us driving into the barracks, and stopping at the gatehouse, where they saw the guards being respectful to me, but they didn't put two and two together, and possibly didn't realise that this was not part of other people's lives, and apart from the uniformed guards, and the buildings of the large base, all the people they encountered at the barbecues were in civilian dress, and, as they grew older and I took them to the

gym and to the diving pool, there was an absence of uniform.

"So what is your job?"

"To keep the public safe."

"How?"

The challenge was not to actually lie, but to tell the truth in as misleading and as apparently boring a manner as possible. Debbie watched with amusement.

"I do research about how to keep the public safe," I started. I moderated my tone to monotonous and attempted to drone. "So I get information from hospitals about how people have safely problems, so that if a child goes to hospital and they have a splinter in their hand, then I will see if there are other people who go to hospital with a splinter in their hands, and if it seems that there is, then I investigate and try and see if there is anything in common with how they got splinters in their hand."

"And then what?"

"Then I tell Uncle Leon, and he goes around and fixes it." (The executive branch!)

Debbie and I played with multiple levels of euphemism. The joke within the joke was that I worked in the `Ministry of Truth' - or we carefully referred to it as such, but within a tightly closed circle. And the `Ministry of Love' with which we work closely, does not exist - never has, never will.

120

Debbie knows that I am a `Deputy Divisional Director of Research' at the `Institute for Public Safety' – or that I have letter-headed paper to this effect. But I also have other job titles, and other euphemistic `employers'.

Debbie knows more than she lets on to. She says that she doesn't want to know, and I'm happy to leave it at that, although when she comes to annual formal dinners at the mess, she can guess at what underlies the euphemisms in the speeches.

The closest that she ever got to the edge– and I forget the exact context, but I had mentioned getting some information out of someone who was reluctant to give it to me. She had taken my hand to examine it, explaining "I'm just looking to see if there is bruising on your knuckles."

I chuckled, but I wasn't going to volunteer any information. "Did you have him tied to a chair, with a light in his eyes?" She teased.

"What about naked and wet?" I asked, not really sure whether to engage or just to remain silent.

I think Debbie also realised she had got further than she wished to. But she recovered really well. "Why would you be wet?" She asked. We changed the subject.

*

Roman was a gymnast - understandable - he liked the different experiences that his body could give him, the sensation of swinging, and somersaulting, while T-Roy was

121

more percussive, into football, and probably would have enjoyed the tussle and brutality of rugby if I had allowed him - which I have tried to delay for as long as possible.

There was something tragic in my love for Roman - I couldn't show it to him enough. I wasn't jealous of the exclusive bond between Debbie and Roman, but I wished that, in comparison with the ease of my bond with T-Roy, that Roman knew that I did not love him less, or that I was not holding any of love back from him. `How can I show you my love, Roman?' I never asked. How could a nine-year-old answer that?

Roman was aesthetic. He delighted in the touch and stroking and massage that Debbie did with him. Almost like a cat, he would go into a trancelike state of bliss. I was happy to stroke him in that way, but I was more geared to how active T-Roy was geared to be. I enjoyed having tickle fights with Roman and T-Roy - T-Roy enjoyed them more than Roman, and he was like a little puppy, lying on his back and writhing as he giggled - and every now and again when I went to the effort of overpowering him, I would then blow `tickly prickly raspberries' on his tummy, which he loved, despite his giggled protests.

Occasionally Roman would forget himself, and enthusiastically enter the fray, when I was manhandling T-Roy. Then he would realise what he had done, become scared of what he had entered into, and he would wish to withdraw. T-Roy always wanted to complete the wrestling which he saw Roman getting involved in - long awaited

involvement from his older brother. We had to calm or distract T-Roy while Roman extracted himself.

When I was tickle-wrestling with T-Roy, Roman preferred to be clamped onto my back, having a ride as I moved around with the tickling, and occasionally - a rather sneaky way - he would reach out and poke T-Roy from behind the safety barrier of my body.

Rather like a small animal, he would freeze if he felt in danger, although he knew that I would never hurt him. He didn't really like having a raspberry on his tummy or elsewhere and would ask me to stop. I took on board not to do this to him, except if he joined in when I was doing it to T-Roy. I would then look to him to see if he wanted me to at least try, before he said `no!'

Generally, Roman preferred to watch, but when he did join in the play, he disliked the being beaten into submission and the forfeit, when he was (I couldn't always let him have no consequences to joining in!) I gave him the option that of having a `vampire bite' on his neck - which was essentially just a kiss, but without the betrayal of masculinity that calling it such might indicate. Debbie would usually be watching - and I preferred her to be there - so she could warn me if anyone got overexcited. As often happened, I would speak to the kids, but what I said was aimed for her, like the time when Roman had submitted and was about to get a vampire bite when I asked him "On a hot summer night, would you offer your throat to the wolf with the red roses ...' which had Debbie burst out laughing.

Both boys turned to look at her. "Romey, ask your Daddy, `Will he offer me his hunger?'"

Roman would do whatever his mum told him, so he asked; "Will he offer me his hunger?"

"Yes!" Debbie was playing as well. This was fun!

"Romey, ask your Daddy; `and will he starve without me?'"

"Yes!" I told him, and remembering that there wasn't anything more in the introduction to the song after this, I then leaned in and nuzzled and kissed his neck.

Of course, T-Roy wanted to try this, but inevitably he wanted to be big stuff, and put his own slant on things. When challenged with the image of the wolf, he reverted to Little Red Riding Hood, and `what big teeth you have?', which was enough for me to playfully rough him up with pretend nipping and biting, while he rolled on the floor giggling and attempting to defend himself.

So, with children's love of repetitious rituals, this became one, but no royalties were ever paid to Meatloaf!

I was amused, when I heard T-Roy briefing Colin, his little friend, before Colin first became involved in the tickle fights; "If he traps you, he either blows a farty on your tummy or you get `wolf' where he bites your neck!" Had the circumstances of Colin's time with us been different, I could expect having to try to explain to slightly concerned parents what was meant by all this.

T-Roy was always tantalised by secrets. He was fascinated by, and somewhat suspicious of, my `security pack' –I never call it that. He noticed how I would generally have it with me when I went jogging and he accompanied me on his bike, or when I went to the park and at other times, no matter how much I tried to downplay it. He didn't buy that it was the equivalent of his mummy's handbag and would always want to explore what was in it. Fortunately, I don't think he became aware of the sleight of hand, such that when I agreed to let him explore it, provided that we did it in the study, the bag that I handed him, though identical, was not the same one that I had safely locked in the safe in my bedroom wardrobe. Debbie said that she generally had the policy of not wanting to know about aspects of my life and work that I thought it best for her not to know, even though she knew bits and pieces of what my profession involved, that parts of it were secret. This, after all, had been part of my ability to protect her, which had led to her approaching me for help, leading us to the very pleasant consequences of where we were today.

I was sure that she preferred not to know that in our bedroom, I had a loaded pistol, several spare loaded magazines, a location smoke flare, and ... other things! I kept it from her, and the boys that I kept up my shooting practice at the army range, as was required and signed off, but I didn't want to encourage the boys to have any more interest in guns than the ordinary plastic toy rifles and pistols that all boys require as toys.

It was a calculated risk for me to live outside of the barracks or the army camp, amongst the general population, amongst whom we knew that undesirable people and people who might harm others live, and so my security pack and other security drills were a part of my life – parking the car in the garage, rather than leaving it on the driveway where it could be interfered with in any number of ways. There were secrecy aspects to my work, and my name and identity were unlikely to be known by people with the capability to be a serious threat to me and my family – if there were, then the freedom with which we mixed with the general population would be reviewed.

The threat was not from the `big departments' that mirrored ours of `countries who did not have our best interests in front of mind'. It was low level operators, self-starters and rogues that we had to be concerned about. There was a gentleman's agreement between the big players. Although we would seek approval before any arranged meetings, supposedly informal ones, at which each party would play the game of trying to recruit the other, and if approached, we would report this as soon as possible to the appropriate authority.

Part of the security, which I was perfectly willing for, was to have me and my family surveilled as training exercises for trainees in my wider organisation to practice with. I was confident that they would not come across deep dark secrets, but – while we were not always being surveilled, and as it is said that terrorists and suchlike only need to be lucky once while people defending high-profile targets need

to be lucky all the time – I liked the idea that there was the possibility of people who would be `helpful and friendly' and possibly on hand, should the need arise. With Debbie's general policy of `not wanting to know', I didn't get around to telling her of this, but certainly if she noticed things, I would inform the necessary contacts that their trainees had been observed. This may sound strange, but it seemed reasonable to me.

Along with my security pack, I would always have my pager with me when I was out and about. With the technology we had in those days, if I received a call I would go to the nearest phone and phone in, but it did not have the capacity for me to be able to make calls or even signals from the `pager'.

This brings me back to my curious younger son, and his enjoyment of the ritual of checking the contents of my mysterious pack; the ritual of it having to be done in the study, and not in any other room. He didn't quite have enough knowledge to be able to seriously question why I might find it necessary to keep close at hand items with no apparent use, and I also needed to make sure that he did not have the idea that I had with me at all times things that he might reasonably want to have access to while we were away from home, such as soft drinks or chocolate bars, paper towels (which would be a euphemism for toilet paper should there be an urgent need), so I had tried to make up a pack of objects which would seem to make out roughly the same shape as he was used to seeing with the actual security pack.

127

I included a book which was roughly the dimensions of the pistol, a book that would be of no interest to him so that he could not suddenly decide that he wished me to read him a story, and other objects as padding, hopefully boring enough not to be of interest, although he enjoyed the ritual of looking through it in the study, probably more often than not, when he knew that I was wearing it. , this was separate from my pager, which I did not lock away, and which, while equally tantalising to him, was tamperproof by numerical codes, and he knew that it was from work, and not a toy, though he would often attempt to negotiate being involved in its use.

*

A little anecdote which follows on from me having volunteered our family to be surveilled for training purposes; back when Roman was about five years old, the training supervisor made an appointment with me. Sat opposite my desk, he took out a brown envelope, and from it extracted a couple of black-and-white photos – in the inevitable style of those taken by surveillance staff. I saw that they showed me, with Roman bent over in front of me, naked from the waist down. I remembered the occasion, some weeks before, at the park, when Roman had an accident and soiled himself, which he was mortified about. I had taken him aside, into a copse of bushes, thinking we were unobserved, and I cleaned him up as best I could with paper towels. One photo had Roman looking in the general direction of the cameraman with my face obscured, and in the other Roman was looking away while my face was clear.

128

"My compliments to your team," I commended. "Please buy each member a drink on my tab."

The training officer smiled. He tapped the envelope which he left in the table in front of me. "The negatives are in here. There are no other copies."

That evening I locked the envelope away in the filing cabinet in the study.

*

It's probably worthwhile explaining my relationship with the military. Having been raised by the State, and I need to emphasise 'well cared for and nurtured' by the State, there had always been the expectation that I, Kevin, and Leon would become part of the State as adults, whether in the military – probably most likely in the military! – or in other branches of the State. There was minimal expectation that we would start up our own businesses or anything of the like.

From early on I had known that although I could do the parade ground stuff - what Debbie called 'ballet' - and the weapon stuff and the things more commonly associated with the military, that I was best suited to and attracted to the more understated sides – the parts that most people take for granted exist, and are quick to blame if we missed something that it was our job to stop. We didn't see it as a job, and certainly not 8-to-5, but rather as a vocation, and to some extent, we were always on duty.

I still had my uniforms, and they were contemporary, although I didn't have the problem of needing to get larger sizes as I was fortunate to not gain weight as some of my colleagues battled with. (Poor old Leon!)

I had worked mostly in civilian clothing since before Roman was born, and with me having taken the decision, with the necessary permissions to move out, the base was a place still very familiar to me, and although it was only one of the different places that I worked, depending on which specific projects I was working at the time, I had full access to the base, and privileges. The base was very large, with a small subsection for my department, surrounded by many other more conventional military units and departments, but it was not a training base so there were no columns of troops being marched around and commands shouted.

*

I had the strange status of being something of a celebrity in military circles, being pointed out to others in hushed tones, that I had been the lead in `The Ferguson Case' which was unusual, as usually we chose to and were happy to remain anonymous about what we did; our successes and failures. It would have been decisions taken higher up to cultivate this mystique about me, making me a legend, and maybe I would learn their reasons for doing so in time. I don't think this reputation was deserved, as it was my job, and I had been lucky – with the caveat that `the harder I worked, the luckier I got'. It seemed as though there was a good match between my work role, and spotting patterns that begged

130

questions, and sometimes led to answers – very useful answers. I was aware that my identity, beyond my name, rank, and unit on my identity card, which I showed to the guards when entering the barracks, was mentioned in hushed tones to those who did not know.

*

From when our relationship had started, Debbie had known that I was wedded to the military – and probably could have presumed this would be the case from our school days. National service was still a feature then, so it was expected that all of the men would end up in uniform in their late teens, which was resented by many, enjoyed by a few for the opportunities it might present, while probably most would just do their bit and get over it. Those raised by the State saw the military as their vocation, and it rewarded us well.

I didn't want Debbie to be a military wife, to feel that she needed to belong to the community of military wives, with their get-togethers, the status according to the rank of the husband, and their focus on military matters, and the gossip about each other. I liked that she had her own job, and career, certainly respectable in the eyes of the military, and with her own friends and work colleagues, although both of us were home bodies, even more so if anything now we had the children to delight in and be amused by.

There were military functions where Debbie was required to attend, like the annual formal dinner, a very bizarre affair

amongst the formality, with speeches riddled with banter and 'in the know' comments, which would make no sense to anyone who didn't know the background being referred to, always euphemistic variations on the theme of discovering leaks – in the context of plumbing – or finding unpleasant things, with little emphasis on seeking them out, and then references to 'taking out the trash', 'tidying up' and references to tenpin bowling et cetera, during which the speech makers, of which I was one, would try to outdo each other with the dark humour. 'Look what I found!' and 'Don't touch that!' Debbie never complained about attending these events and never made little digs at me before or after. During socialising time, the few military wives associated with our unit – and I was the only one to have married of my particular department, the developing of formal relationships being frowned on as possible divided loyalties, not dissimilar to the requirement of celibacy of priests in the Catholic Church. Debbie would play the game, and talk to them as though she was interested, but would never follow up on the invitations from them to get together with them and meet up outside, and, grateful that she was doing what I needed from her, I didn't ask.

Less formal by far, and including the young junior officers who had just started with our unit, were barbecues held at the recreation centre of the base, to which the organisers had specifically told me that the boys were invited, from when they were babies. For my colleagues, the children were novelties, as most were lifers like me and most did not expect that they would ever have proper families, so for

132

them, children were a novelty and curiosity. With Debbie and my approval, these young officers took the chance to play with the children, lining up to give rides to, chase and be chased by the boys, who loved every minute of it!

The Officer Commanding would always put in an appearance. , he attended all the formal dinners, but it would be a substantial but token presence at the barbecues, knowing, that as it should be, his presence added formality, and inhibited some of the festivities. , I knew him well, respected him profoundly. I was his protégé. It was he who had authorised me to get married, but, only after a long and concerned almost father to son chat with me, about how my actions would curtail my promotion opportunities and possibly limit my future in the organisation. He had been sad when he had done this, but I understood, as I had grown up in the world he represented.

He was always very gracious with Debbie and would always make a point of coming over to greet her, and chat with her, always having remembered what she had told him previously, and so showing an interest, and a growing fondness. I knew that it could very well be that after his chats with Debbie he wrote up notes in a file which he would refresh his memory with before his next meeting with her, but he made it look seamless.

He was the keeper of secrets. He knew my secret. He knew Debbie's secret. If he chose to do so, he could learn much more about Debbie's secret than I could. But having access

to secrets, I knew, often meant that there were some secrets one did not wish to delve into!

After several meetings with her, in an informal moment with me he decided to share; "I'm starting to understand why you took the decision you did."

And, following on his acceptance of Debbie, from a distance he had a fondness for the boys. He would always speak to them, having remembered their names, but would always call T-Roy Troy, even though T-Roy would patiently correct him each time. (Had he not updated the dossier?)

Standing beside me with a drink in his hand, he invited; "It would please me if you let them call me Uncle Kasper, if you wish."

"Thank you, Sir," I replied.

"Is Uncle Kasper your boss?" Roman asked when he found us standing together at such a function when he was old enough to understand.

"He tells me what to do," I told Roman.

"I ask your daddy what he's doing," the officer commanding corrected me.

There was a long established game of finding euphemisms to describe our work, trying to make it sound as bland and boring as possible, and avoiding any indication of what was actually being referred to. There was the euphemism about Leon and me and our respective departments; I set them up,

and he knocks them down! The overseas job was to stop people from bumping into each other, meaning that separate teams with the same search agenda did not start investigating each other, thereby wasting tremendous resources and possibly leading to – accidents!

Having worked under him for so long, and fortunate at having been successful in my work, there was a familiarity and even fondness between the two of us, but I was aware of the rank difference, and it was never an issue for me to observe this. A ritual, which I subjected him to, was, whenever called in to meet with him in his office would be that with the slick choreography of a soldier who had just completed basic training, I would do –Debbie's `ballet' – of marching into his office, snapping to attention, saluting, and standing at ease, proud and erect in front of him – which he always flinched at, an exaggerated flinch. I didn't do this to him in public, certainly not at the barbecues or the formal dinners.

The officer commanding was an old hand, who I respected profoundly, and had been mentored by him from my start at the unit. He was what, if Debbie hadn't intervened, I probably would have become, never married, living in admittedly luxurious senior officer accommodation in the base, and indulging in solitary hobbies of bird watching – he had a boat that he would take out onto backwaters to watch birds for hours and hours, and when he came home he would whittle, usually making figures of birds. No, he didn't drink excessively!

I formed the impression that the OC envied me in some ways, specifically that I had taken the decision when I had taken it, to opt out of the mainstream military career, by getting married, and then – well it was Debbie's decision - to have children. I would never address it with him, but I think he would have loved to have been a grandfather, and Roman and T-Roy became a focus to him of what grandchildren could have been if he had taken a different route in his life.

In an understated way, the OC started bringing along presents for my boys, statuettes of birds that he had whittled, and Debbie and I had to immediately become involved to show the boys how to respond to this, to look at and explore and value what the OC had given them, when in reality being given a lump of wood that looked like a bird would have been of no interest to them. I think we got away with it. Well, the OC did the same the next time, and then asked the boys what their interests were, and what they might like him to carve for them, which is not an easy task for young children to think of things they would like carved. Clearly the OC was thinking of either types of birds, or conventional objects like a racing car, an aeroplane et cetera. T-Roy wanted a statue of Spider-Man, which the OC put his mind to and delivered at the next barbecue, and Debbie and I coached T-Roy in how to show his appreciation. Truth be told, T-Roy would rather have had a plastic figure from the official merchandise range, but he did understand the significance of the OC's gift.

I checked with the OC if it would be acceptable to him for the boys to bring him drawings in reciprocation, and in an understated way he indicated that it would be acceptable; "I would like that!"

We would get the boys to draw pictures for Uncle Kasper, from early on, Roman would draw space scenes, with rockets and planets and comets, and T-Roy's pictures would all be very animated, with Spider-Man themed adventures with things blowing up and chases et cetera. He would sit on Uncle Kasper's knee and tell him exactly what was going on, in a well-meaning but indecipherable way, the adventures continuing way on beyond those portrayed in his picture, powered by T-Roy's bubbling enthusiasm.

The OC valued these pictures, and I noticed them on display in a discreet corner in his office, new ones being added as they were accepted. "You've been spring cleaning, Sir," I observed once, when I noticed the older drawings were no longer there.

"They have been transferred home," he told me. "I have a gallery of early artworks by great masters."

*

At the barbecues, Debbie was used to being the only lady there with any degree of consistency, apart from the female staff members, who were mostly in administrative roles, and who tended to keep their distance. Leon could have been seen as a ladies' man, and inevitably he would have a lady on his arm, who would be aware of how after possibly a

small 'excuse me a moment', he would lift up and cuddle and embrace Roman and T-Roy as they rushed up to him with a delighted cry of 'Uncle Leon'. These ladies would seek to bond with Debbie, considering that she was already established in a special society into which they were being introduced, and they hoped and expected that they would be seeing a lot more of Debbie as they joined this world, and they hoped that they would be close to her. Debbie was enchanting as always, but had little in common with the vacuous Barbie dolls that Leon seemed to choose and find, and she knew the pattern that such a girl that she met at such a barbecue, would never be seen again, but that the next time Leon would be accompanied by a different woman with the same characteristics.

Debbie asked me if I would be that way if our relationship hadn't developed, and it had developed in a way that had taken both of us by surprise, based on understanding and integrity. I reminded her of what she remembered of Leon from our school days, and of how he paid attention to his appearance, to the extent of some vanity, and that he would have been a ladies' man if he had had the chance. But we were limited, as we didn't really have anywhere to take girls we were interested in, and I don't know how the staff at Ferndale Hall would have dealt with this if we had tried it, – boys that they had raised to be normal from an unusual environment, so it never happened. And, although it would be denied, we knew that there was prejudice against us, with the stereotyped view of children who were in care,

being somehow of questionable moral integrity, caused by perceived deprivation.

"I don't think I would have put the same energy in," I shared. "I probably would have made the effort from time to time, but I'm not sure how I would have come across woman that would be interesting enough – and who might be legitimate for me to become involved with." I think Debbie knew what I meant by that; okay, none of us were James Bond--type figures, but our professions were our vocations, and which would have to come first, and as had happened with me – which hadn't been compromised because it was what I wanted – developing my relationship with Debbie, getting married, well before having children was a career limiting move, which more career driven people would not make. The culture, generally, was of 'love them and leave them' but it would be frowned on to have left them pregnant. While contraception could be insisted on, we knew of the risks of being trapped, so had an awareness of 'is sex with this woman of sufficient value to risk putting a ceiling on my career at this stage'?

These were the rules of the game, and, sadly for them, the only people not in the know were the vacuous bimbos who Leon and others presented as their dates. These ladies, taking it all in; the obvious camaraderie between the men, and their acceptance of and fondness of Debbie would have been seen as what they, too, could enjoy. They would have seen the love that my boys openly showed with Leon, and his obvious active affection back for them. 'He's good with

children!' They would have noted, and this would be another 'tick in the box' of Leon being a suitable partner.

If I hadn't been ambushed by Debbie, I probably would have been fairly content as a drone, paying lip service to the idea of having some female partner, who would know her place as secondary to my career, and who would accept this, but I probably would have followed the drone lifestyle that I saw around me amongst colleagues senior and older than me. I would have read much more, studied much more, possibly mastered chess to a greater degree.

"Any regrets?" Debbie asked. It was a tease, and there were plenty of things that did not need to be put into words. I exchanged a long, meaningful glance with her. She broke off by sticking her tongue at me, after which we shared an embrace that might appear sarcastic, but which was genuine.

*

Leon was an ideal uncle for the boys. Somewhat mysterious, somewhat anarchic with them, ever indulgent, and slightly dangerous, in a conspiratorial way. , they didn't know how dangerous he was to some people, and I was sure, how dangerous he would be to anyone who hurt a hair on their heads. He was stronger and bigger than me – always had been – and although now in my mid-thirties I could pick them up and carry them, Leon could pick them both up and carry them at the same time, which he did, taunting me at the length that he was able to do this for.

He would not have held back on making them familiar with military skills, as Debbie and I did, and he would have taken them shooting, and bought them pellet guns and made them comfortable with the military, but he respected and honoured that Debbie and I did not want this for them. If they chose military careers after their national service, so be it, but I also wanted them to have a free choice to follow entirely civilian careers if that is what they chose.

Although Kevin had been nineteen when he died, and it would be difficult to project him from that age to how he would have been if he was still with us. He would have been an uncle to encourage and nurture other aspects, leaving Leon to the roughhousing and boisterousness. Kevin had been a wordsmith, delighting in language and communicating, and resources had been poured into him to encourage this, with his involvement in school magazines, Scout magazines, creative writing competitions, and speech and drama classes. For obvious reasons, he had not graduated from the military skills and combat career stage, and had not started at Military Academy, but I envisage he would have been successful in communication operations, possibly public relations and what are now called being a spin doctor, or less kindly, propaganda.

As much as I could imagine him still at my age, I could project his enthusiasm to involving the boys in making up stories, using their imaginations and fantasies, making storybooks with them, encouraging them, and sharing and developing his passion with them.

141

He had been well mentored and coached, and knew the importance of completing/finishing projects. He knew to work out the goal and endpoint early on in any of his projects. `See it through,' was a phrase he had taken on board – or been indoctrinated with. I had a flash of imagination of, if he had been the uncle that I imagined for my boys, Roman, when showing off his room, would stand at the bookcase, in front of a row of lavishly covered exercise books bulging with illustrations, describing; `these are the books that I have made' indicating the volumes, `and those are my brothers'!'

Kevin had loved reading even more than I did, with him having a great interest in stories and fiction, and being encouraged to develop his talents, it had become a routine at Ferndale Hall that he would read bedtime stories to a younger cohort of children, which he did so well, and with such enthusiasm, that Leon and I would tend to drift in to enjoy it as well, as would our house parents and other members of staff. I would like to think that I would have done it anyway, but our routine of me reading bedtime stories to the boys was, in part, my tribute to Kevin.

His belief in the need to complete things was juxtaposed with his death, though this was far outside of his control. All of us, on the helicopter, had thought that that particular chapter was over, and our return to base would be routine. It wasn't even as though our combat phase had ended by the time he died, as we still had the requirement of one more combat jump to do. We don't always know when something has ended, but in those days there were more

definite endpoints, or transitional points, than there are in my life now, with Debbie and my careers continuing – accepting the ceiling on mine – as we mentor and support our boys as they grow up and reach and pass their life stages.

*

The succession of women, with whom Leon had his generally brief relationships, soon learned that he would prioritise spending time with his nephews, if asked, over them, and those that challenged it found that that action ended their involvement with Leon there and then. He was a very physical man, bigger and bulkier than I, and he always had been from childhood before time spent working out in the gym magnified him more. I enjoyed watching him playing boisterously with the boys on his hands and knees on our lounge carpet, with both of them riding on his back, me wryly observing that it was quite possible that the boys would never know that playful tickly and indulgent Uncle Leon was much feared by other people who came across him – generally on the receiving end – when he was in professional work mode. He would have enjoyed being likened to 'The Grim Reaper', even though those who encountered him in this role didn't face immediate death, and in most cases lived on for years afterwards. But, for those finding themselves looking into his face – or what they could see of his face through his balaclava – it would be a turning point in their lives; that their world would change beyond recognition. The boys would not know this, as they clambered over him, and beat him with their fists, having no

concept that adults feel pain, and he indulged them and he loved them – he was allowed to love them, because they were mine.

Debbie never felt quite at ease with Leon. She knew that he and I loved each other as brothers, but that was not quite enough. Possibly she remembered the slight bullying phase he had gone through at school, but that was long ago, and was certainly not a part of him now – but he knew how to make himself look intimidating if he wished. Despite her protestations that she wasn't going to ask and didn't want to know about my... our work, I think she suspected that there were more things about what Leon did that she would feel uncomfortable with than what I did, even though she knew we collaborated.

"He would step in front of a bullet to protect you," I told her sincerely. "... and that's nothing to what he would do for the boys."

"I know he's devoted to the boys, and I trust him with them," she clarified. "But there's just a feeling I get about him sometimes that I don't feel comfortable with."

"But not like `Bobby'!" She clarified emphatically. "Not like `Bobby' at all!"

*

There would be times when I would go to work out at the army gym, which was located within the confines of a much larger and more general army base. I had humbly asked

144

permission for my boys to come along with me if they wanted to, from my officer commanding, who, I was partly surprised to find was always very accommodating to my requests about the boys. He had forgiven me for choosing to get married and have a family, and my acceptance that this would place a ceiling on my military intelligence career. T-Roy always jumped at the chance to come along, not least because of all the attention that he would get from the young soldiers who would likely be exercising, and who he would commandeer as his audience. His charm would have them eating out of his hand, and I do believe that it was this aspect of him, rather than him being the son of one of the senior officers that made him a focal point when we went to the gym – and, sorry guys! – that his presence might distract you from your exercise routine.

Throughout their lives they were aware of the civilian lifestyle that we lived as a family, but that I had a role in the security services – certainly nowadays I am reluctant to refer to myself as being a soldier, or being in the army.

The military is structured and hierarchical, strongly disciplined. I know this, understand this, and I have no difficulty in playing the game. I don't mean that cynically. I have chosen to work in one of the least structured and what would seem to be the most casual branch within the military, yet, after the military police, one that makes people most uncomfortable. Although my unit were almost exclusively lifers, all male citizens were still required to do two years National Service, with follow-up, and though it was still a long way off, this would be required of my boys.

When the time came, I would encourage them to do interesting things, but apart from the glimpse they had into my world, I didn't want them to be too enthusiastic about the military.

I am aware of the arrogance of many officers and NCOs towards national serviceman, many of whom would have preferred not to be there, and I would like to think that it was because I am a nice person that I behaved in a positive and friendly manner towards the most junior soldiers, within what is acceptable within the military structure. It is also not lost on me that kindness and politeness, leads to respect and loyalty, which can pay unexpected dividends in my line of work. Obviously, during basic training, I had had to do guard duty and I knew how mind numbingly dull it was, and although I am sure that my stream was privileged even at that time, I was sympathetic to those doing guard duty.

On our way to the base, we would stop off at a bakery and get a tray of doughnuts, which the boys took in turns to hold, always seeming to want to lift up the sides of the cardboard platter to stare at the doughnuts for some reason, even though they had seen them when we were buying them and they would see them again. As we approached the checkpoint at the entrance to the base, I knew that many people, especially in authorised cars such as mine, would merely wind down the window to show their identity to the guard who approached the vehicle, but I was in the routine of indicating to them that I would park in the inspection bay, where I would then lead the boys back to the guardhouse. With the number of soldiers rotating

through this duty, it was seldom that I knew any of the people on duty, or they knew me, and although I was wearing civvies, when I handed them my ID card, the guard commander would always snap to attention, commanding his subordinates to do the same, and flashed me a salute. Often these guys were fresh out of basics, so there was a lot of energy and style in their salute. Not being in uniform, I braced in acknowledgement, aware that my boys were trying to do the same thing.

I asked him to stand easy which he did, as did the guards.

"My boys are civilians," I said to the guard commander, in earshot of the guards. "With your permission I would like them to introduce themselves to your troops and learn their first names, if that is acceptable to you."

It never happened that my request was declined. "My boys are civilians," I repeated. "They do not have rank." So my boys worked their way around, introducing themselves and shaking hands, and making sure they heard the names of the guards, knowing that the game would be that I wanted them to remember the names, so they could greet them by name when we departed. I signed into the logbook, and got my boys to sign in after me. This wasn't required, but I liked it, and the boys liked it, and I would like to think that it was reasonably pleasant for the guards to have the company of my boys for a while, who , as their proud father, considers that everyone would wish to spend time with them.

The boys were immediately attracted to the rifles, and wanted to touch them, wanted to handle them. I allowed them to touch, while the rifle was securely held by the guard, but I didn't want the boys to handle the weapon. The excitement could make them silly. In time I would take them to a range, and teach them and let them try, but a firearm is not a toy, and should never be played with.

The boys had always asked and pleaded to be allowed to hand the tray of doughnuts over to the guard commander, but there was a line there which most people would have ignored. Maybe I over think! I felt that it could be seen as patronising for the guard commander to find himself in a situation to accept the present from a young child, and despite my assertion that they were civilians, all present would have been aware of them being the children of a senior officer. "We've brought you some doughnuts," I told the guard commander, handing him the tray. "Would you mind if my boys each had one before we leave you?"

There was always a response of; `Not at all, Sir' or similar. To me this little ritual was important. It wasn't as though I had bought the doughnuts for the boys, and I was offhandedly giving the remainder of the doughnuts to the guards. Maybe no such thoughts ever crossed their minds, and along with the relief of having a senior officer leave their presence, they enjoyed the doughnuts.

On the way back, we would do the reverse, we would go in to the guardhouse, sign out again, and unless they had been a shift change of the guards, I wanted the boys to show that

they had remembered the guards names. I usually I had helped rehearse with them, handshaking, signing out again, and followed by ice creams on the way home in reward for their hopefully good memories of the guards names.

It followed me into my line of work to consider it to be very important to know people's names, which affects people's relationship with you. I am wryly amused with people who consider themselves to be too important to ever remember, or to make any attempt to remember names of people. But that's just me!

*

When I drove into the base, the boys were used to seeing the soldiers on guard snap to attention when they recognised and saluted me, which the boys appreciated, waving back at the soldiers standing rigidly to attention, with large grins on the boys' faces, and enjoying the waving. I had to explain to them that the soldiers were not allowed to smile or wave back, and that they were not being unfriendly or rude to them.

I have an exercise routine, which I mostly do at home. Not only is it expected as part of a military career, no matter that it is under another guise, but it is a routine part of my life. It has always been a fascination to my sons, in their different ways for as long as they were mobile. When they were little, the obvious action was of them riding on my back while I was doing push-ups, and the other was having them singularly, or each sitting on one of my feet as I did sit-ups,

leading to the action of me tickling their tummies each time I was in the forward position of having my head at my knees. This led to giggling and squirming, which made it difficult to concentrate on completing my exercise regime, and often I prioritised tickling and haggling and roughhousing with the boys until they grew tired of it – or more realistically Debbie intervened to say that I was making them overexcited. This did mean that later I would need to find an occasion, possibly after they had gone to bed, when I would be able to actually do my-work out to my satisfaction. It was mostly cardiovascular work that I did, and as the opposite of Leon who loved pushing mega weights and maintaining his exaggerated bulky upper body strength, but this difference was similar to our difference in personalities – and to our work roles!

Although we lived in a suburban house, I had the right of access to the unit gym at its barracks discreetly within the larger army camp, and there are times when I would go there, although generally I didn't like the exhibitionist attitudes of many of the people there. My boys loved going there, and they would often nag me to take them.

*

Right next to the gym was the swimming pool, an interesting pool in that it was functional rather than intended for family entertainment, and was used by the various water polo teams, had diving boards for the diving team, and would be used for some training and testing of scuba equipment. It was deep, and wasn't as long as would be required for the

relay swimming teams. The teams practised in the evening, and usually we had the pool to ourselves, which the boys thoroughly enjoyed for a while, although seemed to time-limit themselves. I didn't quite understand it, but it seemed that if we were the only people there, and even if we had Colin with us, they missed not having other children playing and splashing around. This seemed to make them suddenly want to finish with the pool. I made sure always that I had discussed in advance with the boys that if we went to the pool, they had to be prepared for us come away if there was anything official going on. That was part of the deal!

Anticipating we would have it to ourselves, I took inflatables along with us, and with the equipment for compressed air for the scuba-diving, I got an adapter so that I could inflate the toys in record time, without exploding them. With us being there alone, and the obvious privacy, the boys had enjoyed skinny-dipping, but Roman was growing out of enjoying this. After time in the gym, he was content to shower naked in the shower area, which was general rather than having cubicles, but he was at the age where he preferred to wear swimming trunks at the pool. T-Roy, ever the show-off, would enjoy running around naked and flaunting himself – in the showers as well as the swimming pool, to the amusement of any of the other military personnel who came to shower while we were there.

Towering domineeringly over the pool was the set of three diving boards, of whatever the standard heights were. Each time I took the boys to the pool, there would be a time when, with great solemnity, they would spend time on the

boards, seriously considering the magnitude of what they were doing, before they finally jumped. This was confined to the lowest board, though, and I was happy to watch, in the pool with my elbows on the edge, ready to swim to retrieve them should this be necessary. The boys were confident to dive off the edge of the pool, but not from the actual diving board, and they jumped instead. Roman was content to do this, but T-Roy, ever pushing the limits, went up to the middle height board. Looking down at me – our eyes locked – and I could see some fear. Had he realised that he had set himself a challenge too far? I was confident that he was perfectly safe if he jumped from the middle board, hoping he wouldn't do a belly flop, which would hurt like hell from that height, but there was little chance of this with their habit of jumping.

I decided to give him a way out. "Do you want to put your trunks on for this?" I asked, although realising that the thin fibre of his Speedo would probably not do much to protect his (not so) privates. But, if he came down to fetch his Speedo from my gym bag, I could try to distract him with some other activity, so he would not lose face – and he certainly wouldn't want to lose face while his big brother was watching. But no, he stayed there, wrestling with his fear – his eyes still locked to mine. In my experience of parachuting, which I suspect is shared by those who don't progress on to skydiving, the actual step passed the point of no return is where one faces and overcomes one's fear. Passed that hurdle, and exhilaration kicks in!

I decided to save him – from himself – and was about to instruct him to come down, and he sensed this, and before I could finish my request, he jumped!

Still with his eyes locked on mine, I saw the beam of exhilaration shine from his face before he vanished in the splash of the water. T-Roy triumphant!

Chapter Three

Colin

My career was a vocation, rather than a job, and although I usually had regular hours, around an eight hour day, I would be at work for the hours required, which could be unpredictable, depending on what projects were ongoing at any particular time. I don't generally see that coming home late was a part of my life, although it usually seems to have been that way in the events I am describing here. I really enjoyed my time with the boys, and would certainly do my best to be home in good time to at least have a chat with them before bedtime, and to read stories to them.

It was on the night in question that Debbie was waiting for me in the hallway when I had put the car away in the garage. The timing was such that I expected that the boys would be ready for bed, if not already in bed. After a greeting embrace in the hallway, Debbie suggested; "You can go and do what you enjoy doing most!"

I thought of replying; 'What? Getting a massage from my beautiful and loving wife?' But I picked up that there was something conspiratorial in the way she said it.

"What? Mowing the lawn? At this time of night? What will the neighbours say?"

She stuck her tongue out at me. "Being a dad!"

"You'd better go and settle your younger son, or we are going to have some very tired and grumpy boys in the morning." She followed me to the boys' room, and added "We've got one more than usual!" As we approached, there was the brief mad scrambling sound as children who were not in bed hastily bounced into bed and pretend to be fast asleep. As if!

Award-winning little actor, in a few seconds, T-Roy moved from pretending to be so fast asleep that he was snoring, to waking up with stretching and yawning, and then a delighted cry of `MyDaddy' on seeing me standing in the doorway. Then a squeal of `fighty time!' or `wrestle time!', but it was too late for that, so he compromised to `story time!', but it was too late for that as well. He introduced me to Colin who was lying next to him in the nest, puzzled about what he should be doing, or how to react to T-Roy's dramatics.

I knew who Colin was – Colin Harrison – that he was one of T-Roy's classmates, me taking an interest in such things – old habits die hard! I hadn't thought that Colin was in T-Roy's inner circle, so I was surprised that he was here, although it was unusual for the boys to have friends for sleepovers, and this wasn't something that we particularly encouraged. I could vaguely place his mother, Karen, who had struck me as being quite needy, even from the very limited contact I had had with her. I doubt I had given either of them any thought before this evening. Colin was a shy, rather mousy little boy, and it didn't make sense to me that

155

he should be suddenly spending the night with us, but I am sure that all will be explained to me in good time.

I could see Roman with his all-seeing eyes, watching boa-constrictor-like from the top bunk, where he would stay until his later habitual slink to beside Debbie in our bed. When T-Roy got to sleep, he would sleep through an earthquake, whereas Roman was a very light sleeper, and aware of what was happening around him. I went over to him, and he reached down for a good night kiss and for me to stroke his hair.

"You need to settle down and go to sleep," I told T-Roy, and by implication Colin. "We've got a big day tomorrow, and you will enjoy it more if you're not tired and grumpy!" (I did not know what a big day it would be, especially for Colin. In a good way!)

I shifted the little boys apart, in their nest, and lay down on the top of the quilt between them, and cuddled them up to me, with an arm around each set of shoulders. T-Roy cuddled into me with the familiarity of having done so all of his life, but it was pleasing that Colin did likewise, him probably being aware that Debbie was around, and sitting in the passageway outside, leaning against the far wall, watching.

"MyDaddy" T-Roy started in a singsong way, to start a conversation.

"Try to get some sleep now, Sunshine," I said to him softly, trying to sound dreamy.

But T-Roy was far too excited to do that. He had a secret, and he hadn't quite got the hang of keeping secrets, as opposed to broadcasting them. "I'm not really supposed to tell you… "

"T-Roy!" Debbie said sternly from outside the room. "Wait until tomorrow!"

"Ah, but can't I just say a little bit…"

"No. Leave it until tomorrow. Go to sleep!"

"You heard your mummy," I said gently in his ear, hugging him into me with my arm.

I lay there between them, an arm around each, and listened as gradually T-Roy's breathing settled, and I knew he was asleep. I turned my head to kiss his forehead, and as I moved back I was aware of Colin sitting up, to look over me at the slumbering T-Roy. "Try to go to sleep, Colin," I said gently. "Please don't wake T-Roy. It's nice to have you here," I added, naïve to what was going on. I tousled his hair, and careful so as not to disturb T-Roy, I stood up and padded out of the door, where Debbie stood up, to walk back with me.

I raised my eyebrows to look inquiringly at her. "Wait until morning," she teased. Hey I am an adult! Okay, I won't claim to be the (only) breadwinner! But as an adult, don't I get a preview of the secret? Apparently not!

She kept her secret during the evening, and during the massage and more that she gave me, and I asked several times, knowing that she was enjoying the secret, and I was

amused to see that in a profession that involved gathering, keeping and using secrets, I could wait. She was happy, if not slightly conspiratorial, and the boys were happy, and Colin didn't seem to be distressed.

"Can't you just tell me a little bit?" I said, trying to mimic T-Roy.

"Wait until morning,"

"Is there anything I need to do? Anything to prepare?"

"You will know what to do, when the time comes," she teased me. "I know you will do what is required of you." I think she was quoting something, but I didn't understand the reference. "You have been chosen for this task. And I know that you will do the right thing!"

With that, I knew that she would not disclose, as there was something she was relishing, so I left it with her.

*

It was the usual scenario, next morning, of me being awake, Debbie drowsing, with Roman cuddled up to her when the naked ninja bounded, muted into our room, his self-styled karate moves amplified as he showed off to Colin, also naked, but inhibited with his hands clamped over his privates so hard that he seemed to be pushing himself backwards.

I was about to ask Colin to go and put some undies on, but Debbie reached over Roman and shut my mouth with a

couple of fingers. "It's okay," she whispered. Then: "Colin, get in between Romey and Uncle Max."

He did so with a rather clumsy and uncoordinated scramble over the bed clothes, before I found him settled in next to me. T-Roy seem to be slightly taken aback by this, in that his challenging combat moves stopped, and he moved to get in beside me in his usual place between me and the edge of the bed.

"Will you visit me in Prison?" I asked Debbie.

"I just love the look of horror on your face," Debbie chuckled.

T-Roy was in bed beside me, his legs covered by the duvet, but he was sitting up to participate as there was an important conversation to be had. I wondered whether he would be resentful at Colin being parked in the position he coveted, of being on the inside of me, but he was distracted by other things. Possibly secret things!

"Why would you go to prison, MyDaddy?" T-Roy asked. He wouldn't let any comment like that pass. He patted the side of my chest, reassuringly, with his hand.

"I could get into big trouble for being in bed with a naked little boy!"

"But you are usually in bed in the morning with a naked boy!" I noticed how he had left out the word little! "And sometimes Romey's naked as well."

159

"That's different. You are my sons. That's allowed. But I hardly know Colin!" Colin cuddled in closer to me, and I put my arm around him.

"If you go to prison, I will come and rescue you, MyDaddy!" T-Roy was already looking forward to the adventure. It was a theme that he was working on, rescuing me, which usually involved him swinging down on a rope from on high, as demonstrated both by Tarzan and by Spider-Man, and lifting me up and out of danger, and taking me home with him to ask his mummy if I could stay.

So, there we were five in the bed – the usual positions – T-Roy between me and the edge of the bed, so he could fidget and chat without disturbing Debbie and Roman too much, and Debbie at the edge of the bed. But the newcomer, with a large beaming grin, lay between Roman and me.

"MyDaddy", T-Roy started, a predictable path leading to a discussion, invariably one for his amusement, but to be fair, usually of amusement to all of us, even though Roman tried to create the impression of disinterest.

"Yes?" I drawled back in reply.

"MyDaddy, you know Colin …" Okay, T-Roy was going somewhere with this, but in a time honoured manner, I would frustrate him slightly, but as he had my undivided attention, T-Roy was generally a very happy child.

"Could that be Colin Young, the three times Olympic gold medal winner for carrying 17 hamsters and their wheel up Mount Everest ..."

"Noo!"

"Would that be ..." I could keep this up for a while, running through a range of surnames and then a more fantastic set of achievements that could lead to the fame or notoriety of hypothetical Colins other than the one cuddled up next to me, T-Roy's guest for the weekend.

Debbie got involved – slightly amused, slightly irritated. "Good cop, bad cop, and the cop that will get anyone to confess anything just to stop the endless mindless verbiage..."

If the boys hadn't been there, likely to ask questions, and possibly to quote what they heard to others, I might have quipped; "It saves wear and tear on my knuckles!" in a game that Debbie and I played, but now was not a good time for that game.

"Its not mindless ..." I chided. "Its quite hard work trying to be original and not repeat myself. You'd be surprised! Many people I talk to really want to sing 'Ten million bottles hanging on the wall ...'"

"Ten million?" - Roman suddenly whirred into life ... "That would take forever ..."

There was a 'not in front of the children ...' exchange of glances between Debbie and me.

"Let T-Roy get where he wants to go ..." Debbie instructed.

"MyDaddy – you know Colin Harrison..."

"Would that be the ..."

"Max!!"

"Would that be Colin Harrison, the little rudey-nudey cuddled in next to me?" I finished hastily to placate Debbie.

"You're a rudey-nudey," T-Roy challenged.

"Hey! This is my bed. I'm allowed to be naked - ask your mummy. All was fine until a horde of little goblins came bouncing onto my bed and disturbed us all."

"Enough," said Debbie. "Carry on T-Roy ..."

"MyDaddy, Colin's willy is the same as yours. The doctor also took the skin away from over his acorn."

Oh, dear. The `acorn' word. Although he said it himself, T-Roy, gigged. Roman wanted to be big stuff and not be amused at the things that amused little boys, but he had to work hard perfecting this, but he couldn't stop himself from giggling. Colin looked confused, maybe embarrassed, but he realised that this was something deemed to be funny, so he joined in the giggling.

I shot a sidelong glance over to Debbie. She caught it and with a nod of her head indicated that this was all fine, and not something that needed to be stopped.

"Colin, are you okay with what T-Roy has just told me about you?"

"Yus," Colin replied, with the husky deep little voice which always surprised me, coming as it did from such a small body.

"MyDaddy, Colin asked if he can see your willy ..." T-Roy said loudly and deliberately basking in the spotlight of attention.

"No I didn't!" Colin denied frantically, shrinking visibly and bright red with embarrassment.

Another look from me to Debbie with some anguish, but I got the same reassuring nod back from Debbie.

"It's all right, Colin – T-Roy," Debbie reassured.

Now what? It didn't seem right for me to do what T-Roy was always so willing to do – to pull down the covers and show his privates to anyone who had given him the slightest excuse to do so – within very tight confines of family and very close friends.

An obvious possibility occurred to me. "Colin, it's not a problem. In a couple of minutes I'm going to get up and go for a wee. I'm wearing the same as you and T-Roy are wearing ..."

"He's also bare ..." T-Roy explained as though there was any need whatsoever to clarify the matter ...

"If you also need a wee, you can come along as well and have a wee at the same time. Does that sound like a plan?"

"Yus!"said Colin.

"And I'm coming too …" T-Roy announced. I'd just exchanged another glance with Debbie, who smiled and nodded her approval.

"If you come, you have to wee as well," I told T-Roy. "And you, Colin, you have to need a wee …"

"Roman …"

"No, I'm all right …" I didn't want him to feel excluded, but I certainly wasn't surprised that he declined my invitation.

So there I am, walking down the passage to the toilet, followed by two naked little boys who supposedly also need a wee, but it's a viewing that they want.

We did the necessary, standing around the bowl and I told Colin: "You can look. You don't have to be shy …" He had a look, but then I found him looking up at me, wide-eyed. He started to look worried …

"I can't wee …" he told me, T-Roy and I having finished. He looked worried.

"Its all right," I assured him, ruffling his hair with the hand I hadn't just used. "You tried. That's the main thing …"

And so the naked trio of us walked back to the bedroom, and T-Roy dived into the bed, and Colin followed his lead,

with me getting in between them at a more sedate pace. Again an exchange of glances between Debbie and me. How did it go? Fine! Good – thanks. "I'll explain later," she told me.

The three boys had some discussion about something that interested them greatly, and about which Debbie and I had no knowledge. We were warm and relaxed and enjoying the company of our boys, and amused at the effect of the newcomer on them – Roman working hard to be aloof and older, and T-Roy excited to have a new playmate.

Above their heads, Debbie gave me some more information. "Visitor's (a camouflaged reference to Colin) mom asked if he could at least talk about it with a good role model," she started. "Anything more ..."

"Do I get to meet this role model? I think I would like to ..." and Debbie stuck her tongue out at me. I love that little tongue. I love the way she sticks it out at me.

" ... she said to treat him as one of our own, and I told her of the usual routines, and she's happy for him to be included in anything that's on offer ..." Quite a lot of information – thanks Debbie – but presented in a way that went over the heads of the three boys. Well, two of them. Roman carefully monitored what was said between Debbie and me.

Then Colin looked up at me with a slight hint of apprehension ...

"Uncle Max ..."

"Yes, Colin …?"

A long awkward pause. "I have to go and have a wee …"

"Not a problem, Colin. …"

An awkward pause. "I'm sorry I couldn't wee when we all
went …"

"Not a problem. Just go now. … "

"I'll come with you …" T-Roy volunteered, already out of
bed. (T-Roy, why so interested?)

Colin got up out of bed, and made his way over the bed on
his hands and knees, before standing up, where his hand
hovered over his privates. Was he fighting between the
habits of a lifetime to keep his privates private by any means
possible? Even with a group of people he liked and who had
all seen him naked, Debbie and Roman when the boys had
bathed the previous night. "Colin, on your way back, you
can fetch your undies if you want to wear them …"

That seemed to confuse him. "Do you want me to?" in the
little gruff voice that still surprised me.

"Debbie?" I asked. (You're the boss!)

"You can choose, Colin. You can wear your undies like
Romey, or you can be like T-Roy, and we see your cute little
bottom." Quite flirtatious from Debbie, and he wasn't our
child!

"Bum," T-Roy challenged.

166

"Arse," Roman ventured, followed by the sound of an admonishing slap on an undies-covered arse.

So, two naked giggling little boys wandered down the passage to the bathroom where the giggling continued, and they stayed there much longer than it could have taken for Colin to have had the wee that he hadn't managed to do when he had been there with me.

Vowing Roman to secrecy, and he was not to repeat it elsewhere ... We trust the boy with too much information! Debbie explained that Colin's father had been circumcised for whatever reason and so, `like father like son', Colin had a routine infant circumcision. And then, having left his indelible mark on his son, before Colin had any strong memories of him, his father left, and contact swiftly decreased and ended completely. Not very long later, stepfather comes on the scene – who had no interest in Colin on any level, and then along comes Colin's little step-brother, and `like father like son', junior gets to keep his foreskin. Which Colin gets to see on a fairly regular basis with nappy changes, and junior getting to toddle around naked in the back garden.

At school, the willies that Colin gets to see are intact, and he knows he is different, and when he complained to his mom, the fact that his status was in honour of his father who had buggered off wasn't a major reassuring factor. It remained a sore point (did I really say that?) to young Colin – being told to accept it and that it was no big deal. Until one of the strangest `short term pain for long term gain'- situation

when a big mouth child with a special interest in willies, especially his own, extended his interest to Colin and announced to Colin; "Your willy is just like MyDaddy's!" (Ladies and gentlemen of the audience, may I introduce you yet again to my younger son, Troy Russell Maxwell!)

Any attention to his penis was unwanted from Colin, and he blushed and ran out and burst into tears. The duty teacher realised that T-Roy had said something that upset Colin. Colin wouldn't say what had been said, and the teacher told T-Roy to apologise. T-Roy was incandescent! He found himself having to explain to them that being like his MyDaddy was a good thing, that his MyDaddy was a good thing, "Better than Batman ... almost as good as Spiderman ...", and that T-Roy loved his MyDaddy more than anyone else in the whole, big, fat world – except of course for his mom. (Debbie, this is your version of events, I understand, but I believe it.)

"I'd settle for Batman," I confided to Debbie, with the image of me driving the Batmobile along futuristic roads, with Debbie as Catwoman beside me - though she wouldn't have liked the Lycra suit one bit- and in the back seat behind us, both boys dressed as Robin the Wonder Boy, as we pursued our mission to make the world a safer place.

"What about Superman?" I asked, before remembering T-Roy's standing answer to such a question. Debbie and I said in unison; "Superman isn't real!" Jinx!

Colin was placated that T-Roy was trying to be nice. T-Roy was generally seen as being nice. Colin was pleased to learn that there was a good man around whose willy was the same as his. He wasn't the only one. Colin told his mummy, and she too asked if T-Roy was being nasty, and learning about T-Roy's Dad, who she knew by name, and saw as a positive role-model. So as a mother attempting to be a good mom while under a lot of stress, Karen approached Debbie, explained the situation as she understood it, and finding Debbie receptive, asked if I would have a chat with Colin and reassure him about being circumcised.

Debbie agreed to make this happen, and suggested that Colin spend a weekend with us when convenient.

*

Then she thought that it might be nicer and more relaxed all round if Colin came to spend the weekend with us – we have a Scandinavian acceptance of nudity behind closed doors, and our boys, although intact, know about their dad being circumcised, and so their attitude could also be helpful to young Colin if, with his mom giving him permission, he wanted spend time nude. Debbie would alert me, and with Karen's agreement, we would treat Colin as one of our own while he stayed. And so it came to pass – except, Debbie – I can't help noticing that I could have had some warning, rather than suddenly find a naked little boy that I don't know well clambering down beside my naked bed-sheet-covered body.

"I love to see the expression of terror in your eyes!" she repeated.

"Thank you, love of my life! Is this the shape of things to come, that you will pimp me out for what you consider to be worthy causes."

Oh, the scowl I got from her! "If I was to pimp you out I could turn a much bigger profit than to offer you out to reassure little boys whose willies have been cut!"

I won't go there. The two naked gigglers returned to the bedroom – Colin's hands still uncertain whether to cover his privates or not, but he decided not to. "Colin, was it your choice not to wear your shorts?"

"Yus!"

"T-Roy didn't persuade you?"

"No."

It was comfortable for me to stretch my arms down beside the two boys who were snuggled up to me, and I enjoyed Colin gradually relaxing and moulding against my chest.

A good place to end this story, expect it doesn't end there. Two significant further developments coming up.

Over to Troy Russell Maxwell, my source of great joy and great embarrassment!

"MyDaddy …"

"Yes?"

"Are you going to shower?"

"Yes?"

"Can I shower with you?"

"If you want to."

"MyDaddy…"

"Yes?"

"Can Colin shower with you?"

Whoa! Okay, let's work this through. "Colin, nothing bad, but will you cover year ears and not listen while I ask Roman something?"

"Yus", and his hands went over his ears.

"I'll help," says T-Roy and from his position, he leans over my chest and clamps his hands over Colin's hands which are over his ears. Colin will still be able to hear – I sort of know why I do the `don't listen' when I know they can hear, but it's probably too hard to explain.

"Roman, is it okay with you if I let Colin shower with me?" Okay, I am asking permission of my 9-year-old, but I am their father, they have some say over me, and they will be my priority. I know that Roman is reaching the stage that while he loves sleeping in our bed, he now wants to wear shorts, and recently he has stopped wanting to shower with me. He

was never quite as enthusiastic as T-Roy, but now he prefers not to, though he is fine with being in the bathroom when I am showering with T-Roy. I make sure that he does not feel excluded. He's growing up, and that saddens me because I have loved him as a `little boy', and while I am sure I will love him as a `medium boy', that is the great unknown to me – and let us not even think of his teenage years and what adolescent hormones will do to his charming disposition.

"That's okay." I think he had the gist of what lay behind much of what was happening, and I don't know whether Debbie had briefed him, but I think he understood that Debbie thought it was a kind thing for Colin to spend some quality time with me. He would generally do what he believed Debbie wanted him to do.

"Okay, hands down," I instructed, and the boys took their hands from Colin's ears. T-Roy sat up straight in his place, as I rolled back, so he could look over me and see Colin, Roman and of course, his mom. Decisions were to be made, and he liked what he thought the outcome would be.

"Okay, Colin. There are ways that we do things in this family that might be different from other families. Your mom told Auntie Debbie that she wants to treat you as though you were one of our boys. Did she tell you that?"

"She told me to do what you and Auntie Debbie tell me to do."

Whoa! That's a bit heavy!

"I have a shower every morning. On weekends or holidays, when we have time, Roman and T-Roy shower with me if they want to. Its their choice. Roman is getting older and doesn't want to anymore, and that's fine. T-Roy wants to and that's fine. If you want to, you can shower with me."

"Yus!"

"First I'll shower with T-Roy, and you watch. Auntie Debbie will be there, and Roman if he wants to. I wash T-Roy and then I kneel down, and T-Roy can wash my back. Just my back."

"Then we get out and I dry him, and I have a cuddle with him. He doesn't like that -"Okay, this is not true. T-Roy loves that as much as he loves the attention and the contact as I wash him, and as he washes my back, but then there's just so much that T-Roy really loves. But a warning to Colin in advance, that a cuddle while he's freshly dry in Debbie's characteristic big fluffy white towels is a possibility – and to alert my boys that I am offering Colin a cuddle. Debbie will be there throughout as reassurance to me. But they don't need to know that.

"Okay, so you watch me shower with T-Roy, and then you decide if you want to do the same or not."

"Yus".

Colin Harrison; A lad of few words, but many `Yus's.

So it was that the party decamped down to the bathroom – Debbie in her shorty pyjamas made a nest for herself to be

comfortable and insulated from the coolness of the tiled floor and walls, Roman still in just his shorts sat in front of her leaning back against her, and she enveloped him in her large white fluffy towel. She massaged his shoulders.

I washed T-Roy's neck and shoulders while he had his back to me. Colin stood watching - fascinated. Debbie had put a towel around his waist. I think I understood that it was okay to be naked in bed, naked in the shower or naked while doing some task, but it was better for him to have some temporary privacy. The towel had slipped from Colin's waist leaving him naked, but he hadn't noticed.

"I can see your willy," I teased him. Instantly he clamped his hand over his privates, pushing his groin back, and his bare bottom almost into Debbie's face. She immediately pushed it, not hard, but he jerked forward again. Poor little boy, he couldn't move!

"Colin," Debbie called to him, and he looked back to her. "Max is teasing you. You can stick your tongue out at him."

We had forgotten how mind blowing this morning had become for him. "You are allowed to if Debbie says you can," I encouraged him, my hand rested on T-Roy's shoulder, paused in washing him.

Tears started to well up in his eyes. "I don't want to," he stammered.

"It's all right, Colin," Debbie reassured him, with a hand on his back.

I continued washing T-Roy, including his privates and his bottom, and he held onto my arm while standing on one leg so I could wash that foot, before changing over. I glanced over at Colin, who met my gaze. He was looking into my face – any wish to see another circumcised penis had worn off.

Having washed him, as was our custom, I knelt in the cubicle with my back to T-Roy, and he was allowed to wash my neck and shoulders and back, but no lower. He followed his ritual of suggesting that he should wash more of me, which I declined, and he pointed out that he allowed me to wash him all over, so it was only fair that he should be allowed to wash me all over. No, that wasn't going to happen! Then I dried T-Roy with one of Debbie's trademarked fluffy white towels, a cuddle being intrinsic to the process. Then it was done, and T-Roy, chose to remain naked – or more likely, the thought of covering himself with anything did not occur to him – put the towel on the tiled floor next to Debbie and cuddled into her, watching...

Still naked, I looked to Debbie with raised eyebrows, indicating Colin, whose eyes remained locked on me. Debbie asked him; "Do you want Max – Uncle Max to wash you like he washed T-Roy?"

"Yus!"

"Come on then," I said adjusting the water. Colin stepped into the shower with me, looking up into my face. It was straightforward to wash his hair, face, ears, neck and chest

175

and tummy "Are you sure you want me to do exactly like T-Roy?" I said with my soaped hand hovering at his privates.

"Yus," came his reply, without missing a beat. I wasn't surprised. I washed him, as I had washed my younger son, and at the end I asked – fair's fair – if he wanted to wash my back, which again got a `Yus', so I assume the position. Colin was nothing if not thorough, and my back must have been the cleanest – if not waterlogged – it has ever been in my life! Then it was the drying with the white fluffy towel with the integral cuddle. I knew that he was enjoying it.

Then it was job done, two clean little boys, and my fingers and toes were wrinkled. Debbie gave me an approving smile.

*

"Will you chaperone me?" I asked Debbie. "There's still something more I want to tell Colin." We moved to the boys room in convoy, T-Roy stark naked, followed by Colin with a towel around his waist, then Roman in his undies with a towel around his shoulders, then Debbie in her nightwear, and me now wearing a towel.

There, Roman slunk up to the top bunk, and his watchful position. I asked T-Roy and Colin to sit close up next to each other on the edge of the bottom bunk. I crouched down to be at their level. I explained to Colin how a foreskin, like the one sported by T-Roy next to him made it pleasanter to hold and touch ones willy, and how without it, the acorn was less slippery.

"You need to start getting ready for church," was the next item for the agenda. Yes, you read that right! Church! We attended Sunday church services regularly. The boys had grown up with it, as something that the Maxwell family do, even though they didn't find it particularly enjoyable, but they, well T-Roy in particular, enjoyed the socialising with other children afterwards, invariably involving a lot of running around.

Colin attended with us, within the remit of us treating him as one of our own for the weekend, enjoying sitting between me and T-Roy on the pew, and mirroring what we did, though he was slightly confused when I handed him a coin to put in the collection box when it was on its way around, and I had to whisper an explanation to him that the coin had not been a present specifically for him.

*

I noticed that Colin seemed to become quieter and retreat into himself as the time drew nearer for us to take him home. Debbie confirmed when I asked her that she had the same impression. "I like him," I told her. "Do we invite him again?" Debbie was ahead of me, as usual. She had sounded the boys out about inviting Colin again, and both were keen. T-Roy was very enthusiastic – him having a brand-new playmate, and one who was going to be fairly compliant and follow what T-Roy wanted to do, which Roman, as the older brother, sometimes had to make a

178

stand against doing what T-Roy suggested. Roman was happy for Colin to come again, not as enthusiastic as T-Roy, but said he would like Colin to come again. There was no discussion that while Colin was welcome in our house, our boys would not go to stay at Colin's house overnight.

I felt it was important for me to hand Colin back to his mum – and stepfather? – and Debbie was content for me to do so. Both boys wanted to come along.. Karen opened the door to us. She looked tipsy before I smelt the drink on her breath. Her toddler had followed her to the door, with a bottle of milk in his hand, wearing a nappy that needed changing.

"We've brought Colin back," I stated the obvious. "We enjoyed having him!"

Karen leaned forward to hug Colin, who responded. "Have you been a good boy?" She asked, and he nodded.

"Yes he has. He's been a credit to you!"

"Debbie explained the background to me," I added. "That was fine. I took him into the shower with me, and he was fine with that."

"Lucky boy!" She said, stroking his hair, and with a flirtatious glance at me which looked grotesque through the influence of alcohol.

"Colin, tell your mummy what you did when you were visiting with us," – what at work we would call a debriefing – while I was there to explain or clarify anything that a six-year-old might have difficulty articulating. Colin did quite

well, telling of the toys that they had played with, and the games that they had played which, despite knowing them, I would not have been able to understand from Colin's description. Then there was the bath the previous night with Roman and T-Roy, and then the cuddles in bed this morning, the shower with T-Roy and me, church, and playing in the park in the afternoon, before the wind down to bringing him home.

Little toddler boy was holding onto Karen's leg, looking up at me with fascination. Beyond her, within the house I saw her present partner moving across the visible area, with a sidelong glance at me, reminiscent of a shark showing its presence. Cue the *Jaws theme*'! Was he stating his territoriality towards another male? (He could rest assured that I would not make a move on Karen, even if Debbie and I had never found each other!) I found this amusing, rather than intimidating! But let him not hurt a hair on Colin's head – let him not dare!

"I've enjoyed you staying with us," I told Colin, kneeling down. "Can I have a goodbye hug?" He almost leapt into my arms, and melted in to me.

"Can I come again next weekend?" he asked, slightly desperately.

"We'll have to see ..." I said, knowing that it would have to be Karen's decision, modified in whichever way by her partner, and it was not something that I, or we, could negotiate with Colin.

I clamped my hands over Colin's ears, and mouthed to Karen; "That's fine with us!" She smiled!

I disengaged from Colin, only to find little toddler staggering over to take his place, with a broad grin, and I hugged him briefly. It would be rude not to. T-Roy gave Colin a rather awkward hug, but Roman - ever the understated - shook Colin's hand.

We walked back to the car, with Karen, one arm around Colin's shoulder, waving, as Colin waved with his free hand, and toddler beamed after us while holding onto his mother's leg for stability. I felt sad that Karen felt the need to be under the influence of alcohol so early in the day, with her two children to take care of.

Early on Monday evening there was a phone call, and Debbie handed the receiver to me. She expected it, but had chosen not to share it with me. It was Karen, sounding sober, which was a relief, thanking me for my input with Colin, and saying that he was a very happy boy. She partly apologised for having been `tired' when I had bought Colin back, and I murmured `no problem' and withheld my disapproval.

When she felt the time was right, Debbie briefed me that Karen had already thanked her, and again said that it had been very good for Colin. Debbie outlined that he had fitted in well, that the boys had been consulted, and all of us would like him to come and stay with us again, as soon as it worked out for everyone. Debbie suggested that Karen

might make this a reward for Colin if he did his chores, was pleasant to his (step) brother et cetera, and next weekend was entirely possible if Colin had earned it, and if Karen and her partner agreed.

On Tuesday, Debbie handed me a 'thank you' drawing from Colin which Karen had given her when they had fetched the children from school. It stated; '*I love unkil Max, I love arnty Debbbie, I love Teeroy, I love Rummy*' and a picture of two stick figures in a shower, and of 5 stick figures apparently in bed. There were also some hearts, a rainbow, and some birds in flight, which I thought was very sweet – did he think that the more work he put into the drawing, the more likely it would be that he would be allowed to visit again?

*

If, after having come to church with us, Colin had decided to try praying for what he wanted, then he would have found his prayers answered, as he did come to stay with us for the whole of the next weekend. Debbie told me of the poignant conversation they had had. Karen was grateful, and said that she was sacrificing some of the pride she felt in being a mother to Colin, for his best interests – but there was a shadow over the conversation which Debbie thought was that her present partner was quite keen to have Colin out of the house. Karen would not go so far as to admit this.

I was home as early as I ever came home that Friday, to find, as expected, that Debbie had brought Colin with his extra suitcase home from school along with our two. I took them

182

along to the park where we played until it was time to go home for tea, after which we had a pleasant evening of playing games on the floor. Debbie bathed them, although I thought that T-Roy and Colin would want to shower with me in the morning, and, for the first time, Colin got to join in with our bedtime story reading routine.

I was woken by a small child cuddling in with me. I knew it wasn't T-Roy. It was Colin, sneaking into `his' position on my inside side, into the gap between where I lay, and where I was aware that Roman was asleep – if he did sleep. I cuddled Colin, pulling him closer to me, and said "I'd best take you back to the boys' room!"

He was fairly dreamy, and as he cuddled into me pleaded; "Can't I just stay here for 10 minutes?" Then there was a brief silence where through his sleepiness he tried to negotiate; a sad desperation in his voice. "Even for just five minutes? Please!" I was tempted to just let him stay. I was snug, and I had a growing affection for him. My loyalties were to my own sons, and I expected that T-Roy would be unhappy if he found that Colin had cuddled in with me, and in the sought-after place between me and Debbie, with Roman being the inevitable barrier.

"You can for five minutes," I told Colin. "But then I'll take you and settle you back in the boys' room."

"I love you Uncle Max," Colin declared, building up his negotiating case. I didn't doubt that he was sincere. "Please can't I stay just a little longer? Please?"

I knew how important I was to Colin, and it was sad how his needs meant that I was the person needed to fulfil them. "I'll let you stay for 10 minutes," I told him. "Then I'll take you back to the boys' room, and I'll settle you in. T-Roy wouldn't be happy if you found you slept here, and I don't want him to fall out with you!'

I knew he was there, and I know that he is a very light sleeper, but I was surprised when Roman spoke up, quietly and clearly; "It's okay. We discussed it. T-Roy said its okay for Colin to sleep next to you!"

What? Now even my sons are pimping me out? Now wasn't the time to indulge my curiosity about what conversation had taken place, and whether T-Roy really was that generous in sharing out the asset of cuddling in with me, or whether some fiendish bargaining had taken place.

*

The original remit was that I would be helpful to Colin about being circumcised, and despite what we had done the previous weekend, there was something else that I thought might be helpful for him, and amusing to my boys, although I hoped it would prime them to be compassionate. So there we were, five in a bed, Debbie in her T-shirt and shorts, Roman in his undies, me naked, with a little rudey-nudey cuddled up on each side of me. The conversation returned to willies but, surprisingly, it was me who initiated it. Given longer, I'm sure that T-Roy would have got there...

Roman was right, and T-Roy was okay about finding Colin cuddled up next to me, but it was important for him to know that Colin was naked. I confirmed this so that he didn't have to check. T-Roy would see for himself when we got up. T-Roy; an evangelist for nudity!

"I'm going to use a rude word," I started, "which your Mummy will allow because of why I am saying it. You're each allowed to say it once, and then not again." I said inquiring of my two. Then back to Colin; "If anyone teases you about you being circumcised, you can say to them 'Why are you so interested in my cock?'" Giggles from all three boys, and a clandestine smile from Debbie. "Understand?" Colin nodded. "Now you say it."

"Why are you so interested in my cock?" Colin repeated, with that smile of enjoying permission to say a prohibited word.

"Okay, your chance, T-Roy."

"Why are you so interested in my cock?" and then immediately he varied with "Why are you so interested in my cock-o-doodle-doo!?" He was triumphant! Again giggles from each boy, and Debbie and I found it funny.

"Your turn, Roman!" I knew he could use this chance to show off that he knew ruder words. "Don't use the 'p-word'!" I qualified.

"What? Don't say `penis'?" he asked, with mock innocence. I knew that he knew the word `prick', but I didn't want that said in the sanctuary of my bed with those I love.

"Well done! Good joke! Please don't say the rude word I know you know."

"What? The one that rhymes with bri ...?" The boy was on form!

"Don't do that, Roman."

"Why are you so interested in my dick?" he asked if, pushing the boundaries, but I was okay with him going that far.

"Will you remember that?" I asked Colin. He nodded `Yus."

"Or you can say; `My willy is just like T-Roy's dad's willy. He's seen mine, and he says it is good."' "What about my willy?" T-Roy was not going to be left out!

"Your willy is good too," I told my youngest son. I didn't want him to hijack the conversation, so speaking to Colin I added; "Or you can say; `My willy is just like Jesus Christ.' That's true. Jesus was circumcised. We can show you where it says that in the Bible if you want."

"Did someone tease you for being cir...?" And I knew T-Roy was going to struggle with the word again.

Roman looked at me with an expression which said `I know the answer to this', and I presumed he'd remembered what I had confided to him about my experience with Deep Heat.

I didn't want him to prompt the story, as I really didn't want Colin to learn about that. In Roman's sight only, I shook my head slightly, briefly, with the deliberate glance back towards T-Roy, and fortunately he understood.

I don't know how to deal with these situations. I prefer to answer questions and satisfy curiosity, rather than shutting it down, and if I say too much I hope that I do not cause damage. T-Roy can't keep secrets, so anything I tell him is likely to be broadcast, especially for effect, and especially if there is any suggestion that he could show knowledge of a secret. So let me tell him, all three of them. Maybe it will be helpful for Colin, and help develop compassion in my two.

"When I was at Ferndale," That was probably unnecessary to specify, as it had been my only home until I started with the army. Roman knew that the story I had told him about Deep Heat had not taken place within Ferndale, but away from it. The story I was about to tell happened within Ferndale, within my childhood home.

"Who teased you?" T-Roy demanded, and I gathered that he was planning to go and avenge me; probably in the way that Spider-Man would deal with the situation, which would have to be more dramatic than just a bullet in the back of the head at short range. But let me rather encourage Spider-Man-like retribution!

"No one you know," I lied. It was acceptable to me to lie to the boys on trivial matters, but my agreement was that I would not lie to Debbie, on serious matters.

"Who was it?" T-Roy was starting to show off, encouraged by Colin's presence! "You always tell us that names are important!"

"Okay, okay! It was Nelson Muntz." None of the boys picked up on the reference, but Debbie did, with a chuckle, which T-Roy had to investigate.

"Do you know him, Mummy?"

"Yes, he was in our class at school." This was an in-joke between Debbie and me. Long ago, we had watched an episode of *The Simpsons*,[1] where Bart forms an army to neutralise and capture the school bully, Nelson Muntz, leading to a peace treaty, and aware of Nelson being able to wreak retribution when he is released – as he surely must be – the treaty makes allowances for Nelson to remain `a figure of menace in the neighbourhood.'

Debbie had chuckled at the time. "Who does that remind us of?" She asked.

"I'm a pussycat," I assured her.

"I was thinking of Leon," she clarified.

"You can't let Leon loose in the neighbourhood," I chided. "It would be bedlam!"

---

[1] SE01 E05 - Bart The General

"I'm sure Leon would like to hear the description," I told Debbie. And Leon loved it when I told him, surprisingly responding; "I'm a pussycat!"

"A sabre-toothed tiger more like," I corrected him.

So, for what it was worth, Debbie knew that I was referring to Leon, who had been my best man at our wedding, and who minded our children when they had the choice of a child minder, and Debbie's poor old mom didn't get a look in if Leon was on offer.

"So what happened?" T-Roy probed sensing 'blood in the water', or that there was going to be a story involving willies and discipline, and he had great expectations of this.

"Do you want to hear?" Enthusiastic responses from T-Roy and Colin, a murmur of ascent from Roman, reserving the option of plausible deniability.

"You can't stop there," Debbie admonished me. "That would be cruel to T-Roy!"

"I can't remember the exact details, but... Nelson was teasing me about my willy being different from his, and from the other boys, and I got upset. Yes, Colin, I got upset, like you did when T-Roy first told you that yours is like mine..."

"I'm not upset with T-Roy anymore," Colin reminded.

"And I wasn't teasing you," T-Roy confirmed, two six-year-olds having an earnest conversation. "I said it was a good thing!"

189

"… and my House Mother saw that I was upset about something and asked me and I told her, and she told my House Father, and he got me and… Nelson together in his office."

"Did he spank him?" As a child who had never been spanked for real, apart from very likely in play, this was tantalising for T-Roy.

Now, committed to telling the story, I realised how completely inappropriate it was, though meant with the best of intentions by a clumsy man, and yet it had worked.

"He told us to both strip, which we did."

"So he could see your willies?"

"He was our House Father, and he was used to seeing us naked. It was a house of just boys, and it wasn't unusual." And as I was saying this, I remembered that the house rules were generally stricter about wearing clothes than we allowed in our house, with T-Roy's nudity being indulged – as with my own, and until very recently, Romans as well.

"The whole thing was that he was teasing me about being circumcised, and he wasn't circumcised, so the difference was that he had a foreskin. So my House Father – also his House Father - suggested that if there wasn't a difference between us, then Lee… Nelson would not be able to tease me. And he made Nelson agree to this. Then he asked Nelson if he thought I could get or grow a foreskin, and Nelson knew enough to know that this wouldn't be possible.

So then our House Father said he thought it would be a nice thing if Nelson gave me his foreskin, so I had one. And Nelson said that that would mean that I had a foreskin, and he didn't, which meant that there would still be a difference. And the House Father told Nelson that the operation would be very sore, and told him that if he teased me, he could be circumcised. He asked Nelson if he wanted that, and Nelson said that he didn't."

"Really?" Debbie looked at me wide-eyed. "That really happened?"

"Yes, I find it hard to believe, but I remember it clearly. And after that he made us shake hands and make up..."

"And you were both still rudey-nudeys?"

"I still am, and so are you!" I teased, as I reached down and gently squeezed a pair of buns on each side of me. Colin squeaked in surprise, but not distress.

"Yes. But it worked, and Lee... Nelson never teased me again, and he stopped anyone else from teasing me. We grew up together, and we were sort of like brothers."

*

I enjoyed reading bedtime stories to the boys. Unless I was working too late, or there was some specific activity that we were involved in as a family, I would spend at least half an hour reading to them, and quite often Debbie would come and join us. Usually I would be sitting in T-Roy's nest, leaning against the bottom bunk, with T-Roy cuddled up beside me

191

and turning the pages, while I had my arm around him. Roman either watched from the top bunk, or if Debbie had arrived before he had climbed up, he would be cuddled up with her, her probably stroking him while they listened. When Colin was with us, he would be cuddled up to me on the side opposite T-Roy, with my arm around his shoulders as well, and the boys took it in turns to turn the pages. I made sure with Roman, as Debbie did separately with him, that he didn't mind Colin being with us, and with me extending my affection to Colin.

One of the books that I would read to them from time to time was *"The Little Prince"*[2] which had special significance to me, remembering from Ferndale Hall that this had been one of Kevin's favourite books, and which he would read to the court below us as bedtime stories. This was a tribute to him, which eventually I would explain to the boys but, while they knew that Debbie's real father had died, I wanted to keep the idea of death as far from them as I could. Antoine de Saint-Exupéry wrote: *"If I am attempting to describe him, it is in order not to forget him. It is sad to forget a friend. Not every one has had a friend."* From my childhood, I was fortunate to still have Leon around and as actively involved in my life, and with my family. I did not feel that there was any risk of forgetting Kevin, as I had many happy and vivid memories of the childhood and teenage years we shared. In time, he would become a character in the lives of my children as well.

---

[2] Antoine de Saint-Exupéry: *"The Little Prince"*

T-Roy liked the character of the Fox, and he would develop the friendship between the Little Prince and the Fox to the adventures that they would have together, which involved a lot of running around, while the more contemplative Roman enjoyed the idea of the sheep in the box, though he enjoyed the con trick he recognised that the hero had played on the Little Prince, but that the Little Prince was content to go along with the deception.

Roman and T-Roy had grown up with us, and we were a secure and dependable basis from which they could explore the world, them hopefully being unaware of the occasions when Debbie and I had been baffled about how to deal with situations which presented themselves, but somehow we had always managed to muddle through, happy to work as a team.

Much as I cautiously extended my affection to Colin, the words from the book *"One runs the risk of weeping a little, if one lets himself be tamed..."* resonated for me, as I knew that if for some reason it was no longer possible for Colin to spend time with us, I would miss him. And much as I might try to hide it, I would weep. He and I had tamed each other. He had burrowed his way into my heart.

*

It's not the word I would ever use to him — sadly for the expectations it might raise in him, but it did not take long for me to 'love' Colin. Difficult not to, when he idolised me, and so desperately craved my attention. T-Roy and Roman are

193

my sons, and though I try to be just and fair with them, they take me for granted, and push limits with me more than Colin would ever dare. We all knew that if he fell out with T-Roy, then it would not be possible for him to spend time with us, or with me – unless there was some very specific and probably time-limited reason. To some extent, Colin was at T-Roy's mercy. Fortunately, T-Roy has a good heart, and he enjoyed having Colin around, and his dominance over Colin, and as Roman had always had him as a younger brother, he now had essentially a younger brother – power wise – even though Colin was a month or two older than him.

I felt that I needed to intervene, on Colin's behalf, when T-Roy came up with a little stunt which he thought was very amusing; he would say; "Come on Collie dog," at which Colin was required to say "Woof!" , T-Roy came up with this when Debbie wasn't around, so I didn't have the chance to confer with her, and check whether I was being too sensitive, but I told T-Roy that while I could see the humour in it, I didn't want him to do it anymore, because it was being disrespectful to Colin.

"Colin doesn't mind," T-Roy argued back. "You don't mind, do you, Collie dog!"

"No," Colin said in a way that I understood his feelings to be exactly the opposite of what he had said. But he had to make sacrifices to stay in T-Roy's good books, and he wasn't sure how much he would have to put up with.

"I know that it seems funny to you," I said, crouching down to their eyelevel, and put a reassuring hand on each boy's shoulder, "But I don't want you to say that."

"I said it in front of Mummy, and she didn't mind," T-Roy started the time-honoured tradition of playing the parents off against each other.

"Okay, when your mummy is back, we can ask her what she thinks. But please don't do this again until we've discussed it with her?"

T-Roy wasn't quite comfortable enough to leave it until then. "What's wrong with it? His name is Colin and a collie is a type of dog, and dogs go woof?"

"Yes, but it's a sort of teasing, and I don't feel comfortable with it."

"Dogs are fantastic! I'd like to be a dog! I wouldn't mind saying `woof' if I was a dog."

"Colin didn't choose his name himself. So I'd rather you didn't do things that look as though it's teasing him."

"But you heard him say he doesn't mind."

T-Roy didn't want to leave it, and although it was my impression that Colin didn't enjoy it, he wouldn't admit to this in front of T-Roy. It will probably have been best to wait until Debbie got back, and let her have the final say, but I had T-Roy waiting for an answer, and he wouldn't let go.

"You'd be the same if people made fun of your name. And you chose your name yourself."

"How could people tease me about my name?"

"Can you think of anything? I can."

"What?"

"Something starting with T – maybe like... Teabag? "

Colin burst out giggling at this. T-Roy was not amused – if looks could kill! – For a split second. T-Roy glared at him, and Colin immediately stopped and put a lot of effort into keeping a straight face. T-Roy did not pursue this further, and did seem rather reluctant when I raised this with Debbie, with him and Colin together. Debbie agreed with me – phew! – And T-Roy didn't do this to Colin again – well, not that we overheard, or got wind of.

I don't know whether my boys did capitalise on their power; that Colin had to do what they told him in order to continue visiting and staying over with us, and I would like to think that they didn't do this anymore than would be normal for boys finding they had power over someone relatively disadvantaged. I had a chat with Colin at some stage, with Debbie there but when my boys were out of earshot and speaking generally, told him how we liked him, that he was a valuable person and shouldn't allow people to push him around, which he listened to wide-eyed, but I don't know whether he took this on board or not.

*

Young Colin had his demons. I was working in the study — yes that did happen sometimes — when I became aware of his figure loitering outside the doorway, looking in at me but not wanting to make the actual step of entering the room or calling me. I looked up and was puzzled by a look of sadness on his face. T-Roy and Roman weren't around, presumably still at play in the boys' room. I turned to face him and reached out my arms in an invitation for him to cuddle in, on my lap, in the chair. He was mournful for some reason, and I cuddled him, and rubbed his back. As he didn't say anything, I asked "Is something wrong?"

He didn't answer, but his breathing became staggered, and I thought he might be crying. I continue to stroke his back hoping to reassure him. "Do you want me to do something?"

I was used to the pattern of him becoming quiet mid-Sunday afternoon as the time to return him home drew near, but this was Saturday, and we were fully expecting that he would stay for the night and most of the next day as was becoming routine.

T-Roy strode past, when, looking in he saw Colin cuddled in, and he jerked to a halt. I gathered he had noticed Colin was missing and was tracking him down. "What's wrong?" T-Roy asked.

"I don't know," I told T-Roy gently, as he came into the room and stood behind Colin.

"What's wrong Colin?" T-Roy asked him directly. Despite all his excitement and mysteriousness, T-Roy was compassionate, and aware of distress in others.

"Have you had a disagreement?" I asked as neutrally as I could.

"No!" T-Roy asserted, as though slightly insulted by the question. "What's wrong Colin?"

"That's fine, T-Roy," I said apologetically. "Please just give us a couple of minutes, and then we'll come back to you."

T-Roy was very reluctant to do so. Not only was there his natural curiosity for secrets and not wanting to miss out on any, but he had seen the implication that he might have done something wrong.

Speaking into my shoulder, Colin said through his difficult breathing. "T-Roy hasn't done anything; he's been very kind to me. And Roman." And then he paused, trying to get his breath. "I just want to ask you something."

I really had no idea what was coming, but I knew it would be best for T-Roy not to have a ringside seat, at least until I knew what the issue was. T-Roy did not have any comprehension of privacy, or of keeping secrets, and at his age he was an open book. He might have known that there was a secret for why Debbie and I would lock ourselves into the study for half an hour or so after he and Roman had gone to bed, and before Roman migrated to Debbie's side, but that would be about it.

198

"I'm happy you and Roman haven't done anything to upset Colin," I told T-Roy. "But please can you give us a couple of minutes, and then we'll come back to you."

Even if what was troubling Colin wasn't confidential, I knew that T-Roy didn't have the hang of quietly observing a conversation, and that it wasn't always intended that he would be an equal status participant in the conversation.

T-Roy went into Martyr-mode, heavy and reluctant footsteps taking him away, but I knew that he had the integrity and honour not to stop within eavesdropping distance.

"What's the matter, Colin?"

I don't know whether I ever understood what was happening for Colin at that time, though with its mysteriousness I have thought back to it, attributed meanings, and explored hypotheses. I have not resolved it.

"If I did something bad..." Colin said, taking his courage, "could you not take me home and tell my Mummy. Could you spank me instead?"

What on earth do you do with this? You want to know what bad thing we are talking about, and we want to know this before we consider a suitable punishment to be. If he had done something, I wasn't aware, and nor was T-Roy.

"I don't want to hurt you Colin. I hope you know that. Has something happened that you know I'm going to find out about?"

199

"No."

"Do you want to talk to Auntie Debbie?"

"No."

"Or Uncle Leon? He would listen to you."

"No, it's you."

"So are you wanting to talk about possible punishments for things you haven't done?" I didn't want this to sound as absurd as it probably did, but there was something worrying this little six-year-old, who tugged at my heartstrings.

As if you had forgotten it for even a moment, my skills, leading to my vocation, and my apparent success there in, are in gathering information, working out what it means and how we might use it. My job involves gathering information, determining why I was given that information, why was it presented the way it was. Was it reliable? Was it true? Was it slightly true, but to distract from a bigger, more dangerous or useful piece of information? And here I was being bamboozled by a six-year-old, a child who might wish to avoid punishment – or negotiate the type of punishment for an unspecified crime, which I suspect had been committed. Did he just want to explore the limits that he would never dream of testing, or was this somehow a request for reassurance?

"You know that your mummy told me that I should treat you the same way I treat my sons. Did you hear her say that?"

I heard a slightly muffled yes.

"So," – I could see the stretching of the logic, but it could help Colin. "If T-Roy did something bad, would I take him back to your mum?"

This did seem to work, and Colin pulled back a little to look in my face. He smiled at my suggestion, but there were tears washing his lower eyelids.

"Is this a talk that T-Roy can listen in to?" I asked. As always, there were calculations and possible compromises to be made. Time would drag very slowly for T-Roy as he knew that he was being excluded from something, and collusion between his daddy and his best friend, which might make him sulky with Colin when Colin was back with him.

"That's okay. He can listen," Colin decided. Yes, but how to keep him from trying to take over the conversation.

Putting my arm under him so that he was still at chest height to me, I stood up and we walked to the boys room, with T-Roy and Roman both looking up as they heard us approach. "Colin is upset about something," I addressed the glaringly obvious. "You don't have to tell me what it is, but can either of you think of anything that I will be annoyed with if I find out?"

My sons exchanged glances – which they must have discussed following what I had asked of T-Roy. I sensed some indignation at my implied accusation, undeserved as I accept it was. "No," in a way that I believed them.

"As far as I understand it, nobody has been naughty and there is no need for anyone to be punished," – I can't believe I said that! "Colin wants to have a talk about this, and he's okay for you to be in the talk as well, T-Roy." Then I remembered that Colin hadn't said anything about Roman, so I checked with him; "Can Roman come along as well if he wants to?" Which Colin agreed to, and – what nine-year-old boy could resist a discussion of punishments geared to his age group, but for which he was not in the firing line. It wouldn't be comfortable for the four of us to crowd into the study, and I didn't want to have what I thought would be a fairly grown-up discussion in the boys room, with the focus of fun and childhood around it, so we migrated to the lounge, me on the sofa with Colin and T-Roy cuddled up under each arm, and Roman at a slight distance, as befitting his age and status as the older brother.

And there we were when Debbie walked past on her way back from the garden, coming to an abrupt halt at the site of us. "What am I missing?"

"MyDaddy's going to talk with us about spanking," T-Roy announced to her with delight. Thank you T-Roy!

"Okay, who do I have to spank first?"

"MyDaddy," T-Roy sang out in delight, trying to wiggle his hand under my bum. I caught Debbie's eye, did a deliberate sidelong glance down to Colin and clenched my eyes in what I hoped indicated distress. She understood, and ditched the playfulness.

"I'll just wash my hands, and then I'll come and join you," she announced. Moments later she joined us, and Roman cuddled up with her. It was ever thus!

So we had a discussion, opening with me extracting confirmation from Roman and T-Roy that they had not been spanked – ever – and that little pats on the bum... bottom... didn't count as spanking if they had been meant, and taken as fun. And that from what I was getting to know about Colin, I couldn't envisage me feeling that a spanking would be required, and that Debbie and my preferred alternative was grounding which usually meant being restricted to a room which didn't have their books and toys in it, which was usually the study. For T-Roy rather than Colin, there was the threat of not allowing him the use of his bicycle for a determined number of days, and again withholding me going to the park with him. These could be nominal sanctions for Roman as well, but neither of these was as meaningful or as enjoyable to him as they were for T-Roy.

But this didn't address Colin's issue – about the consequences of the unspecified badness – and his request to be spanked rather than sent home. So we had a discussion about different things that might or might not be seen as bad or naughty and whether some form of punishment was appropriate or not. Accidents can happen, and if someone had made a mess in the toilet, then if they let us know, then this wasn't a problem. If an accident was due to carelessness and inattention, then a telling off could well happen, and if something was deliberately broken, then we were into being grounded territory. There were many

things which, at their age, had not become issues yet, and I didn't wish to give ideas. I chose not to talk about fire-starting, or vandalism, let alone smoking or drinking alcohol. We had had the discussion about swearing, and I knew that they would hear and learn words I did not approve of, but they were not to say these words at home, and I would be `unhappy' if I had reason to believe they had used such words other than in hushed tones amongst their mates.

Actual violence —I could go into some specifics here, although I had no awareness of there having been any fighting between the three boys, T-Roy was `fightiest' of them, but that would be mostly with overexcitement and possibly rough play. Roman would withdraw from situations that could lead there, and Colin would probably defer due to the perceived precariousness of still being seen as a visitor.

I could suggest that if T-Roy smacked Colin in his face, and I got to hear about it, I would probably go for a variation on `an eye for an eye', but without faces being smacked, and the suggestion that after we had talked it through and agreed, in such a situation, T-Roy would be bent over my lap and Colin could slap his bum, and then, though I could not conceive of it happening, I spelt out the reverse, with Colin bent over my lap to be slapped by T-Roy, but I just couldn't imagine this happening, as even though boys might squabble, and Debbie and I were sure that although we might separate them if this happened, we would give time for them to settle, remember the enjoyment they got from each other's company, shake hands and make up.

204

Was there more to Colin, and this out-of-the-blue distress leading to a discussion of the philosophy of justice, or had he possibly been channelling some philosopher or Old Testament prophet to get me to declare what I found to be policies that I hadn't seen as such? The issue with Alvin happened before this. I think Roman had kept my proposed punishment secret despite persistent enquiries from T-Roy, and Debbie had been consistent with her policy of not wanting to know. She had seen Alvin suitably distressed but not physically harmed at the end of his ordeal. Roman and I knew that my approach was of `if you do it to him, I'll help him do it back to you'. That had been my guiding principle.

Debbie had been puzzled, and it had been an understanding she had been pleased to reach during our courtship, although she remembered that she had no information from our school years; that I am not impulsive, and do not lose my temper, which can be seen as a positive – and although good for my chosen profession, I can be fairly cold blooded and relentless in the pursuit of justice as I – and my work – see it. I could be temporarily distracted by a desire to understand, to comprehend how the different pieces interacted with each other, and any cause and effect.

Being the person I am, and developed by the profession that I gravitated towards, I look for patterns, at multiple levels, and I try to see through camouflage and fog. I know that sometimes there is no pattern; `shit happens'; random and unpredictable which can be catastrophic.

I was to wonder later, after what happened ... happened, whether there was some way that was to punish me for the biggest secret that I had kept from Debbie. Try as I might, I can't see how there could be. If God is watching over us, and keeping score, then I know that he has given licence for me to do what I did, and therefore no punishment for me was in order. Its not just the `eye for an eye' justice of the Old Testament, its covered in the New Testament, clearly explicit in support of my actions, involving millstones, deep oceans, and people whose continued presence is not in the benefit of society. But in my experience, having such a person in the presence of both a deep ocean and a millstone does not happen. Something I should take up with our logistics people.[3]

Colin seemed to be reassured. Discipline was seldom an issue for us. I know that at times Debbie struggled with T-Roy, and much as I tried to explain to him that Debbie and I were the unit of his parents, he wasn't able to hide from her his preference for me. We could deal with any cheek and defiance that he showed Debbie, by sanctions from me, and it was rare for him to cross the line enough for this to be necessary.

I told Colin that I could not imagine any crime that he might commit that T-Roy or Roman might not also commit, and that as we would deal with this at home for them, I would

[3] Max is thinking of *Matthew 18:6*, which is often interpreted as referring to child abusers, but actually condemns people who cause children to stumble, or cause children to fall into sin; the children referred to being God's congregation, not necessarily children age wise.

offer him the same, but with him being able to opt to go home instead if he felt he wished this. That all sounds very heavy, but it had been worrying him. Debbie confirmed the same thing, and while I invited him to challenge us with examples, which he couldn't, and I invited Roman and T-Roy to suggest examples, and I asked T-Roy to keep it vaguely realistic.

I could see a final point to end on, with a delightful way to raise the mood.

Debbie briefed me that she had spoken to T-Roy and Roman, in a careful discussion so as not to give any sound-bites which – thinking of T-Roy in particular – might be repeated and cause offence, and possibly consequences for vulnerable people – thinking of Colin. A discussion of how they were used to our family life as they had grown up in it, that not every family had as much love for each other as we did, accepting that petty and soon-to-be-forgotten squabbles between Roman and T-Roy – which didn't happen often – did not detract from the love we shared. We had fun, and played, and giggled together, we had bedtime stories and we had friends, like Debbie's mum and Uncle Leon, and although we didn't have a dog and didn't tend to go on exotic holidays, we had a good life. By contrast there were other children – `no names, no pack drill' – who might not have things as good as we did; who might be sad to see what we had and they had not.

"Are you talking about Colin?" Roman asked.

Debbie tried to salvage this, without giving them a sound bite. Not that they would say things vindictively, but T-Roy did not have it in him to keep secrets or be discreet.

"Colin might be a bit like that," Debbie conceded, with a meaningful glance to Roman and a sideward glance indicating T-Roy, which hopefully Roman understood. "You have your daddy, and you know he loves you. Colin's real daddy isn't around…"

"Colin hates his step daddy," T-Roy announced proudly. There was no point in having a secret if you couldn't tell people that you had the secret!

"You mustn't say that," Debbie told T-Roy.

"Colin says it!"

Debbie decided to have a quiet word with Colin, and to warn him that if he made his stepfather annoyed, his stepfather could make it difficult for Karen to allow him to continue to come to us as often as he did.

With this knowledge, I added, looking at Colin who was still cuddled into me and looking up at me; "When I take you back to your mummy, I should tell her if I have found it necessary to punish you," and I could see the sadness return to his face, but I continued; "but I have such a bad memory, I could forget… so you might have to remind me!" I could see it dawning in Colin's face as he interpreted what I said. A conspiratorial smile returned to his face. "You will remind me, won't you?" I said, shaking my head to indicate `no'.

He smiled again. "Yes!" He said, shaking his head 'no'.

"Do you understand me?"

"Yes!" This time he nodded 'yes'. I reached forward and kissed his forehead, and his smile increased.

"I'll remind you, MyDaddy," T-Roy felt he had been left out of the conversation for too long.

I think it was mission accomplished. I think I had assured Colin that I could not think of circumstances under which I or we would send him home as punishment, and between Debbie and I, we would hopefully come up with a suitable civilised punishment if it was ever needed, but it was obvious that he valued the time that he spent with us so much that he was fearful of doing anything to jeopardise it, which might have underlain his question.

I think the point was made, so I could join in with T-Roy as we raised the mood.

"Remind me of what?" Trying to feign an expression of bafflement.

"Of Colin being naughty!" T-Roy knew that the game was on.

"What did he do? Who is Colin?"

"You know!" T-Roy said, but he had already grabbed one of the cushions, and was beating my shoulder with it.

I looked over to Debbie. Roman had sat up, knowing that very soon I would have T-Roy and Colin as giggly wiggleys on

the carpet as I tickled them, at which stage he would join in. I am sorry that I am so predictable! "Pretty lady sitting next to handsome boy, do you know who this little person is who keeps hitting me?"

It was rhetorical. "I'm T-Roy!" Said T-Roy, and increased the ferocity of his cushioned assault on my arm.

There was a little bit more byplay, touching on whether I would forget which child I had to bring home with me, and which one to leave behind – but I realised this could get too close to the edge, and that Colin might say that he wished he could come back with us to stay for the week in between weekends, or something more permanent, and I knew it wouldn't be helpful to him, given the circumstances, for him to articulate this. Then there was a follow-up on the theme of spanking, and with T-Roy assaulting me whether that constituted grounds for a spanking. From across the room, with mocking seriousness – and with `the bravery of being out of range', Roman stated his verdict of; `definitely a spanking', and as I pulled T-Roy over my lap to do the necessary, in between his giggling he quoted Queen; "Mamma Mia Mamma Mia Mamma Mia let me go." I gave him a couple of quick light pats on his buns, which was something we had done plenty of times before, but I realise that I don't think that Colin had seen this.

Across the room I saw Debbie signalling to Colin that he should punch my shoulder on his side, and with this encouragement from her, he did so, gingerly.

"I'm being attacked from both sides," I observed, T-Roy's standing up as I had released him, rubbing his buns as though to soothe them, as if he had received a painful thrashing. Little fibber! Then he wiggled his bottom, to add emphasis, as he triumphantly stuck his tongue out at me, grabbing his cushion, and launching another attack. I pulled Colin over my lap, so he was in position for – he knew what. I leaned forward and whispered in his ear; "Are you okay, Colin?" I looked across to Debbie, for instruction, at the same time Colin said "I deserve it!" morosely. Debbie nodded assent, (she could see his face!) Colin turned round to look up at me and gave me an exaggerated wink. He was catching on fast!

("What you deserve, little boy, is to be loved and cuddled and valued! But I'm still going to pat your buns!" It would be rude not to!)

I had to fend T-Roy off, as he was getting excited, and was willing to help with the spanking, but a couple of softly patted buns later, I scooped Colin and T-Roy to lie side-by-side on the carpet as I got between them, making sure they didn't bash heads, as their tummies got tickled, and they writhed and giggled. We knew that Colin wasn't quite as ticklish as T-Roy, but he was perfectly happy to put on a good show to be included, before Roman entered the fray, wanting to be wrestled with rather than have the indignity of being tickled, and become incapacitated with giggles in front of the two little boys.

I remained tantalised about what undiscovered `crime' Colin had in mind to prompt the discussion, but nothing emerged during the week that followed. It remained a mystery to Debbie and the boys, but not something they gave much thought to. The next time he stayed, I had a chat with Colin, by which time it seemed he had forgotten. I took the unprecedented step of offering him a complete amnesty on the rime if he would only disclose it – he could have milked that for all it was worth, but he wasn't like that. The conclusion I reached saddened me more than if he had owned up to having broken and hidden the evidence of something. I concluded that his great fear was that for some reason his chance to spend time with us would be taken away, and he wanted to try to offer anything – accept any punishment – not to be deprived of his part time membership of our family. Touching though this was, his insecurity saddened me, but there were no assurances that I could give him. We could let him know that he would always be welcome, but we had no control over whether Karen's partner would ever control her into stopping his visits, or that they might move away. But now, in the moment, I gave him an extra long cuddle. I wish that I could have made everything all right for him.

*

Debbie spent quality time with the boys, but this mostly happened when I wasn't around, but I delighted in watching her when she did. As she had comforted Roman when I had brought him back from camp, she practised her aromatherapy with them, and essential oils, and would

212

massage them, to which they responded in the same individual styles that they had shown when they were babies. Roman would go into his trancelike state of ecstasy when Debbie massaged him, but although he tried his best – I believe – T-Roy was always too ticklish, and I knew sadly that things were strained between them sometimes, Debbie was content to moving on to tickling him, which he wanted more, and there were precious moments that I saw between them, him squirming and writhing in delicious delight, and not lashing out – even in fun – as he did with me.

The 'treat him as one of your own' mantra was happily adopted by us, and Colin took his turn on the massage bench, and was easily pleased, soaking up all of the attention and affection that he found so abundantly with us. With us having a Scandinavian attitude to nudity, our two were used to being nude while massaged, which Colin seemed fine with, and when while massaging his chest and tummy, Debbie offered that he could have a towel to cover himself – although he was used to being naked in the bath with the other two when Debbie bathed the three of them, which was most nights – with her giving the option of 'or like T-Roy...'

"Like T-Roy!"

It probably wouldn't be long before Roman started to want modesty, and we would respect that when he wanted it, but we wouldn't prompt it by asking.

*

I will get to Debbie's issues, as I gradually got to fully understand them, but as a paediatric nurse, she had plenty of exposure to naked children, which was not an issue for her, and ours were delightfully healthy. Though sometimes, T-Roy's fiddling and jiggling annoyed her to the extent she would tell him to stop, she knew – we agreed – that he did it because it felt good, and we thought through and decided that this was not 'disgusting' or any other words that others might associate with it.

It was different for me, as an adult male, and my nudity was a battle that she chose to engage with, but it made it easier for her to massage me and 'make me happy' with me being relatively passive on the massage bench, in a fairly clinical environment, where she was stressed and she was standing and she was in control and she could ask me to be still, and – although she never felt the need – she could always unlock the room and leave. She never spoke of it as being her duty as my wife to satisfy my needs, but on the rare occasions we spoke about it, she described it as 'making me happy' and she was glad that I could accept what she was able to do to 'make me happy'.

*

I am something of a year-zero child! I have a date of birth which could well be accurate, and there is a file on me from my time at Ferndale Hall, with the date that I arrived there at less than a year old and a little bit of information about my birth; normal delivery, normal birth weight, healthy baby, no jaundice, routine infant circumcision – except it

wasn't truly routine even in those days – but no information about my parents, why I had arrived at the home, or anything else. It was the equivalent for Leon and Kevin, minus the surgery, but there was no information about our backgrounds available to us, and we were not encouraged to ask. There was the philosophy that, expressed in variations of the theme seen as appropriate for our age, to say that the state looked after us, and loved us and would provide – what more would we need?

There was the philosophy of us being self-made men, with the assistance and nurturance of the staff at Ferndale Hall, on behalf of the State, and it was more subtle than I am describing it here. I was amused when comparisons between us and the so-called baby farms in Germany during the period of the Third Reich, but from the information I gleaned, we were born elsewhere, and not as wards of the State.

There were the questions which those we had contact with didn't know and didn't wish to encourage our curiosity. At the time we didn't know who would know, where this information might be, or how to access it. The three of us did not look like brothers, with Leon being thickset, Kevin being tall and slim, and me being – well, perfect! We were encouraged to think of each other as brothers, although we had different surnames, and it dawned on me that these, as our initial names, might have been chosen for us, and on reflection, were unlikely to be any link to our actual parents. There were other children at Ferndale Hall, of different ages, but tending to be in clusters of between three and five of

roughly the same age. I don't know if it is a clue, but Leon, Kevin and I were bright, and did well at school, and at sport; the virtues of achievement being emphasised to us at Ferndale. All possible assistance was provided, but with the trace of bureaucracy, such that our nominal home parents did have two fortnights of annual leave away from us each year. They did not come on the holidays that we were treated to, which inevitably meant meeting up with other children of our age range from places like Ferndale elsewhere in the country.

Although he could certainly hold his own academically, Leon was particularly skilled with practical things, and under other circumstances might have been channelled towards a career in engineering, and whereas I was seen as good at analytics, and extracting information – even at that age – and Kevin was creative and good at making things up, stories and so on. We knew that we were guided to expectations of a career in some branch of the civil service, and that we would spend time in the military, longer than the two years National Service that all boys faced, and we expected that we would graduate from the Military Academy, after which our career paths would be guided by our actual and perceived strengths and abilities.

We discussed, amongst ourselves, whether our parents had been seen to be intelligent by the state, but unable or unsuitable to raise the children they had produced themselves, and whether the state had intervened to give us the optimal upbringing, and we probably did not want to think much further about whether we had been taken from

our parents, with varying degrees of coercion, or whether something unfortunate had befallen them.

I know I can't leave the subject alone, but there was an added puzzle of me having been circumcised. It's possible this had been for medical reasons - I have read up on this - but that didn't seem to be particularly likely from what I had read. Although Roman and T-Roy only shared fifty percent of my genes, neither of them had had such issues from birth. It had been suggested that I might be of Jewish heritage, and that it might have been done at eight days of age while presumably my parents still had me. We could not discount this, except I look Aryan – but then so do many Jewish people

So I wondered, whether, like Colin, it had been a `like father, like son' decision from my parents, indicating an interest in me, and possibly going against voluntarily giving me to be raised by the State. I understood this to mean that they had hoped and expected to have raised me, but then there was the evidence to the contrary of how Colin's biological father had wanted to leave his mark, and having done so left, apparently without looking back.

*

As Colin become a "plus one" to our family, I requested my officer commanding to permit him to join us at Directorate barbecues, and for the use of the gym, the swimming pool, and possibly the dining hall.

I knew that my OC would authorise this, but he enjoyed the question; "I'm no expert in this, Max, but don't children usually spend a long time in their mummy's tummy, and then start off as a little baby, rather than suddenly arrive as a six-year-old, with a different surname? If you can skip the whole shitty nappy stage, maybe more people would go down the family route?" He was being rhetorical, as he had signed my application form as he asked this.

"What are ...-" he looked back at the form... "... Colin's interests?" I suspected that another woodcarving would be forthcoming.

At their meeting at the next barbecue, there was a strange bonding between Uncle Kasper and Colin. I wouldn't want to say `two lost souls found each other' but it was somewhere in there. The OC had become aware of his deficit of grandchildren, beyond what he enjoyed of the contact with the children of his protégé, and Colin had found someone with more to give him, than the crumbs of me he got from T-Roy and Roman's table. After their quality time with Uncle Kasper, and the exchange of gifts, when released, T-Roy and Roman would bounce over for roughhousing with the young officers, but Colin would stay and be interviewed by Uncle Kasper and I fetched a chair so that Colin could sit next to him in comfort.

The context didn't fit, but looking at the two of them, it was a classic image of a grandson listening with rapt attention while the grandfather regaled him with stories of his youth. The OC stayed longer than usual that night, enjoying his

conversation with Colin and becoming oblivious to the surroundings, until he remembered his role, stood and announced his retirement for the evening and wished all present an enjoyable evening onwards.

One of my junior officers, returning from a deployment elsewhere, met Colin after Colin had been to several barbecues, and the officer asked without thinking – which I would probably tease him about later:

"Is Colin also your son, sir?

"No," I confessed. But, drawing him close to me I added; "if I was allowed to choose a third child, I would choose him!"

Colin looked up at me and beamed! The young officer was too polite to have asked, even if he had noticed my suggestion about being allowed to have children, and at his age and stage, he wouldn't yet have been affected by the policy of being married to the state and not dividing your loyalties by commitments to another person. There had never been a question of Debbie having another child. Neither of us ever approached discussing the possibility. I think we knew that we had two children –one each!

*

When Colin first came along with us to the swimming pool, this again created another dilemma for him, with T-Roy pressurising him to skinny dip, and me pervasively telling him that he could do as he wished – Roman and I wore trunks. I knew that he felt the need to keep T-Roy happy

219

with him, and that T-Roy wanted a naked companion, but while he was seemingly content with nudity within our home, his trained inhibition kicked in at the idea that other people might walk in – but he too, like Roman, had been content to shower naked in the communal area. While T-Roy was out of earshot, busying himself with choosing which inflatables he was going to play with, I offered Colin that in front of T-Roy I would tell him that I wanted him to wear his trunks – to give him that opt-out, that it was my instruction – but if he decided he didn't want to wear them I was perfectly happy for him to not comply with my instruction. He also had the option of leaving his trunks very close to the side of the pool, so that if someone came in, he could reach them and put them on, and as seemed to be the pattern, with those assurances, we ended up with two little skinny-dippers, with Roman making an exaggerated statement about them being childish, but this as an aside to me.

It was a proper diving pool, and therefore deeper, which Roman and T-Roy were used to and not put off by, but Colin was a bit freaked out about the depth, and required me to swim around with him hanging on to me for a while until he got used to it. I knew he had many worries, and that swimming in deep water might have been one of them, but he might also have used it to get more attention from me, my boys preferring to show their prowess by not needing me. If this was his game, I was content to play along.

*

220

Colin became a regular part of our family, and happily so. A permanent playmate for T-Roy, who for the most part was willing to share with him, and he seemed to get on well with Roman, although probably the main advantage to Roman was that Colin occupied T-Roy, and gave Roman space. He stayed most weekends with us, possibly with the pretence of so he would be able to attend church with us, and I kept my amusement at this to myself.

There was also a little irony which I kept to myself which was that if it were not for Colin's biological father wishing to leave his mark on his son, by circumcision, before losing interest and leaving some six years ago, it would never have happened that Colin was welcomed into our family, and became a valued member. And how although this led to our introduction, it seemed that what he really wanted was a male role model who would care for him and take an interest in him!

Debbie did all the liaising, which was fine with me, and, uncharacteristically, she gave me notice that due to some reasons that she would explain if necessary, she had agreed that we would have Colin's little stepbrother, the toddler still in nappies with us for the weekend as well. I gathered that there had been some awkwardness from Karen, until Debbie had just upfront offered that we would have him as well as Colin.

We agreed to invite Alice to stay and to be an extra adult to help with Denzel, and Alice was delighted to – in her deferential way, always glad to be invited so that she did not

feel that she was intruding, and she loved little children, even if there was no biological link. We loved Colin, with whom we had no biological link.

I wasn't working that weekend, which was just as well, and Colin was oddly quiet when Karen dropped him off at ours, and handed over Denzel, with the bits and pieces necessary for a toddler still in nappies, and for a while we all watched with amusement as he tottered along exploring the house beaming and giggling in delight. He did a lot of beaming.

Colin seemed to withdraw a little, so I took him to one side, and cuddled him into me with him sitting on my lap, it made sense when he reluctantly explained that he didn't want Denzel there. Understandably, he saw us as `his', and for reasons that we could understand, he resented Denzel anyway, and now Denzel was not only encroaching on his haven with us, with the novelty of it, Denzel was being the centre of attention. He became tearful, and I cuddled him and he cuddled back and I told him that he was special to us. I reminded him what I had told that awkward junior officer, that if I could choose an extra child I would choose him.

*

Cuddled into me, Colin looked up with tears in his eyes – and sadly I remember him like this on many occasions. "It's unfair!" He sobbed. "He spoils everything..."

I understood, from what he said, that he had liked it better when it had just been him and his mum, and then he had lost out when he had had to share his mum with her new

partner, and then he was pushed out further when Karen had had her partner's baby, Denzil. Colin had found a refuge with us, and now his stepbrother was following and encroaching into his refuge.

I offered, that while Denzel was with us, if he wanted to, Colin could come into my bed at the same time that Roman came to cuddle in with Debbie, rather than having to wait until T-Roy woke – or he woke T-Roy – in the morning for them to come through. This concession seemed to please him, and I added another treat, although it was a treat that he sort of knew was always there, that he could wear shorts or undies when he came through if he wanted. A bit more of a cuddle and a hug, and he dried his tears and went back, and I prompted T-Roy to involve Colin in some activity that they could do together, at a time that Debbie was settling Denzel down.

I was aware that it was two boys, rather than one that slunk into our bed that night. Roman was routinely wearing his shorts by now, and I noticed that Colin was wearing undies, as he cuddled in beside me and next to Roman. T-Roy had played ball, and as previous, I knew that he was generous in allowing Colin to have some of my time. I explained to him about Colin being put out about Denzel being along, and I was proud of T-Roy with him saying that he accepted this.

For a little while, this routine stayed, and then I noticed Colin was back to being a rudey-nudey as he cuddled in. I observed this, and we again had a conversation from

223

previously that he could wear undies if he wanted to but he decided that he wanted to sleep naked like me.

*

As with my own two, I changed Denzel's nappies, when they needed to be changed, if anything, trying to do it more than Debbie. Okay, one doesn't like the smell, but I enjoyed interacting with babies – or I had with mine, and I found Denzel also endearing. Of course, as `the curator of willies at Number 9', if there was a new willy in the house, T-Roy needed to know about it. He would come to watch, always making a point about the stink, dramatising it, but deciding it was bearable if I told him to keep away until the smell cleared.

I'm not an expert on foreskins, but Denzel's seemed to be the longest that I had seen; certainly longer than I remember my sons having been at that age. I commented to Debbie, her having the specialist knowledge on babies and young children and she agreed that it was long, but not that there was necessarily anything wrong with it. He would probably grow into it!

T-Roy was fascinated. Denzel was aware of everything around him, enjoying the attention, and had no inhibitions. "Can I touch it?" T-Roy asked, indicating Denzel's penis. Interesting. Should one say; no, it's private, or something else regarding Denzel's privacy of which Denzel was completely unaware? "Be gentle," I told him. "Don't pull it, or push it, or pinch it, but you can touch it." I had touched it,

along with the rest of him as I had put powder on him, and had carefully cleaned pooh off. Denzel beamed even more, when he felt T-Roy's touch. T-Roy asked the questions that I had asked Debbie, so I answered some myself, and referred others back to Debbie. Should I have banned T-Roy from watching, or should I have told him not to touch, when it seemed to do no harm? While Denzel stayed with us, T-Roy was a constant presence as he `helped'!

"Can I look at his acorn?" I liked the honesty of his question, and I hope that his straightforwardness in matters such as this was restricted to home, and that we had inculcated into him to hide his interest in such things away from home.

"I'll show him mine!" T-Roy offered. Fair's fair!?

I told T-Roy `No', and explained to him the medical reasons why, that it could hurt him if his body wasn't ready, and that it would be up to him as he explored his body for him to be ready, and he wouldn't hurt himself as others might hurt him. T-Roy's curiosity was not important enough to risk causing Denzel pain. "Willies are for good feelings," I told him.

"And for weeing!" T-Roy reminded me. It was his specialist subject after all!

"And for weeing!" I confirmed.

I told T-Roy that I didn't want him doing any investigations when he was alone with Denzel, which T-Roy seemed to accept. As far as I was concerned, any combination of the

boys could bath together – although that was Debbie's department. All T-Roy had to be was patient, if he wasn't distracted by other things. Oh, he would be distracted by other things, but he had a pervasive interest in willies, and I knew that his interest would return.

*

When whatever the problem had been was resolved, and Karen could look after Denzel again, we had become fond of him, and our normal life of having Colin with us each weekend resumed.

In the fullness of time, and after what happened... happened...

... sadly for her, Colin's mom found herself abandoned by yet another man, and was struggling to cope, so Colin spent more and more time with us, which we all enjoyed, and after some discussion – and being aware of the need – I discussed with Debbie that we could also look after little Denzel, explaining to Colin that he was the elder, and his place in our affection was established. Denzel was too small to be any competition really, and as he settled in, he seemed to always have an incredibly wide smile and beamed all the time that he was with us.

Chapter Four

Debbie

I had enjoyed putting the boys to bed, and reading them bedtime stories, with T-Roy cuddled up to me as we sat in his nest, with Roman, boa constrictor-like looking down on us from his post on the top bunk. Although T-Roy had nodded off, and was doing his soft snore, I knew to add a summarised ending to the story, for the sake of completeness to him, and Roman knew what I was doing. Gently, I extracted myself from T-Roy, and settled him out in his nest, kissed his forehead. I stood up, and gave a good night kiss to Roman's presented cheek, and I stroked his hair. Leaving the door slightly ajar, so that light could enter from the passage, I padded out.

*

After a satisfying day at work, and the quality time that I loved with my boys, I settled down to treat myself to listening to some music in the lounge. At the time Debbie was due, I boiled the kettle.

Debbie drove up, and parked outside the garage, and I walked out to open the garage door. Instead of driving in, Debbie switched off and got out. She was very distressed.

"I've seen him", Debbie told me as I embraced her, knowing that this is what she wanted or needed, enveloping her in my arms, and flexing my arm muscles to increase her sense of being protected by how hard my biceps were or could be!

I held her, hoping this would comfort her, standing outside the front of the house, the darkness giving us some privacy.

"Who?"

"Bobby!" She spat out his name.

"It can't have been him," I tried to reassure her.

She pulled away from me, feeling contradicted. "I know what I saw," she snapped. "I was there, and you weren't!"

"I'm sorry," I said, requesting forgiveness, opening my arms to embrace her again. She cuddled in.

I knew that I had words that could comfort her. "He's dead," I told her.

I could feel and sense the penny dropping in her head as she digested what I had told her.

There was a long pause, and her hug eased. She was withdrawing from me.

"How do you know?" she asked in a hollow tone that I had not heard from her before.

"I saw it in some documents ..." I answered.

"And you didn't think to tell me?"

"I thought it was better not to remind you..." Yes, I could have told her, but knowing that it would be impossible for her to bump into him, I had hoped that no situation like this would ever happen.

"As if I don't remember him ... every night ...?"

I didn't say anything. I couldn't think of what to say for the best. There have been plenty of times when I have learned that remaining silent was the best course of action,

"What documents?"

I knew that this was not going to end well. "His autopsy report," I explained. "I put his name on a list of people of interest, and it turned out that he had died." This was broadly true.

"I would have told you if the subject ever came up. ... But it never did." Until now, that is.

"I wouldn't speak to anyone about him..."

"Did you have anything to do with it?" I don't know how to answer this. I could deny it, but I don't think she would have believed me. Now I knew that it would have been better for me to have let her know soon after he had `died'.

"Did you?" she asked again, as she saw that I had paused.

"You killed him, didn't you?" She accused.

I stayed silent. I know that an answer of; "Well, yes and no!" would not be helpful.

Suddenly she started pounding my chest with her fists, expressing her anger, a sort of drumming rather than aimed close to cause pain. Different perspectives – I was impressed at the power that she put into these blows, and I have to admit, it hurt!

Paraphrasing little Colin; `I'll accept any beating, just don't send me away!' But I didn't say that.

It was best for me to stay silent, concerned at her distress, while she thought through the facts that were falling into place, and her emotions. I know about `Stockholm Syndrome' so I could understand that for her it was far more

complicated than the straightforward removal of threat it had been for me.

I would accept what she decided. I did not have a choice. I am convinced I did the right thing, and this was reinforced because my actions had made my wife and my unborn child safer. I could not, and would not undo it. `Bobby' was dead and cremated. He isn't coming back.

There were many things that I knew not to say. If I said anything amounting to; `I did it for you...', this would then make her feel guilty, and angrier. It was best to take it – whatever was coming – on my chin, or shoulders, or wherever...

"Why didn't you tell me?" I stayed silent. I could have reminded her of her philosophy regarding my work; `don't tell me! I don't want to know!', but that would have been too big a responsibility to put on her.'

"Couldn't you have just scared him off?" Again, stay silent, and don't try to explain how sometimes this works, but it can go spectacularly wrong where the person threatened decides to `go out in a blaze of glory' and take innocent people with them, or causing severe damage to those from whom we had tried to scare him off.

"Would you like me to go and stay in the barracks tonight?" I offered to remove myself, in case she felt this might help, rather than finding my presence provocative.

She didn't reply. She was thinking, thinking in multiple dimensions. I would wait. I would give her the time. All the time she needed.

"Was he a threat?" Again, don't remind her that, 20 minutes earlier, she had thought that he was a clear and present threat, which is how this conversation had started.

"Yes."

"How?"

I was on fairly firm ground here. "He was taking an inappropriate interest in us. He was observed – photographed – trying to peer in at our house. This house!"

"And I suppose you have the photograph?"

"Yes."

"And I suppose it's locked up in your mysterious cabinet in the study? Or in your mysterious lockbox in your wardrobe?"

"In the study," I confirmed. "Do you want me to fetch it?"

She buried her head in her hands and sobbed.

With the benefit of hindsight, I would have done things differently. Although he hadn't been mentioned in years, and I am sure that she had put him out of her mind to the best of her ability, he had remained a demon in the back of her mind over the last 10 years – which I had the knowledge to exorcise him for her. But I had known that it would be distressing for her, even if I had presented it to her as information I had come across, which she might have believed if I had indicated that I had used my position for there to be a standard request for information about him.

She didn't seem to doubt that I had the photo – the photos – from several occasions. If asked, I could explain that yes,

he was being followed, and yes I had been involved in arranging that, rather than to tell her that we were routinely observed by trainee officers, and it was him that had walked into their view.

"Do you want me to ask your mom to come over?"

"No."

"Unless you say `stay', I'll go and sleep in the study tonight," I told her. I watched her, and she didn't respond. "I will always love you," I told her. I tried to reassure her, but this didn't have the effect I desired.

"Just go!" she snapped back through her hair and tears. She moved away from me, moved into the house, and I know she went straight into the bedroom and shut the door. I understood – or chose to understand – that she wasn't telling me she wanted me to go to the barracks for the night.

*

I put the car away, and went to the study. I settled in the chair, knowing that I would spend the night contemplating, and that I would not sleep. If Debbie did, then hopefully in the morning we could see what needed to be done. Hopefully before T-Roy woke up and sensed that anything was amiss. There wasn't a way to prevent Roman from realising that something had happened, with the routine of him slipping into bed beside his mum in the small hours, and he would see that I was not there.

The study had much more emotional significance than what we chose to call it would indicate. This was where Debbie and I had spent much intimate time, and Debbie had fought

psychological battles greater that any I had faced. It was where both boys had been conceived.

This had been the most angry or upset that Debbie had been with me in the 12 years we had been together. I knew she might want it changed – reduced – or I don't know what.

I could find regret that Debbie had seen someone who had reminded her of `Bobby' and that this had startled her. I did not regret my role in `Bobby's' death. He had made himself a realistic threat, and what I had done had led to his removal, for the protection of my wife and her unborn child. She had hated `Bobby', and on the very rare occasions that she referred to him, she made this clear. I hoped that this perspective would return, and that she would anchor this thought during the night.

Despite knowing that I had caused distress to the woman I loved, I did not believe that I had made a mistake. I had not done the wrong thing. Part of what had attracted her to me was – in her words `my strong arms' that could protect her – and she knew some of what I had done in the military. No matter how much she switched off to, clues still seeped out about my work. She had met many of my colleagues, many of whom loved her as my wife, and the mother of my children, and who were probably envious of my decision to limit my career prospects by renouncing my single status and to marry.

We had been in the same class at school; rivals in a way, in that we were always in the top three pupils in the class, across the board. Leon and Kevin were in the same class, but didn't excel in academics as we did, though Kevin gave us a run for our money in English. I had tried to be friendly to Debbie, who was pretty, but she always seemed aloof and

disinterested. I accepted this, and didn't try very hard, spending more time with people who were more responsive to my friendship, who were many. I gathered that her father – later I learned that he was her stepfather – disapproved of me, and of Leon and Kevin, as being the children from Ferndale Hall. There was some form of stigma there, although looking back that was an unusual and inaccurate view to have, because although we did not have parents that we could call our own, and were raised by the State, we were loved and nurtured, and wanted for nothing – apart, possibly from a more conventional family life. The three of us had the same House Mother and House Father, who were in a happy and loving relationship, and provided us with affection, while emphasising the importance to us of being independent; we would serve the State, as the State had looked after us. In no way were we deprived of material things, or mental stimulation, and we were encouraged to develop our hobbies and interests – Leon with his sport and technical abilities, and me with organising, leadership and chess, and Kevin with creative projects even including unexpected things like speech and drama, which one would not have expected the State to encourage. It was expected that we would spend time in the military, longer and more committed than our peers doing military service.

*

I can't say that I thought back to Debbie at all after finishing school, and going to the Military Academy. It was probably five years after I had last seen her at school when I met with her again. I was browsing in a bookshop when I heard a voice to one side; "Max?" I recognised her, of course, and took in that she was wearing a nurse's uniform, probably having popped out for lunch. I was surprised that she looked pleased to see me. I couldn't remember her ever having

looked at me in that way before. I smiled in recognition.

"You look very much like a soldier pretending to be a civilian," she observed.

"And you have put a lot of effort into preparing for your fancy dress party," I countered. Had this conversation happened when we knew each other better, she would have stuck her tongue out at me, but it was a strange encounter between people who knew who each other was, but had not been friends.

But she was being friendly, and I was willing to respond. We got talking, catching up with each other, as much as I was prepared to share with her – me finding myself talking to a familiar but far pleasanter person than I remembered from our school days. There was no sign of the haughtiness, the looks of disdain that she would give to Leon, Kevin and me, or the way she seemed to feel affronted when I had better grades than she did at any of our school evaluations. I could tell her bits and pieces about my military career, being very aware of what not to tell; what to avoid. I didn't tell her of Kevin's death at that time, me being protective of his memory, and not trusting how deep this unfamiliar friendliness extended.

She had not been idle in her life either. She had qualified as a nurse, and was specialising in paediatrics, with the plan of being in a community clinic rather than in the hospital working on wards as she was doing at that time. I was surprised to find just how pleasant I found our conversation, and I was pleased when she immediately accepted my suggestion that we go for coffee.

I was on leave, and the day was my own, and I never did find out how, with her still being in uniform, she was able to

spend the couple of hours with me that she did. Conversation flowed freely. I was enjoying being friendly with her, finding that she had a compassionate personality underlying the pretty `Ice Princess' I remembered from school.

We arranged to meet up again, with her seeming to take the initiative with this more than I would have ventured, and we had a meal together two days later. She was married, but felt that the marriage had passed the point of no return – she was reluctant to go into details – and it was becoming a messy divorce. Fortunately, there were no children. People would have suggested that I should have had a big neon sign flashing `rebound' in front of my eyes, but with having been encouraged most of my life to expect to remain single and unattached; to do what was required of me without conflicting interests, made me less wary than lads who had grown up in conventional households where there was the expectation that one would play the field for a while, find the right girl, settle down at the right time, career and education wise, and start a family. I, and those like me, did not give such a future any consideration.

Many unfamiliar things were happening, and I was enjoying myself. Suddenly things seem to reach a pinnacle; after taking in a breath to increase her courage; after a hesitation she blurted out; "Please would you pretend to be my boyfriend?"

"What?"

"Sorry! I shouldn't have said that!"

"What do you mean?"

I was puzzled. I was very intrigued. I didn't have personal

experience, but from books and films, I was aware that the usual protocol was that people gradually became increasingly attracted to each other until they fell in love at which time they would eventually decide to declare their love.

"It doesn't matter! I'm sorry I said that!"

"I didn't mean `no'!" I was just surprised. "Please tell me what you mean."

I could see that she was struggling. She had taken a step that was obviously difficult for her, and my reaction had made her falter. I had never seen her like this before. At school she had always been remote, never uncertain and never struggling to decide what to do next after having put a foot wrong.

"I'm being stalked," she confided, dropping her voice. "It's becoming very difficult. ... Then I saw you, and remembered you .... I have enjoyed the time that we have spent together now, and I was just too tempted not to ask you..."

"By your ex-?"

"No!"

"You don't want to go to the police? Take out an injunction or something?"

"It's more complicated than that!"

"I've enjoyed meeting up with you again as well," I shared, "I'm willing to help you if I can, but I really don't understand."

"Would you just trust me that I need you to be seen to be

237

someone I am close to? It may only need to be for a week or two. I'm sorry that I was so bitchy to you when we were at school, but I always knew you were decent and honourable – we all did!"

Sounds like words that I would like in my obituary!

"Are you sure you shouldn't get the police involved if you are concerned for your safety?"

"Yes, I'm sure."

"Can you give me a hint?"

"I'm sorry, I think I misjudged this. Please can you just forget that I ever asked this?"

But I was hooked. I had been enjoying her company – rather marvelling at the situation of us enjoying each other's company – I thought – after she had been so dismissive of me at school. Somehow we had picked up a sort of intimacy – it didn't seem to be the camaraderie that I was used to with my – for want of a better word – comrades, as with her being female and attractive, this changed the dynamic.

I managed to calm her and reassure her that I wanted to help her and that I didn't want her to take flight after her first step, which I could see had been brave of her. "What do you want me to do?"

"Nothing difficult. Spend some time together, where we can be seen together. I need to tell you something more about this, but if you could pretend that we are affectionate with a hug and kiss when we meet, and when we separate?" And then a slight change as I saw a hint of confidence which she hadn't been showing when she added; "I'm sure you would be able to manage that!" Despite the seriousness she

implied about her situation, she could still poke fun, and I liked that.

I paused for a while, wondering how to respond. It wasn't difficult – I could use her words! "I could manage that!" I confirmed. "Or I could give it a damn good try!"

So it was that we appeared to be dating for a while, and as she alerted me, she was very tense when I embraced her in greeting and was very tense as we kissed, which she explained would be very difficult for her. I was pleased to go through the motions knowing that she really wanted me to, even if she found this difficult. I understood that this behaviour would have been due to bad experiences that she had had, and I was aware of the messy divorce and that she was being stalked – but mysteriously not by her ex-, but by someone else?

My Rest and Recuperation ended, but I was due to be based at the barracks for the next three-month cycle, which I explained to Debbie, which didn't seem to be a problem to her. It certainly was not onerous to meet with her regularly. Conversation flowed; it came easily, and would have appeared natural to anyone who might be watching. We ate out at ordinary restaurants, and Debbie had offered – in a very businesslike way – that she was willing to pay for everything as I was doing what she had asked and needed. This wasn't necessary and I felt more comfortable with me paying – me earning a good salary by this time, and in any country and at all times nurses are never paid what they deserve.

I was enjoying the time we spent together. I expected that this arrangement was going to be time limited, and at some stage she would tell me that the mission had been

accomplished, that she believed that her stalker had lost interest – or might have been scared off. If she had wanted to be seen with someone to scare off the stalker, she would have been better off with Leon than me!

My military career was developing in a way that secrets would be important; what secrets to keep, what secrets to investigate, and what secrets to expose. There were, and would be, secrets that I would have to keep from Debbie, if our friendship developed, and there were some secrets that at present she continued to keep from me. When Debbie finally and bravely confided to me what the problem was, I understood and accepted it without question. As our relationship gradually developed in the strange and deceptive way that it did, I did things that I felt needed to be done.

*

It was accepted, or even encouraged, by our organisation – the State – that young men would take an interest in young woman, and that was fine, as long as it was done discreetly and did not draw any unwanted attention or lasting commitments. There were strong reasons why non-personnel should not be brought onto the base, and so while the young cadets could not bring young woman home with them, there were a number of hotels and motels dotted around where our personnel were given discounts for soldiers – in its broadest sense. Substantial discounts. The advantage to the State was that they – we knew who the staff were, had been checked and vetted, and the rooms were swept for recording devices of all kinds. As an organisation, we could state that there were no recording devices of any kind to be found in those rooms, and any such devices that were found – were ours!

So, having been in all three positions myself, as a young lieutenant guided towards and self-directed there, into the world of intelligence gathering, evaluation and flagging for action, I made a request for an interview especially to report the `unusual' proposal when Debbie had asked me to visibly stay overnight at her home, despite – and again she was being cryptic and evasive with her request that she wanted the impression to be created that we might sleep together, although in reality she made it clear that she wanted us to sleep in separate rooms – with wry amusement – that she would give me her bed and she would sleep on the couch! Just as I would have done if I had been the intelligence officer I described the situation to, my impression was that he thought I was overly concerned, but he followed the party line of treating all reports of strange behaviour respectfully, and not suggesting that the informant was being oversensitive. Having also had the role of supervising the intelligence officers taking such reports, I can look back with some amusement at the thoughts that would have gone through the intelligence officer's head. I fully understand that one should always treat such reports seriously, so as to encourage the informant not to self-censor and to report things in the future that might be of interest to Intelligence or Counter Intelligence.

With me having provided our intelligence people with more information than they needed to know, and with them asking more questions than they knew they needed to know, I agreed to Debbie's request to stay over at her apartment, on the terms she had stated. She had a relatively small apartment, which she had told me that she shared with her mother, her father – or stepfather I now learned - was no longer on the scene, and it was obvious that he was someone that Debbie did not wish to talk about at all.

I recognised and remembered Debbie's mother, Alice, when I saw her again, from odd social occasions from school, although she had always been in the shadow of Debbie's father – stepfather! Debbie's mother was quite gushy when we met, and seemed to remember things about me from when I was at school with Debbie, which surprised me, as I was aware of Debbie's father - stepfather - seeming to disapprove of me, if not be hostile towards me. Any thoughts that I had had on this, I had attributed to either the stigma of me being a child of the State or as a possible intellectual rival of his daughter. Debbie's mom was complimentary saying – as mothers do - that I had grown into a handsome young man, that I looked fit, and she squeezed my biceps in greeting – measuring my strength. I noticed, but didn't think much of it, although it was dawning on me that I was seen as a protective figure; someone who could look after himself, and those around him – an impression I understood was intended for the stalker, in the hope of scaring him away.

I am aware that one does not always know how much different people know, or are playing roles, and what ordinary behaviours are. We had a meal together in Debbie's apartment, after which Debbie's mom retreated to her room with an obvious `good night' and the implied but not stated; `I'll leave you two lovebirds together!'

"You do accept that nothing physical can happen?" Debbie asked, seeking reassurance.

"I understand!" I told her. She relaxed, and we had a pleasant evening chatting, with no specific content, until it was bedtime and she offered to sleep on the couch in the lounge, but of course I would not hear of that.

I didn't know then how much Debbie's mother knew of what was going on, about the harassment and stalking, and how Debbie had asked me to play the role of a love interest in the hope of scaring off the person stalking her. Her mother joined us for breakfast the next morning, Debbie mouthing a silent 'thank you' to me, and we repeated the arrangement several times that week. I asked several times if she wanted me to see what I could find out, or see what I could do to stop the stalker harassing her, but she seemed to look nervous about this and asked me not to. She told me that I was doing enough by what I was doing. I was willing to do more, and she knew it.

We would hug visibly on greeting, and on separating. Debbie would always squeeze my biceps as an afterthought, checking my strength as her mother did. Did it run in the family? I didn't mind. Having firm biceps is easy. If anything, I was more proud of my six-pack, which I think is more difficult to achieve, but they had not seen this yet. I didn't feel any need to draw attention to it.

My stay at the barracks was extended, and so my availability to help Debbie. I didn't know if this would go anywhere, whether there would be an endpoint, at which time she might decide that I had served my function and scared off her stalker; she might thank me and formally end our strange relationship. It didn't really need to go anywhere. I was enjoying what was happening day by day, and as we knew from school, we were probably intellectual equals, and I found our conversations interesting, and I enjoyed her playful sense of humour which I had not come across at school. Sadly, she showed no interest in learning to play chess.

The fact that I was spending less time at the mess out of

hours was noticed by my comrades – shall we call them. Most of them knew me to be relatively quiet and `an ideas man', but one who could hold my own when we did macho, manly things, there was some interest in who I was spending my time with. I deliberately taunted them by telling them that I had reported everything to intelligence, who monitored the situation, leading to some conversations attempting to draw out more detail - suggesting that it appeared as though I was really enjoying my work! They were right. I wasn't spending as much time in the mess. Although, except for my birthday, I would never initiate going out for drinks or a meal, or other activity during our down-time - I would usually go along to such activities. Otherwise would be interested in engaging people in games of chess, or in the various strategy games that we seem to have in the mess, or I would be known to study or read.

I could read Debbie's body language to a certain extent; how, when she wanted to ask something significant, that might change our relationship – as before she had taken the step of asking me to pretend to be her boyfriend - she did this again with a pause, intake of breath, and then a rather awkward start to the question; "Are you straight?"

"Yes ..." I didn't ask her to explain, but looked at her showing my curiosity.

It was awkward. She didn't know how to explain. So I asked; "You thought otherwise?"

"You haven't made any moves..." She blurted out.

"I understood very clearly that you didn't want me to."

"And that's it?"

"Did you want me to?"

"No," I think we were both puzzled by the way the conversation was going.

I tried to make it easier for her. I would not mention some of the well-intentioned teasing from my comrades who suggested their suspicions of me making mad passionate love all night ...

"Do you mean that you think that most men would have tried it on, even though you asked them not to?"

"Sort of."

"Of course I mix with lots of men from – the military – who probably would have. I am enjoying the time that I spent with you, and you asked for help. It would not be right to take advantage, when you asked me for help..."

"So you're being honourable and disciplined – an officer and a gentleman?" I knew she was teasing me. "If we had met, and I hadn't asked you for help?"

"How could that have happened? You seemed to despise me when we were at school. I was surprised that you seemed to be interested in spending time with me when we met. Then I understood that you needed help..."

"'Despise'? Is that what you think?"

"I think that came through loud and clear."

"I didn't despise you! Definitely not! I was interested in you, but you didn't seem to have any interest in me."

"We weren't encouraged to show much interest in girls. It was drummed into us that the priority was to do well at
245

school to get into the right stream for our careers. Getting enmeshed with girls could spoil our chances." "IF THE ARMY HAD WANTED..."

"And you went along with that?"

"It made sense!"

"And I certainly got the impression that your father – your stepfather treated me with contempt."

"Yes he did. Not just you, any of the Ferndale boys! I don't know what was behind that."

"But he's away now – he has no influence on my life!" Why did she suddenly sound less convinced as she said this? "And I never want to see him again! He is evil!"

"I hope he rots in hell!" She added.

I raised my eyebrows to her, but she was clearly upset. I changed the subject to something neutral and cheerful, and she seemed grateful to follow me.

*

I had switched off the ceiling light, and left a reading lamp on the desk. After about an hour, Roman emerged from the shadows, tears running down his cheeks. I opened my arms to him, and he cuddled onto my lap in the chair. "Mummy sent me to see if you all right," he sobbed. "She said that I should give you a hug." I was getting a cuddle. A cuddle is worth much more than a hug!

"What's happening?" he asked me, through tears and sniffing.

"Your mum and I have just had a bit of a disagreement. But don't worry. I'm sure we will sort it out." I tried to reassure

246

him. I was hoping for the best.

"Have you been having an affair?" That took me by surprise. But then I remembered that in the limited experience he had of classmates whose parents had separated, that had been the usual cause.

"No, definitely not!" I said, stroking his back. "Your mummy is the only woman I ever wish to be with. She's the mother of my children."

He seemed to be soothed for a little while, and then suddenly he spoke again; "If you do get divorced, I will stay with mummy," he told me. "But T-Roy will come with you." How had they ever got to have this conversation?

"No," I told him. "Both of you will stay with your mum. I don't think we will separate, but if we did, I would stay close by so I could see you every day!"

He started to cry again, and I held him that much tighter. "Don't worry. I'm sure it will be all right," I told him again. "I'll do anything your mum wants that I possibly can." He seemed to be slightly reassured by that. "I want you to go back and look after your mum now," I told him.

He gave me an excellent tight squeeze, and then turned to go. I don't approve of involving the children – not that it had ever happened with anything serious before – but that something serious was happening. "Please tell your mummy that I'm very sorry that I upset her," I said to him. He nodded, still tearful, and disappeared into the darkness of the hallway.

*

I was spending all of my free time with her now, still with

the same terms and conditions of appearing to be in a relationship, but separate beds in separate rooms at bed time. I enjoyed her company, living it day by day, and ~~not in a hurry or tempted elsewhere~~. She had started ~~to navigate a course~~. Again, I noticed her pause at the end of one conversation, her intake of breath, and the faltering start of a significant and emotionally loaded question.

"Okay, `Mr Lord of Discipline...' Would you still be able to control yourself if...?" And here, the brief confidence she managed, suddenly evaporated. She had taken the plunge, and soldiered on – to coin a phrase!

"Will you control yourself if ... if I `examine' you?"

I could see it was difficult for her, and I tried to ease things through gentle humour. "I thought you were a paediatric nurse? Aren't I a bit old...?"

She stuck out her tongue at me! This was the first time that I remember her doing this, the first time of many of how she teased me as our relationship developed.

The second burst of her confidence ebbed away, leaving her feeling awkward – and me feeling awkward, despite her playful reaction when I had teased her.

Let me help her again! "You can `examine' me if you wish," I said gently. "I will let you, and I won't do anything. You can be the boss, and I will obey. `Lord of Discipline', hey?" I had no doubt that she referred to exploring my body sexually, even if pseudo-medically, and I liked the idea.

"Are you sure?"

"Yes," I wanted to encourage her, and held back any humorous observations about playing `doctors and nurses'!

I wasn't entirely surprised at what was happening. Although I knew that I was enjoying our friendship, I suspected that it was a transitory stage, and would end or transform in one of a number of different ways that I could hypothesise.

I knew that I could always get out of the situation if I wanted to, by indicating that I was required to stay back at base, or that I had been transferred to a different location or sent on some task or similar. This could be an outright lie if I felt the need, and as long as I did not go to the places that I knew she frequented, she would be none the wiser. I knew that she was going through a messy divorce, and although I offered to let her talk about it, she chose not to. I gathered from snippets that I picked up – as I do – that her estranged husband had been a nasty piece of work; that he had been initially very pleasant, while wooing Debbie, but shortly after she was committed by having married him, he started to become controlling, and when she resisted, he would become violent. She had tried to overcome this, tried to tame him, initially accepting his supposed remorse and promises never to do it again, until the next time. I had also assumed that the reason that she had asked me to pretend to be her love interest was that he might be stalking her, and she wanted to scare him off by seeming to have a new partner, and apparently a military one as well.

I probably learned more from the occasional snippets that her mother let slip, as Debbie maintained she didn't want to discuss it, and didn't want me to do something more active to scare her ex away. Initially I wondered if there was a rebound desire for a replacement, but her reluctance for any physical contact, like cuddling up together on the sofa if we were watching television suggested this was not the case, despite the greeting and departing hugs which she was keen on, especially if they were in the doorway or

somewhere visible to people outside. I assumed this aversion to physical contact was a legacy from her marriage. Other thoughts had crossed my mind, like that she might prefer the 'company of ladies' (strange that she had the equivalent question about me!), and that at some stage, if I had served my purpose, she might disclose this, along with my marching orders. Again, I would not have lost anything; it was not as though if I was not spending my time with her, I would have been seeking another romantic attachment – not at that stage in my life and career.

I thought that with her aversion to physical intimacy, bad things might have happened in her marriage, that, traumatised, she was being very careful with any future man, and possibly with us having known each other from school – although a very different relationship – she considered me to be a safe pair of hands.

My comrades enjoyed the idea of her being a nurse – I had not revealed her name to them – and despite some inappropriately intrusive questions, I was choosing not to answer about to what extent our relationship had become physical. Most of them professed at least to a 'love them and leave them' approach to woman, which held little appeal to me; there didn't seem to be much attraction to having sex with someone one hardly knows, or knows little about – which, when I mentioned this to them when they tried to encourage me after regaling their sexual exploits, suggested I was just using this as an excuse. Their behaviour did not encourage me to explore whether I might enjoy things differently. That Debbie was a nurse, led to the inevitable teasing about her nurse's uniform being an integral part of our presumed lovemaking, extending on to suggestions about her putting on her rubber gloves.

"I can control myself by not moving," I offered. "But I can't promise that I won't become – aroused!" I knew this, as the way that the conversation was going was arousing – physically.

She took this in a very matter-of-fact way; "That's okay. I can cope with that!"

We established that as long as I was passive, she would `explore' my body and I was perfectly happy with this, and I expected to enjoy it. I hypothesised that she might have been raped within her marriage – terrible thing to think of for a girl that I was becoming increasingly fond of - and not that I had ever disrespected her. I had great respect for her, and wanted good things to happen to her. I understood that she would need to be in control, and not have me do anything that might startle or frighten her. I presumed she was working on overcoming the trauma she had suffered.

She seemed not quite sure how to develop things. I have only had the childhood I have had, as a child of the State, and then into the military, where privacy has seldom been a high priority – expected or available. "Do you want me to ..."I had been intending to say strip, but I decided to finish with "undress?"

I was aware that there were many things going on in her head; I could not see the cogs whirring, or the rapidly churning feet under the serene swan's visible body. I could be patient and I was happy for her to take her time.

"Yes... but leave your underpants on!"

Had I read more into her word `examine' than she intended?

She was sitting opposite me, and as I stood to remove my

shirt, she stood as well, which I only understood later. I flexed my stomach muscles. "Nice six-pack," I prompted.

"Please sit down," she said rapidly. Suddenly she seemed to be particularly tense again.

"Just give me a minute or two," she said. I sat down immediately, and folded my shirt before resting it on the arm of the chair. I watched her as she wrestled with her anxiety.

"We can stop if you want to," I said. "I can put my shirt back on. I can leave now and come back tomorrow if that's best for you?"

"No, it's okay."

Later I learned that with me standing up and being taller than her, and so seeming to dominate was a problem for her at that time, despite my average height, being part of what she wanted to scare off the unwanted attention. Also having innocently flexed my muscles had exacerbated that. In the early stages of her curing herself of the effects of her trauma, she needed me to be passive – almost dead? And certainly lower than her, supine or prostrate.

She regained her composure. "I'll go out of the room for a moment," she suggested. "When I come back, can you be lying flat on the sofa, in just your underpants?"

"Yes." I said gently, and so it happened.

I don't want what happened over the next hour to sound like erotica. On a film it might appear to be so, but I was very aware that much was going on in Debbie's head, most probably therapy for herself, as she explored my uncovered body touching, and at times massaging. This was before she

252

trained to do professional massages, which she developed as a skill, as well as an adjunct to our later lovemaking. This was all done in silence – no television on in the background, no background music played, making it clinical, which I think might have been helpful for her, even though it was in her living room in the apartment she shared with her mother, and not on the standard issue massage table we later bought and used in the room in our home that we referred to as the study.

I took a breath, about to say something, which she picked up on, and stopped and lent back to straighten her spine. She raised her eyebrows and looked at me, encouraging me to speak. My hands had been at my side. "Do you mind if I put my hands behind my head?" She assented, while keeping her distance, and when I had done so, she took a few moments before resuming her massage.

"You look as if you're enjoying yourself," she accused, but not with anger. Teasing!

"I am!"

"So I see," she said, and pointed to the obvious bulge in my underpants. This was the first time she actually acknowledged that I had a penis.

She had never questioned my masculinity, and she – and her mom – had taken that interest in my biceps. She had asked me about my history of girlfriends, serious ones, and knew that there hadn't been many. She seemed to be satisfied that inevitably I had found that I didn't have much in common, much to talk about with them. She hadn't asked much and I hadn't volunteered much about the physical aspects of these relationships not having been satisfying enough for me to want to continue with them.

"I'm glad he's enjoying this," she said, pointing at the bulge, with a slight mischievousness – which I had last seen when she had stuck out her tongue at me earlier. She had been terribly serious since then.

"He doesn't get as much exercise as the rest of you," she said, gently – having taken the hint – massaging my six-pack!

"Don't you believe him? He gets as much exercise as he needs, just not always with company."

So, once again in my life, things were back to front, and the wrong way round. Here's me, an elite soldier, in supreme physical shape, and the lady that I am with is doing to me, what most males would be tentatively and cautiously seeing how far they could get with intimate touching and beyond with the woman they had chosen. A question for them would be whether this would go any further than a one-off encounter or not. The irony was not lost on me!

"Are you okay?" She asked, and I raised my eyebrows inquisitively hoping to suggest `how could I not be?'

Several times I had seen her hesitate before asking some question which could change things; which one cannot rewind and undo. She had gradually focused her attention, and her fingers on my underpants, and – can we say – my arousal was unambiguous. Then she took the plunge, and reached in and took hold of my erection. Oh yes!

If it was difficult for her, her success was great!

She felt for a while, and rubbed, and massaged, and I really hoped that my dick would not respond in a way that could spoil the moment.

"Lift your bum up," she instructed, and when I did, she

slipped my underpants down to my knees, leaving my dick standing proud. She continued to attend to it.

"Oh, you've been circumcised," she observed.

"So I've been told!" What a smart Alec am I? She saw the humour, and still holding my dick, she stuck her tongue out at me again. Twice in one evening!

"Why were you circumcised?" She asked. Just a medical interest? An easy enough question to ask, but more difficult for me to answer.

"I don't know. There's nothing in my medical records about it, other than that it was done, before I started at Ferndale Hall. I don't remember anything before then."

She contemplated this for a while, with her eyes resting on my dick.

"I'm going to try and make you climax," she said. Very clinical, very medical! "Are you okay not to move?"

Still luxuriating with my hands behind my head, I smiled at her and told her that was fine. Then, remembering what I believe the context to be, I offered; "But only if you want to. This isn't necessary for our friendship to carry on... I do understand this is not easy for you!"

"What do you mean...? What do you know?" She stopped abruptly, and then decided; "No, don't tell me now. I'll ask you some other time...!"

She started to stimulate me then, in the age old approach, but it was uncomfortable for me as she was expecting to be able to pull a non-existent foreskin over my glans – should I call it my acorn in honour of my boys who, at that stage, I

had no idea would ever be conceived?

"It isn't working," she announced just as I had taken a breath to ask her to stop.

"We'll need some skin cream, or something like that..." I told her, explaining to her exactly what she had just realised.

She was still cautious, and still seeming a little like a deer caught in the headlights. She was very bravely working on her problems to overcome, with me, damage done to her by others. I asked her if I could show her, and she agreed, standing up and back. She provided some skin cream, from her collection from her growing interest in aromatherapy, and I put some on me and showed her the motion.

"Leave some for me," she said with an attempt at conveying confidence. I replaced my hands behind my head, relaxed and let her continue.

"You're not used to circumcised penises?" It was an unnecessary comment, as I knew that the circumcision was relatively unusual, and my status had made me unusual, and during childhood, a source of interest to boys in the know who remained intact.

"I've seen them, but mostly on little boys. I've seen some in my general nurse training, but yours is the first I've ever done this to."

"I'm glad to hear that!"

She achieved her goal, which coincided with mine! I made sure that I was passive and didn't make any physical movements when I climaxed, she made good use of the towel and then stepped back – distance was important to her sense of safety – and invited me to finish off cleaning

256

myself up.

I commended her, acknowledging that I knew that she had been courageous. She again almost asked what I hypothesised, but then backed off it again. I cleaned myself properly in the bathroom, and dressed. Then we chatted, immediately distanced from what had happened, and almost as though it hadn't happened.

It did bring about a change though, as I had proved to her that I could control myself and that I would honour her wishes, which was important to her. After that she found that she felt able to sit next to me, and allow me to put my arm around her, shoulders at first but later to around her waist and rest my hand on her thigh.

I didn't ask for it, but I wasn't going to turn down what she offered, even though it seemed almost to be offered from a sense of duty to give me such relief each evening. She sensed that I had needs, although she knew that I was perfectly capable of satisfying these myself, and not averse to doing so. Gradually it developed – rather clinically, but our relationship wasn't based on a romantic infatuation, as she bought – or I bought the massage bench, after which that was what I lay on. Our routine was developed so that she would also give me a body massage, experimenting with her aromatherapy lotions and potions which would always reach a `happy ending' – though it took awhile before I used that phrase with her, by which time she was able to take it in her stride.

And that, as I revealed yet another family secret, is the same massage table that we have in our study, where we make love – such as we do – on which both boys were conceived – and there is a warm irony that they like massages too, which

257

Debbie will do for them usually on request. It works best for Roman who goes into a state of dreamy ecstasy whereas T-Roy, who does enjoy it, but wishes to be doing other things at the same time, even when lying face down with his face through the hole at the end of the bench.

*

I kept our intelligence people informed of the situation, which I had always known I would have to do. They knew to always treat such confidences with respect, and though I had the same intelligence officer monitor, I had minimal contact with him outside of such debriefings. I very seldom saw him around the base or the directorate, but I knew how to contact him should the need ever arise. Although I did not have firsthand experience of this, I rather gather that our meetings with our intelligence monitors were similar to Catholics having to make regular confessions with their priests, except that Catholics, if necessary have to do penance, whereas there was no penance from our monitors. I understood that they were required to collect information about us, and the maxim would be that transgressions could be forgiven, but would never be forgotten. I never expected that, transparent as I was content to be, there would ever be anything that I would need to seek forgiveness for.

About three months after I had started staying over at Debbie's apartment, my monitor showed particular interest in what I knew about the stalker. I reported that I had not knowingly seen the stalker, and did not know whether he was still doing this – or whether he ever had. Not that I thought Debbie might have been making it up, but I am aware that she might have believed she was under more threat than she actually was, especially with her ex having been playing power games with her. I had assumed that it

258

was her ex-husband who was stalking her, until my mentor put a dossier on the desk and asked me if I wanted to know who it was. I was slightly surprised that this had been investigated, me being a junior officer at that stage, and having fully informed them. He explained that – always anonymously – it had been decided that this could be a useful training exercise for some of our staff, and so surveillance task had taken place. I opened the dossier, and I suppose that I shouldn't have been as surprised as I was to see the photo of the man who I had thought was her father – but who she corrected me was actually her stepfather – the infamous 'Bobby' – clipped to the front of the report.

"What use am I to make of this information?" I asked. The deal was that although he was my superior, I did not refer to him by his rank or by the more generic 'Sir'!

"As you see fit."

As I was becoming used to, I realised that having information did not prompt immediate action, but it would be useful to store until time of need.

When I deemed the time right, I asked her whether she had evidence that the stalker was still active. She tensed up as I did so, and then thought about it, and then carefully and slowly said that she hadn't. She still had the fear, but she hadn't seen any recent indications – actual signs that he was still stalking her.

"Does that change things?" She asked, suddenly sounding melancholic.

"Not for me. And I hope not for you!"

*

My relationship with Debbie had started with her looking to me for protection, her being vulnerable which I had never imagined her to be when we were at school. I suppose most marriages are like this; she looked to me to be her protector as our relationship developed. Under the overarching view that I was her protector, there was a little rebellious streak - her enjoyment of mocking me, and what I found endearing, of her sticking her tongue out at me as a mild insult.

I had enjoyed our friendship – what had become intimacy greater than a mere friendship, and while neither of us would use the `L' word, and nor would we venture anywhere near the concept of a romance, we had a deep friendship different, but as valuable as, the camaraderie that I enjoyed with my male friends in the directorate, and broader military, who I had trained with and in some cases grown up with. I certainly didn't want it to end, but also I didn't know how practical it would be to continue as things were, me now sleeping over most nights at her apartment, with her mom being around, but making herself discreetly absent for us to spend time together, and especially our particular intimacy.

Probably about four months after the first night I stayed over, I was tasked with the project that meant I would be away for three months, but with a week back at the end of each month. This meant that I was away for three sets of three weeks, and although I could generally phone from time to time, communication in those days wasn't what it is now. Debbie accepted this as being part of my career, that I had chosen as much as I had been directed into it, and said the inevitable; that she would miss me and she would wait for me – and I responded in kind. I knew that waiting for her was not an issue, as although I found that as the intimacy developed, I noticed other woman around more than I had

260

when my ingrained philosophy of `don't even go there' had made most women that I saw or come into contact with not even register. I had been well taught, and until now I had not had reason to question or challenge what had been instilled in us.

Before my chance encounter – or so I thought it was – with Debbie that fateful day in the bookshop, I had assumed that my life pathway would be straightforward; I would complete my qualifications, and challenge myself to advancing up the career path as fast as I could. I was certainly raised with the philosophy of doing one's best, slightly expanded to a competitive element of; do better than all the rest! I was vaguely aware that I might find some aspect of my work particularly captivating and stimulating enough for me to want to deviate from the line to the top, which would essentially mean senior management. The target was clear though, and I have to accept that in my early to mid 20s, what senior management would actually involve didn't sink through my goal direction. I had given no thought to the possibility that I might be distracted by any relationship, certainly with my developing sense of myself that I did not need other people - even though I generally enjoyed company - and I was self-sufficient.

Now, after the break in my routine, I found that my obligatory assurance to Debbie that I would miss her turned out to be true. I found myself looking forward to when I would have the opportunities to phone her, and to meet up with her for the nights of the week when I was back at base, except when I was required for evening functions or duties.

Unaccustomed as I was to such thoughts, I realise that unexpectedly, Debbie had become a very important part of my life. I wanted to have her as part of my life for the rest of

my life.

*

When I had realised that I wanted to develop a permanent relationship with her, despite the damage I could expect it to do to my career, I knew that I should give her some information that I thought she needed to know. I wanted our relationship to be based on honesty, though I would have to explain that there were things to do with my work which I would never be able to tell her about. I had to let her know that as part of my work I would be monitored and observed – 'spied on' is the phrase most people would use, by our own side, and possibly by 'other people'. I had been raised with this expectation, and although it didn't date back to my birth, I was aware that there was a file of my records beyond my medical records and school reports that followed me from Ferndale Hall, and through into the military. There was a certain advantage for the security of the State that they had such comprehensive records of me, and those like me, which those who had had a more conventional childhood of growing up with their parents might not have had.

Before I could propose, I needed to get permission from the directorate. Getting married, and thereby dividing my loyalties between the Directorate and my wife – let alone children – was not encouraged. I had a meeting with the officer commanding, a contemplative man, who did not patronise me by trying to talk me out of it. He did as was required of him; he pointed out to me that if I were to get married, that would probably restrict my utility, and I could expect that I would not be promoted beyond the rank I was already destined for. He knew that I was not rushing into this lightly, and that I wasn't willing to settle for the casual

262

girlfriends and affairs that most of my peers indulged in to satisfy their sexual needs. Probably a large part of my thinking was wishing to commit to a girl whose company I enjoyed – and, although there were no textbooks on this, I considered I loved her. I delighted in her company, looked forward to her company when we were apart and wanted to commit to the relationship which I could rely on to be there; that I could look after her and cherish her.

I did propose, in a rather clumsy manner, which she was expecting. Her sense of humour kicked in, and she teased me with a; "This is a big step! I will have to think very carefully about this! I accept!" And seeing me being somewhat perplexed, she honoured me by sticking out her tongue.

We had a conventional civilian wedding, at the church that we had started to attend, so Debbie could wear a white dress, although she had done this before. It was a fairly small function, with her mother in attendance, who was allowed to `give her away' and some of her friends who were mostly colleagues from work. Leon was my best man. Although I invited various people I could consider friends from my school years and from conventional military units I was surprised to find how many of my directorate requested to attend in a civilian capacity. It was not lost on many of those attending how over-represented young, extremely fit men with buzz cut hairstyles were, portraying the awkwardness of military people conspicuously pretending to be civilians, but not wanting this pretence to be too convincing. Some comrades had girlfriends attached, who might easily have misinterpreted the situation, expecting that they too could marry the man they were with, not realising how exceptional my breaking the mould by getting married, was!

My commanding officer attended the ceremony, discreetly and he did not stay to mix and mingle at the reception. It was a courtesy to invite him, but I understood that he had mixed feelings. I had known I was his protégé, and hints had been dropped that I was under consideration to replace him eventually, but by getting married, a deliberate choice and action on my part now made that unlikely. I could expect that he was disappointed, but he did not change his manner with me and we remained fond of each other across the gulf of our different ranks.

*

We continued to live in Debbie's apartment for a while after we were married, and for a year or two developed a lifestyle which suited both of us well. Neither of us was possessive, and she spent as much time as she wished with her friends and colleagues, as did I with mine, but we became more and more home bodies, enjoying spending time at home, getting to know each other and enjoying what we found.

Debbie took me by surprise, when, after summoning up her courage she eventually blurted out that she wanted to have a child!

I knew that she had issues about sex, which I was pretty sure I understood the origins of – her stepfather, followed up by her first husband! I had never expected that she would have been willing to have the conventional sex that would be required if she were to conceive. I had put two and two together, and with her being a paediatric nurse, I had thought that she might have satisfied what maternal desires she might have had through her work, but it seemed I was wrong!

"Are you sure?" I found myself asking, automatically,

264

wishing immediately I could take back those words. Of course she had thought it through! I could only imagine how difficult it must have been for her to reach this decision.

"I'm not letting that bastard win!" I knew she was referring to `Bobby'!

So there was a variation, which instead of me lying on my back with my hands behind my head while she attended to me, carefully and rather awkwardly she got astride me. I could see her anguish, but she continued. She made an attempt at humour to try to defuse the awkwardness that we were both aware of; "You look as though you're enjoying this!" She accused. I could have made some quip about how `I was obeying orders and that I liked obeying orders', especially like this, but I held my tongue and I was glad that I did so.

In this way, with great courage and strength of will, and with a little input from me, Debbie made Roman inside her - How clever is that? - and she kept him. And then, less than two years later, she put herself through the ordeal again, and she made T-Roy! And she gave him to me!

*

There were other aspects of our life dictated by Debbie's courage and determination `not to let that bastard win!'

Knowing that she was apprehensive about me bumping into her in my sleep at night, although I believe myself to be inactive when I sleep, I had suggested when we moved in together that we could sleep in separate beds if this would make things easier for her. I knew she appreciated what I was offering, but her determination – or stubbornness – kicked in and she insisted that we have a traditional double

bed. We did go for the largest double bed we could find, and I noticed that she had many pillows at her side, and that more often than not a couple made their way down to form an obstacle between the two of us, until Roman arrived and possibly served this function.

I preferred to sleep naked, and generally be naked from the time I went to bed until the time I dressed in the morning. It would have been a trivial sacrifice for me, enjoying the feeling of the sheets against my bare skin to have worn shorts to bed, and it was a sacrifice I was certainly willing to make, considering her bravery in facing some of her demons.

Again, she appreciated my offer but on different occasions, repeated her mantra about not letting the bastard win, and suggesting that my nudity in sleeping was a part of me and she didn't want to take this away from me, and on another occasion, when she was more graphic than usual, she spoke in terms of if I was naked she could assess the challenge or threat and that when I was naked this was somehow more reassuring to her than if it was concealed. Somehow this extended to the boys, and possibly coinciding with her interests in massage and even aromatherapy, `the body beautiful' was something to be appreciated. She couldn't quite manage to overcome her discomfort with T-Roy's fiddling, though, but knew that she didn't want to inhibit him, in the hope that he would soon, eventually, grow out of it. But, when our bed was shared in the mornings with the four of us, she could compromise to T-Roy doing what T-Roy did, providing it was on the far side of me, with, in this case, me being the protective barrier.

*

I wasn't paying attention to the time, being lost in my thoughts and memories. Another hour passed. Roman emerged from the darkness again, and cuddled in onto my lap again. He was still tearful. I stroked his back to comfort him.

"Mummy says she wants you to go and sleep in the bed in my room," he told me. My dutiful little messenger boy!

"I will," I told him, but I didn't move, and I continue to stroke his back, and he continued to cuddle in.

"I do love you, Daddy!" He told me. "I love Mummy more, but I do love you!"

"I know that. That's fine. She's your mummy." And it was fine! More of a problem was T-Roy's evident preference for me, which was an issue for Debbie, and as it would be better for all concerned, I wish that T-Roy loved Debbie more than he loved me. Nothing stopped the amount of love I felt for them, and I was more than satisfied with the love I got back from Roman.

He was still cuddled up on my lap, with me stroking him, and it seemed to be easing him, but then, suddenly he sobbed; "I just want it to stop!"

I cuddled him a while longer, and then sent him back to Debbie, telling him that I loved him and I was sure things would be sorted out. I would move to his room. There was no guarantee that I would be able to fall asleep, though, even if I lay down.

*

Bureaucracies! Don't you just love them? There are forms to be filled in, applications to be made, and authorising

267

signatures to be required. There was even such a paper trail for someone who is to be disappeared. Disappeared, in its broadest sense, the phrase we used for those removed, or neutralised as a problem. Most commonly, they wouldn't disappear, and the body could be produced, with an autopsy report that matched the cause of death. The roads are safer than the statistics would lead us to believe!

I submitted a dossier – really scraping the barrel for what I was prepared to write down – attempting to portray the man as a threat to the State, but I knew it didn't hold water. It would get me an interview with the OC and it was just possible that a face-to-face, off the-record exception to the rule might be made. So it was that my 'presence was requested', and at the appointed time I did my usual brisk march into his office where he sat behind his desk, him feigning mild irritation at my military ballet.

He had been in the business for a long time, and he was wise about the people that worked subordinate to him, as well as those we hunted and watched. Normally, he would have gestured to me to sit in one of his comfortable seats, and he would have moved to sit in the chair next to it, but this time he left me standing before him while he continued to sit at his desk. We knew the games that we play; and his desk was clear except for the dossier containing the documents I had submitted.

"This is not a strong enough case," he told me. "There isn't really enough to interest the…" and here he used a disparaging nickname that we used for the ordinary police, who supposedly protect the public and solve crimes, as opposed to protecting the State and removing threats, as we did.

It wasn't a game that we were playing, but a dance. I was his protégé, and we both knew it. "I understand he is your father-in-law," the OC added, although he knew that this was a misrepresentation. I knew that I had not included this information in the documentation, but I was not surprised that he had done his own enquiries. "You don't think this is a bit of an overreaction to a family dispute?"

"Stepfather!" I respectfully corrected him, which he conceded.

"I believe you are withholding some information, Max," he said calmly. "That is not like you!"

Then, in a moment that was so incongruous that I can't believe that it happened, despite me remembering it clearly, I heard him say; "Trust me, son!"

"It's Debbie! "I took the plunge. "He raped her every night since she was seven years old!"

Even though he might have had an idea of where this was heading, he looked stunned. I felt stunned realising how bluntly I had explained the case to him.

He stared at me for a while in a meaningful stare, but which did not contain disapproval or anger or commendation, and nor was he doing the stunt of pretending that he could look into my soul, or read my mind. It was also not a stare to cover while he was thinking, as I knew that he would have made an instant decision.

"Team Maxwell is one of my most valued assets. I cannot tolerate any impedance that will compromise Team Maxwell in the performance of its duties," He reached for his pen,

and elaborately signed the cover sheet, authorising the removal of a threat to State security.

"It could be useful as a training exercise," he mused – supposedly to himself – but he would never speak aloud anything that he did not want to be heard. He placed the dossier in his out tray, and I didn't see it again. It went into `process', for the attention of the executive branch.

There was gallows-humour about a prank to play on trainee interrogators who were getting too big for their boots. This was to withhold from them the actual information wanted from the person they were interrogating, and leave them to see what they could discover. But for those on the side of might, not expecting to face interrogation ourselves, beyond the routine checks, we joked about the horror of being interrogated for information that one did not know, by interrogators convinced that you knew the information, but were holding out on them! I gathered that this might be the fate that awaited `Bobby'!

After just having waded through many euphemisms, confirmed the death sentence on a disgusting, but still human being, I watched the skill with which my commanding officer lightened the atmosphere again.

"Have you decided on a name for your child?" He showed an interest in family life which he had never had himself. He had prioritised his career, and to some extent looked upon his subordinates as the children he never had.

"I get to name him if he's a boy. My choice is Roman Warren Maxwell. Debbie gets to choose if it's a girl, and the latest is Julia Catherine Maxwell. We'll have to see when the child is born which it's going to be."

"Good names," he said. There wasn't anything else he could say.

The meeting was over. The purpose achieved. "One last thing, Max, would you make an old man happy...?"

"Sir?"

"Just this one time will you please shake my hand and walk out of my office without your bloody parade ground drill moves?"

"Yes sir," I said, in the manner of a recruit at the start of basic training replying to an instructor, but not as loud. He flinched, but stood up, and we shook hands over the desk.

"Thank you," I said. I did not add `Sir' this time. He knew how much I respected him, and I honoured his request for informality.

"It is necessary," he said, and I granted him his wish, and turned and casually walked out of his office.

Time moved on, and a few weeks later I received a file through the internal post which consisted of an autopsy report, indicating a road traffic accident leading to catastrophic head and internal injuries. I knew that there would be photos deeper into the full report, but I knew what I needed to know, and preferred not to know the details.

Those who organise these things work on a need to know only basis, and the official autopsy report would be publicly available to people with the appropriate qualifications for access, which could include any family members and their legal teams. There was no secrecy rating on it, and I knew I was free to take it home and do with it as I pleased.

I knew though, that after he had been picked up, `Bobby' would have been interrogated by a team completely different from my own – one of the teams that one hopes never to bump into while following the same leads, and records would have been kept about the results of his interrogation, and I didn't know, and I didn't want to know whether the OC had alerted them to the real reason why he was to die. I have an idea of the difficulties and frustration for an interrogation team if they are not tasked with what areas to investigate. So, somewhere within the Directorate archives there will be a report on his interrogation, care having been taken that if our regime was threatened, all of this, as well as the document I prepared and signed, and was countersigned by the OC which was essentially a death warrant, would be destroyed.

The autopsy report was signed off by a leading consultant pathologist, who I knew was one of ours. We owned him; he would do as he was told, and he would find impressive wording to complete the documents. I never expected anyone would ever enquire as to how it came to be that this eminent pathologist had done what appeared to be a routine autopsy, this had been thought through in general, and there was a rota for autopsies, and `it just so happened' that it was always one of our people who happen to be on duty when there was an autopsy to be done that we had an interest in.

I had it in mind to drop into conversation to Debbie that I had learned – by chance – that her stepfather had been killed in a road traffic accident, although I did not wish to do this. Debbie did not share my general inclination to want to know endings so one could draw a line under matters. Inevitably, for reasons that I understood, she often wished lines to be drawn under matters, and for unpleasant things

to be shut out of minds as best one could. When I returned home that evening, Debbie was glowing with her pregnancy and so much enjoying the prospect of motherhood, and – she always downplays it to tease me – how we both enjoyed our relationship, which had far surpassed what we had expected from our very businesslike start.

I did not have the heart – or was I too cowardly? – to tell her then, and to offer her the chance to see the coroner's report, fully expecting that she would not wish to read it. I filed it in my filing cabinet, locked it away, and probably because I did not want to do anything more with it, it faded from my task list. I acknowledge that this was uncharacteristic of me.

*

I was lying on Romans bed, still dressed, except I'd taken off my shoes, when Roman reappeared from the darkness. I sat up, and cuddled him onto my lap. I stroked his back which was a natural habit I did anyway when he cuddled with me.

This time he was less upset. He was businesslike. He had a definite task. Hermes, my messenger!

"Mummy says she wants to meet you in the kitchen," he told me.

I still didn't like the way that Debbie was using Roman as a messenger, but I realised that despite what it might be doing to him, she didn't feel that she could come and speak to me directly while she was preoccupied with events in life she hadn't thought possible.

I cuddled Roman a while longer, but there was a course of action to be followed. He knew it, and I knew it, and the

sooner we started this the sooner – hopefully – things might be resolved.

"Please tell your mummy that I'll be there in a moment," I whispered in his ear. "I want you to go back and keep your mummy's bed warm for her. Please stay there, and don't come to us while we are talking in the kitchen. I need you to do that for both of us!" He agreed to that. Though still tearful, he was no longer sobbing.

*

Minutes later I was sitting at the kitchen table, when Debbie walked in and sat down opposite me, wearing a dressing gown. She won't thank me for saying it, but she was puffy eyed, with dark rings already around her eyes.

I offered her a drink, which she declined, sitting, gathering her thoughts. The ball was in her court. I felt as a schoolboy facing punishment, and in Alvin's words, I would accept six strokes of the cane on my bare arse if, for Roman, that would make it stop. But that was all superficial. I was not going to defend myself, I was above that. Part of Debbie turning to me for protection when we had met again as adults was knowing that I was something in the military, and as she got to know me and she accepted not to ask questions. She couldn't not know that I was ever increasingly deeply involved in protecting the State. In my circles, when push came to shove, the normal rules of society – make that `the laws of society' – could and would be ignored if really necessary. I wasn't going to remind her that she knew this when she had implored me – with emotion she didn't need to put it into words, that I would make the problem go away. I would not say as any defence that I had done what she had asked me to – so much

unspecified. Was she really surprised? I wouldn't go into that `he got what he deserved'. I presented myself to her, sat across the kitchen table, willing to do anything I could to ease her pain.

She took a breath, and her eyes climbed my face to meet mine. "Did you kill him?"

"Not physically myself. I put things in motion for it to happen."

After a pause, choosing her words, deciding which questions to ask, she asked; "Were you there when... he died?"

"No. I knew that it would happen, and that is as much as I wanted to know."

Again she was silent as she processed this information, and decided what to ask next. "Did he suffer?"

"I don't know for sure. As far as I know he was removed as a threat to..." (Don't say `you'l) "my family. That was as much as I wanted to know."

After looking me in the eyes as she asked her questions, she dropped her gaze down to her hands classed tightly enough for her knuckles to be white on the table surface.

"My educated guess, though, would be that he was unconscious when he died."

She looked up, indicating that she wanted to know more.

"I fully expect that he was anaesthetised when he died. I know you tease about the reputation of people in my line of work, but we are committed, and we feel uncomfortable having anything to do with sadists."

"Do you want to see his autopsy report?"

"You have that to hand?" She asked, mockingly.

"It's in my filing cabinet in the study."

"What does it say?"

"... *Probable cause of death is road traffic accident, head-on collision at speed...*"

And then I decided it would be best to add; "*the injuries are consistent with...*"

I could almost see the information I gave her being absorbed in her mind. "But that isn't what actually happened to him?"

"I seriously believe that it is likely that he died behind the wheel of a car that came to a very sudden stop. I think he would have been unconscious in the vehicle at the time." I watched her thinking, my insides burning as I felt her pain, and waited to answer her next question as best I could. "When... did he die?"

"When you were pregnant with Roman. When we were starting a family. When I felt the need to protect my family the best way I could."

"So ten years ago! And you didn't think to tell me?"

It is best just to take full responsibility – as is said, it is easier to plead forgiveness than it is to ask for permission – not quite fit, as it would have been unfair and wrong to push responsibility onto her to say yes or no about permanently removing her ex-stepfather as a threat to our family. I wasn't going to quote back to her the way that she had said; 'please just sort it out. I don't care how,' which is what she

had conveyed to me when he had stalked her when she was pregnant and she had seen him. I had verified that it was him. It was best for her not to know how routinely security monitored our comings and goings, which had invariably been so useful to me.

"I never found a suitable time to tell you," I admitted. "I couldn't imagine that there would ever be a good time to tell you, and our life together seemed so good that I didn't want to hurt you. I've kept the report under lock and key in case you ever... needed to see it."

I was not going to defend myself, as that would have complicated the matter, as she became distressed at finding the role that she had played in prompting me to arrange for his death. I remembered vividly her fairly explicit need for my protection at the time our relationship started, though the threat there might have been seen to be as much from her ex-husband as her ex-stepfather.

She wasn't saying much. Her clasped hands stayed still on the table top, but her knuckles were still white. I couldn't tell whether she was formulating another question, or whether she wanted me to say something.

"I can't undo it," I stated the obvious. "I don't regret doing what I've done, but I am very sad about the effect it is having on you. My family means everything to me. I will do everything I can to keep you and the boys safe."

"Was Leon involved?"

"I don't think so. Leon is very professional, and I think he would have ruled himself out because he knows me. I think it would have been done by a different team from a different area."

"Would he have known that it was because of me?"

"No!"

Another silence.

"Do you want me to leave the Directorate?" Although this could be seen as an offer, it was more to assess what she might want. It was certainly not something that I would do lightly, and not offer to make on the spot.

"You wouldn't be 'you' anywhere else," she said, matching my gaze.

"And Graham?" She asked, after another pause.

"That wasn't us. We had nothing to do with that."

"He's dead?"

"Yes. A heart attack. Before you became pregnant with T-Roy."

"And how do you know about this?" She asked with some suspicion.

"Because of my job and my position, there is a department that keeps an eye on me, and possible threats to me... us. They let me know what they think I need to know."

"But you could have..."

"Yes, if I considered him to be a serious threat. But fate took care of him, and I didn't have to."

She looked at me through her red, swollen eyes. "I never asked you to kill 'Bobby'!"

"I know. It was my decision entirely. I never wanted you to find out." After a pause, I added; "It wasn't your responsibility at all!" Put it on my broad shoulders; I'll carry the burden.

"I didn't know you would have him killed," she told me. At least I'm not too predictable!

I could sense that her mood was lifting. She was coming to terms with the new information. "Who else do I know on your list?" She asked, with a touch of humour.

"Who did I miss?"

She stuck her tongue out at me. We would be fine!

She stayed silent, looking down at her hands on the table. I decided to push a little bit. "You are the boss, and I will do what you wish. If you want me to, I will move out. But I ask that you let me have contact with the boys, and…" (The rest of the sentence would be about how I could not compromise my organisation for what they had allowed me to do, but I didn't get that far.)

"For fucks' sake, Max!" She said with irritation. I can't remember her ever having used that word before. "There's no question of that! I love you…" And she started sobbing again, "… and you are the father of my children." She paused again, re-gathering her thoughts. "I'm very angry at the moment, and I've got a lot to get my head around, not least that I should have realised what you would do… have done!"

I gently pushed my chair back and stood up, and started to move around towards her, opening my arms to her, and inviting her to cuddle in. I didn't know if she would, but it

seemed to me the right thing to do at the time, and fortunately it was. She stood up and embraced me, sobbing into my chest as I rubbed her back in an attempt to comfort her.

"Come back to bed," she invited still through halted breathing. She disengaged and took my hand to lead me back to the bedroom.

Roman was at his post in the bed as we entered, sitting up in the darkness, save for the light coming through from the passageway, his eyes wide and tearstained, but the look of relief at the two of us arriving, holding hands made his relief palpable. Truth be told, so was mine!

I got into bed, and reached over to take Roman's hand to comfort and reassure him.

"Romey, I want you to sleep this side of me," Debbie told him. "I want to sleep next to your daddy tonight."

Chapter Five

Max

I was looking into T-Roy's eyes when he died.

We were at the nearby park. He was ramping his bicycle over the various mounds. He was riding towards me after a successful landing, with a look of triumph in his eyes. Suddenly I noticed that there was something gone from his eyes. Although still heading towards me, the bike slowed, and tilted to the side where he fell to the ground, without any movement from him to break his fall. I was at his side immediately, trying to get some response from him, but he wasn't there. I have seen this before.

Things moved into slow motion. I pulled him off his bike and onto a flat area where I started to do mouth-to-mouth and chest compressions. People gathered around. I was aware in my peripheral vision, but I felt very alone with T-Roy. I knew he wasn't there. As I breathed into his mouth, for a moment life seemed to flash back into his eyes, only to fade out again as the breath flowed back out of him. This happened once or twice more.

"Call an ambulance, please!" I begged, pointing to one of the people who had approached, and I saw him turn and move away. I had my pager on my belt, but I could not call out. My vision focused again onto just me and T-Roy as I continued with trying to bring him back to life, but I knew he was gone.

I would have done the chest compressions and the mouth-to-mouth all night and all day if there was the remotest chance of bringing him back. I was still focused on this and nothing else when the paramedic ambulance crew appeared beside me and gradually eased me away from him as they transferred his body onto a stretcher and carried him to the ambulance.

It was something in his head that had killed him. Something that no one could have known about, from a weakened area in one of the arteries carrying the blood around his brain, and his vivid imagination, his cheeky provocative sense of humour and the person he was. They told me later it was a catastrophic cerebral haemorrhage, and I didn't stop asking. His death would have been instantaneous, and he would have felt nothing which somehow reassured me. I had witnessed, in our last exchange of glances, the last moment of his consciousness. No one could have loved anyone more than I had loved T-Roy, and I know that he loved me as much.

*

How do you tell a mother that her son is dead? T-Roy was not there, but nor was I for a while after that. Seeing myself as a distant figure, through my tears and cracking voice, I channelled the ambulance intercom through to my work control room who patched me through to Debbie at home, who through my incoherence could understand that

something terrible had happened, and there couldn't have been anything worse that happened than what I was incoherently trying to tell her. I knew that it would be too cruel to ask her, or to get one of the staff to ask her to meet us at whatever hospital they were taking us as we were driven at speed by the ambulance, me embracing T-Roy's cooling body now that I knew that there was nothing I could do to bring him back and there was no mechanism to bargain my life for his.

Mercifully an emotional mist that spread over me with the sense of unreality which the facts poked through. Despite my tears and shattered voice, I was able to make some statements of what needed to be done. Probably the most sensible thing that I was able to do was to ask that Leon come to take over the situation for me.

Arriving at the hospital, and the time that we spent in accident and emergency during which the staff valiantly went through the motions of trying to bring T-Roy back, but even at the time I knew that they were doing this out of kindness to me and that really he wasn't there anymore.

He was certified dead, the date and time noted.

A work car had been dispatched to fetch Debbie and Roman. There isn't much that can be said about how a mother and a father and their older son meet each other in a hospital near to where their younger son lies dead on a gurney.

My son is dead!

Things were a blur for me after that. I grasped and held Debbie and Roman as much as I could, and we cried until there were no more tears.

*

As it always had, the directorate looked after us, and we wanted for nothing - apart from them bringing my son back!

A young captain, with sad eyes, presented himself in uniform to me and told me he was there to `assist me', and I knew he would have been the duty officer from the general welfare team. Looking back, I appreciate just how helpful he was, even though it was his job, and I remain grateful. He invited me to call him Andy, although insisted on calling me `Sir'.

Leon arrived promptly, brought in from whatever he was doing — I don't need to know! I was glad to have him there, even though there was nothing he could do.

That day or two remains a blur for me. Work did what they could. Captain Anderson was the coordinator, and they provided fully qualified psychologists for Debbie, and Roman, to help with their bereavement, with the offer of more for Alice, Colin and — me! I became aware that Colin had been added as a member of my family, and I realised that this had been done by my officer commanding — and I don't know what liaison had happened between him and Captain Anderson.

The Directorate provided an armed guard stationed outside our house from then until the funeral. There was no point to this at all, which anyone thinking about this would acknowledge, but work thought that this was something that they could do, and so it was arranged.

*

Captain Anderson alerted me that the hospital intended to follow procedures and conduct a post-mortem on T-Roy's body, and while I understood that this was a usual procedure, there was no way that I was going to let them cut up my little boy.

Alerting Leon to what the hospital intended, and with Anderson's guidance, I took on the hospital authorities. The hospital did not back down gracefully, insisting on legal requirements, and they were considering calling the police to have me removed, when a team from work arrived, and with a general authority seized T-Roy's body and transported it with me in attendance to the mortuary within the military base. From some anonymous high authority, it was decreed that no post-mortem was to be conducted on T-Roy. Thank you Sir! It was later that Leon observed that I had my security pack with me, but as I was not in physical danger, the thought had not occurred to me to threaten any of the medical staff.

I don't know if I would have acted differently if I hadn't known that the hospital had intended performing an autopsy, but I felt very determined that T-Roy should be

guarded until he was safely cremated. I find it strange how I can talk about these things in such a matter of fact way. Leon was there, and willing to do anything that he could to help; all I had to do was ask – and he would be grateful to be given a definite task that he could do to help. He loved T-Roy, and T-Roy had loved him, just as Roman did.

I've attended post-mortems - usually with a professional interest. There may be procedures and protocol, but there's no need. Nobody needs to know how much his liver weighs, or the texture of his spleen.

I knew that it would never come to this, but there are plenty of people around who could probably be found, or who would step forward to say what they had seen. Real, genuine people, who didn't need to be... influenced! Anyone who had been in the vicinity would have been able to testify that he had been full of the joys of life, right up until the sudden end. There were no external injuries, and no question of whether he had been abused.

I tasked the medical photographer to take a series of photos of T-Roy lying in state, and he understood that he was to do as I wished, so he took these and I was satisfied with them – satisfied seems the wrong word, but in this situation no word seems adequate, and I could keep these photos securely locked in my filing cabinet for when and if the need arose. My need as much as anyone else's!

There was an acid burning pain at the roof of my stomach, and a great distance through the mist of my tragedy, but

when I saw it, days later I noticed that the autopsy report was signed by a familiar name – and a strange irony that it was the same name and signature as had been on `Bobby's' death certificate. T-Roy's death was straightforward, and I could not imagine that questions would be asked. But we `had' this pathologist, and he would do as he was told. If we wished it, he would have certified cause of death as being `taken by the Angels!' and he would have to live with the consequences of this.

"What happens to him now? I asked Captain Anderson.

"He is taken to a funeral home, prepared, and put in a casket."

Then there was the option that we could take him home …

… that we could take him home with us… until it was time for the cremation… Providing this was less than 48 hours. An alternative was that he could be kept refrigerated at the morgue… Don't even go there! We are taking him home!

The practicalities; when T-Roy is delivered in his casket, where do we put him? It was obvious; on the massage table in the study. There would be no other use of the massage table for the foreseeable future. Not in our bedroom. Not in the boys' room. Not in Roman's room – I expected that Alice would move in for the duration. The study would be the best place.

*

There was much information that I absorbed, and I can't remember whether the information and the choices that we needed to make were presented to me, whether I asked, whether Debbie asked – although I think she left everything to me, but would have had her say if there was anything she wanted differently.

It was not something that we had discussed, but there was no question but that we wanted him cremated. This was the most common way anyway. Captain Anderson had a team of assistants, who could organise things, and there was a decision to be made about how soon we wanted him cremated, and whether we wanted to have a funeral service at the crematorium, or a memorial service later. Again, I absorbed the information that if we wanted the cremation much more than 48 hours later, there were procedures which would – have to be done – which could be avoided if the cremation happens sooner. Intrusive procedures ...

I could imagine that there were things they might have to do to keep a body hygienic for 48 hours, which I could accept as long as they didn't cut him. That would be okay, and for now I didn't want the details, but I wanted to know that T-Roy's body would keep its integrity.

It's strange the things one picks up as part of general knowledge. I knew that in the hours after death, as the muscles relax, the contents of bowels and bladder are released. T-Roy and Roman knew all about the waste products of the digestive system, from conversations we had had – seeming so bizarrely to look back on it, in the

288

family bed, though T-Roy's interest had always been in leading the subject and spotlight back to his willy. If the choice was on offer, I would be willing to spend hours each and every day cleaning pooh from my beloved son, if this would only bring him back. Changing his nappies when he was a baby had not been a problem, and I had always been rewarded with a delightfully clean smelling baby at the end of the process. It had not been a problem for me to help him with his toilet training, and wiping until he had eventually mastered this himself. But I understood that professionals had ways of cleaning out such waste products from the body in one go, which would be much more dignified for T-Roy and his memory as he lay in state for the time we had him back home.

If it was possible to bargain with God, or with Mother Nature, or any entity that could give my son back, thoughts flashed through my head of what I would be willing to bargain with. I would be willing to wash and clean him as he needed it however many times a day for the rest of my life if I could have him back – but then I realised there was a qualification for this; T-Roy was who he was with his energy, his enthusiasm, his sparkling eyes as he plotted benign mischievousness. If he had been brain-damaged to the extent that he had lost his humour, or that he had lost the vitality in his eyes, then he would no longer have been T-Roy, and the deal was off.

Leon agreed to accompany T-Roy to the funeral home, to be with him and to guard him. He agreed immediately, and without question. "Don't let them cut him," I implored Leon.

Leon put a reassuring arm on my shoulder. Leon had never been a particularly tactile person, with the notable and significant exception of the boys, which extended to Colin.

T-Roy had been perfectly happy to be naked in Leon's company when he was alive, as was Roman - although nudity had never seemed to be as entertaining to Roman as for T-Roy. There had been occasions when Leon had minded them for us, and Leon had taken it in his stride that T-Roy would want to shower with him so that T-Roy could see him naked and have the discussions, and Debbie and I had assured Leon that we were happy for him to deal with T-Roy's requests as he saw fit, our trust in his concern for the boys' welfare was unquestioned. Another little anecdote sprang to mind, when, after Leon had stayed overnight to mind the boys when Debbie and I had been out together – probably to one of her work functions – T-Roy confided to me that Leon had 'forgotten how to clean my willy, so I had to show him again. He can never remember how to wash my willy!' (Nice one, Leon! Why didn't I think of that myself?)

*

This was one weekend when Colin wasn't with us, but through our horror I knew that he needed to be taken into account. I asked Captain Anderson to phone Karen as he would be able to communicate better than I could through my tears, and he told her what had happened and asked if I could go around and meet with Colin, which she agreed to.

When we arrived, Colin had tears streaming down his face and leapt up to embrace me and strive as I might to contain my tears I wasn't able to do so we hugged each other, becoming damp with each other's tears.

"Can I still come and stay with you?" Colin asked through his sobs. Did the poor little boy think that our growing love for him would end with T-Roy?

"Of course you can," I said to his face, my face contorted with tears. "We need you! I need you!"

I don't know what the normal thing to do is in such a situation. It wasn't a normal situation at all. Captain Anderson did his best to appear neutral and professional but I doubt that he had to support parents with the loss of a young child before.

I know I've been critical of Karen before, for my impression that she wasn't always able to put her children's interests ahead of her own, for her drinking, and poor choice of men, and the clumsy flirtatiousness she showed to me early on, but she moved over to stand next to me and stroked my shoulder, and stroked Colin's back, trying to offer comfort. The liaison officer sat discreetly to one side, with a look of contemplative sadness on his face, looking at the floor. He did understand the need to give people time, and he did so.

Through my bleary tearstained eyes, I looked up to Karen and pleaded; "if he wants to, can Colin come and stay with us for a couple of days? He and T-Roy loved each other…" I know I had no right to ask this. She could feel that it was

her role as his mother to comfort him with his loss but again, she surprised me.

"Do you want to go and stay with Uncle Max for a couple of days?" She asked him.

Through his sobs and our tight embrace he answered with a very clear `yes!'

"Thank you," Captain Anderson said to Karen.

I sat Colin on my lap so that we could look into each other's eyes. "It won't be fun with us as we are very sad," I told him, not sure how to put my feelings into words, but I knew that I – we wanted him as part of our broader family at this time, and he wanted that too.

"Whenever you want to come back to your mummy, that's fine. You must just say when you want to!" Karen had gone to pack a little suitcase for him, and he hugged and kissed his mum goodbye, and I hugged her as well, finding her to be a genuine but tortured soul under her awkward façade.

I realise, as I write this now, how it could seem that I had lost all boundaries about who was my family, and involving someone else in our time of tragedy. I know that I have said how at Ferndale Hall we wanted for nothing, that we were loved and provided for and defended. But I'll tell you now, that if any of us had had the chance of being adopted or fostered by someone who had tried to care for us as an individual be they as inadequate as Karen, we would have

jumped at the chance in a heartbeat. I wasn't just doing it for Colin Harrison; I was doing it for me!

So I do actually owe T-Roy an apology, which he would find amusing. His plans to swoop down and rescue me – a younger me – and then bring me home and ask mummy if the younger me could stay, which we had teased him about, was not altogether far from the truth, if Colin was that younger me!

*

I found that some kind soul had taken it upon himself to return T-Roy's bike and to leave it to the side of the front door of our house, with his helmet hanging by its straps from the handlebars. One of several little reminders that people can sometimes go out of their way to perform little acts of kindness.

*

Debbie and I were familiar with death. She had seen it as a paediatric nurse when, despite her and her colleagues' best efforts, a child had died. As a combat veteran, I had seen death, or the effects of it, not that I had any desire to look, but most of those were adults – male – of combat age.

Debbie and I faced each other over the casket in which T-Roy lay. Inside, he was wrapped in a sheet – there is another word `shroud', but I'll stick with the word `sheet'. His clothes had been neatly folded, and returned to us in a transparent plastic bag.

Why did I have the feeling that we were like ancient Egyptians, preparing a loved one for a final journey? We had T-Roy with us until his last journey in this state, which would be to the crematorium.

`How do you dress your son?' I don't remember the dialogue, but I conceded the decision to Debbie, as his mother.

"He's your son!" she said.

"He loved you," I tried to reassure her, but I knew where this was going.

"He worshipped you. He adored you," she said, tears welling up in her eyes. We all knew, and probably everyone knew, of the bond she had with Roman, and the bond I had with T-Roy. She and I had both worked to try and strengthen the bond with the other, and to encourage each other's child to be more receptive to the other, but there was plenty of love and it hadn't been a real problem – until now. I knew that it would not have been possible for T-Roy to have loved me more than he did, or for me to have loved him more than I did, and there was some comfort in this. For the rest of her life, Debbie would have to live without the ability to win a greater share of T-Roy's love. It wasn't a deficit of love; it was just the knowledge that each of our boys loved one parent more than the other.

We embraced, and cried into each other which seemed to be how we spent all of our time.

"I want to wrap him in his Spider-Man duvet," I told her. "Stop me if you want to. I don't want him to be wearing anything else. That's how he liked to be. That's how I want to remember him."

Debbie agreed, smiled through her tears. She went and fetched the duvet from the boys' room, and brought it back. I lifted T-Roy from the casket and Debbie removed the sheet, and lined its interior with the duvet before I gently laid him into it.

Fuck convention! This is my son! I placed his right hand over his willy, and then placed his left over it. I think that's what he would have wanted.

We folded the duvet around him, and left his face visible at the top, as though through an Eskimo parka hood. We both kissed his forehead and then I closed the casket lid.

Like Roman had cried into my shoulder; `I just want this to end!'

*

In a vigil, I sat in the study on the massage bench with T-Roy in his casket. Another dark night of the soul!

I remembered back to the beginning of our family, and how bringing Debbie with Roman home from hospital, how suddenly we had an extra little life in our family, who though expected, hadn't existed as a person until he was born, and how we had gone to bed and asleep that night as a three-person family. Now, as the bookend to that, we had woken

295

in the morning as a four-person family, but as we settled for the night, T-Roy was gone, and we were a three-person family, and when we woke – if we slept – in the morning it would be the three of us again.

It was more complicated than this, with my very mixed feelings about my belief that T-Roy was no longer there, while the body he had enjoyed so much life in, and which would be recognisable as him, was still here, in our home, for some hours yet.

There was the issue of whether to let Roman and Colin view T-Roy, and I asked the psychologists what they recommended, and I suppose I was not surprised that they clarify the issues, which I grasped myself, without being able to commit to what they thought was best. There were so many things to consider; that there was a limited amount of time during which they could view him if they wish to, and whether there was any merit for this in terms of `closure' – a psychobabble term I had heard before, or whether it was the stuff of nightmares, now or at some later stage, to see his face with the absence of life, the smart sparkling smile and the mind seeking some opportunity for mischievousness. It was my responsibility – shared with Debbie if she had thoughts on which way to go.

It would be easy to suggest, that with the absence of any physical injury to him, apart from the puffy lips from my CPR, that he was sleeping, and that one could expect that at any stage he would murmur and turn, but that wasn't true.

His spirit was very definitely gone, and – as suggested in
`The Little Prince'[4] which I had read to them several times,
the body was just a shell.

*'You understand. It's too far. I can't take this body with me. It's too
heavy.'*
I said nothing.
*'But it'll be like an old abandoned shell. There's nothing sad about
an old shell...'*

I can't agree! The body that he had left behind was a symbol
of him, his face, the mechanism through which he expressed
his love and laughter, his body, his mechanism for enjoying
the vigorous sensations he loved so much and the warmth
of his cuddling into us; there was something desperately
precious about the shell he had left behind. A mother-of-
pearl!

*

My son is dead! Never again will I be able to look down into
his eyes, and see the love staring back into mine.

Never again will he feign the injustice of him never getting
to wee into my mouth.

Never again will he try to debate how he had the right to
wash me completely in the shower, after he allowed me to
wash him.

---

[4] Antoine de Saint-Exupéry: "The Little Prince"

Never would puberty arrive, and him have the absolute delight of his first orgasm, which would increase by an order of magnitude the delight he got from his willy, and comparisons to bowls of ice cream, no matter how big or fat, would no longer register.

Never would he have the chance to share the intimacy with the girl that he hopefully loved, of allowing her to see his willy, and hopefully she would be graceful, and tell him that she was impressed.

Guessing about his first serious girlfriend was as far as I could project the life he had been denied. He was frozen in time as my beautiful boy just having started in his eighth year of life. Had I been spared the pain of the necessary and normal withdrawal of affection as he reached puberty and adolescence, where he would have to inhibit his affection…?

But most of all, I wouldn't ever again have the joy of having him cuddled in beside me, warm and smooth, and the cherry on the cake of him looking up into my eyes dreamily before sleep finally took him.

*

Nothing made sense any more.

"Look after him, Kevin," was almost a prayer.

"Look after my little boy. Love him for me. Don't let him get into bother!"

And for a brief moment in my mind's eye, I saw T-Roy's arrival in heaven. Mist covered surfaces amongst the clouds, and enough love. More than enough love, and no fear!

"I'm Kevin,' said Kevin, 19 years old, with his head the way it always should have been, kneeling down and reaching out to embrace him. "I loved your Daddy, and he loved me ..."

T-Roy moved over to him, but still looking at the scene that opened around him. "And Uncle Leon ..." T-Roy prompted him.

"And Leon..."

Kevin picked him up and held him to his chest. T-Roy moulded to his body, but was still looking around him. Kevin had never been as strong as me – and neither of us was as strong as Leon, but he was now about half my present age, with the fitness of an operational paratrooper.

"Let's go to God," Kevin said, carrying him there, with T-Roy fascinated, by God and by Jesus at his right hand side.

"Hello T-Roy," God said warmly. "I'm sorry to have brought you so soon. I need you here ..."

Kevin put T-Roy down, and he walked over to be embraced in Jesus' extended arms, and now Jesus was lifting him up.

"You don't look like you do at church," T-Roy told him. "And God doesn't look like that at church either ..."

"So I've been told."

"Jesus ... is your willy like MyDaddy's?"

"Yes," Jesus confirmed.

"Can I shower with you?"

"We'll see ..." Jesus replied.

Turned to God, while Jesus still held him, "God ..." with the whine he used when he wanted something. "Can I have MyDaddy here?" And after the slightest pause, he remembered to add; "And my Mummy, and Romey – and Collie Dog ...?"

"Not just yet, Sunshine," God said softly. "There is still work that I need them to do for me. But they'll come later. "Uncle Kevin will look after you until then ... And we'll be here ..."

"Please don't tell MyDaDee that I called him `Collie Dog'," T-Roy requested.

"Your secret is safe with me, Teabag!" God winked back!

No, T-Roy! Don't stick your tongue out at God! I could see the thought going through his head, as could God and Jesus, but T-Roy thought the better of it. Good boy!

Jesus handed T-Roy back to Kevin, who respectfully braced and was about to move away, when God called him back. "T-Roy," said God, with a twinkle in his eye. "What's better than a big fat bowl of ice cream?"

T-Roy was delighted. Some of the old jokes were still going to work. "My willy!" he giggled with delight.

God and Jesus smiled. They knew him so well. "I thought you'd like it," said God. "I knew it would make you very happy!"

"Can I have my bike?"

"Sorry, no, but we've got something better for you. Come with me."

"Is it a T Rex?"

T-Roy and Kevin started to move off, initially with T-Roy moulded in beside Kevin, with Kevin's arm around him, and then T-Roy pulled away a little so that he could look up to Kevin to ask him some very important question that he needed to have answered but he accepted Kevin's hand. Then both of them turned inwards to look back at me, and waved. I want to say that he will be fine, but I can't bring myself to. Surely he will miss me at least a tiny bit as much as I will miss him? I don't want him to, but yet I do!

Kevin would look after him. Kevin will be good. But it should be me!

"Come to bed Max," Debbie shook my arm. She had come herself, but Roman had followed her and watched from the doorway. With a reassuring pat on the casket, I followed her back to bed, taking our usual places with Roman and Colin

between us. Colin was awake, and cuddled up tightly to me as I got into bed.

*

We woke up gradually on the day of the cremation, no early morning naked ninja to make his presence felt.

"I do want to see him," Roman decided, which helped as I had wondered whether to mention that this would be the last chance, or whether to just leave it to them. Colin was intent on coming as well, and I saw no need to put this into words.

I went to check on T-Roy, just to make sure that it would be okay for the boys to see him, and I decided it was.

There before us, his face looked more like a photograph, due to the captured stillness, stillness which did not suit T-Roy, as in life his face was never still. Even when he slept he always seemed to find a way that he would have his head back so that he would snore, whether aloud, or barely discernibly. The stillness felt wrong. So many things were wrong!

"He looks snug!" Roman decided. I love that! It conveyed comfort and peace.

There was silent contemplation. Debbie and I stood either side above T-Roy's head, allowing the boys to stand next to him, looking down at his face.

"Can I touch him?"

302

"On his forehead."

Roman touched him, gently, for a moment before gracefully withdrawing his hand. I handed him an antiseptic wipe, and he knew what to do. Colin hesitated, but then he too reached out to put a couple of fingers delicately on T-Roy's forehead.

"He's cold," Roman observed.

"He's at room temperature," Debbie explained. "His body isn't keeping him warm, like ours are." Would we ever be able to talk again without it being with halting breath and through tears?

Maybe I over-think things. I was aware that the boys had read and listened to ghost stories, and possibly even some zombie stories, and without wanting to make any links, I wanted to do what I could to prevent them ever having any such thoughts in association with T-Roy.

"I believe he is with God and Jesus, and that Kevin is with him, and looking after him."

"He'll have Kevin wrapped around his little finger by now," said Debbie.

"I believe he will be there to welcome us on board when we get there, which I hope will only be in many many years time."

"I don't believe that he would come back to visit us – I don't believe you can do that! But if he did, he would be the

lovely, beautiful boy we remember. He will still love us. He would be the same as we remember him."

"If he were to come back, he would want to get back massages from Mummy that always ends up with him getting tickled. Roman, he so enjoyed playing imagination games and stories with you. Colin, he loved having you as a playmate of his own age, and he loved having you here – as we all do. But…" Colin raised his tearful eyes to me… "He would still want to see your willy from time to time. And to show you his!"

Colin smiled up at me through his tears. "He can do that any time!" He sobbed.

"And you?" Debbie asked, seeing what I was doing.

"He would wake us as the naked ninja, and then the early morning cuddles…"

We hugged and cried in the presence of the shell of the boy we loved, until Debbie shepherded Roman and Colin out.

"Sleep well, my beautiful boy!"

I sealed the casket.

*

I know I have said that I don't have a temper, or if I do, it is very well controlled. I don't think it was temper related, but watching the ordinary world through the window of the car in which the four of us, and Alice were driven to the

crematorium behind the hearse which carried T-Roy, one couldn't but notice ordinary people going about their ordinary lives though most would stop and stare at the hearse, discreet as it was, as it passed by. For these people, their ordinary lives continued, while for me and my loved ones, it would never be the same again. For a split second it seemed an outrage that their lives could continue with them being unaware.

An unmentionable thought, but if there had been a big red button within reach of me, that would end everything, and take us to a nirvana of nonexistence, where such as we could, we would be with T-Roy, and there wouldn't be anything we left behind, no other people with their lives as we all disappear together. I noticed the thought, but I let it go...

There was a brief ceremony at the crematorium, where the Minister from our church said a few words, which was meaningful, as he actually knew T-Roy, but at our request it was well short of a protocol driven procedure. He referred to "bouncy T-Roy" which I appreciated, as it showed he knew T-Roy personally.

Colin stayed with us as an honourary Maxwell, and I invited Karen if she wished to attend, but tried to graciously suggest that we would understand if she needed to look after Denzel instead, all that – (`please don't accept' I thought) – if she wanted to bring Denzel and her partner along that would be fine – but either she was perceptive and diplomatic, or she just accepted it at face value, she politely declined.

My commanding officer – known to our family as "Uncle Kasper" asked if he could attend. Of course he was welcome, along with Leon, and Captain Anderson in his official role. Debbie allowed some of her closest friends and colleagues from work to come along, and I knew them vaguely from the times that I attended functions as Debbie's husband, but I didn't know them from outside of this context. I noticed, and was touched to see my OC contemplatively walk to the casket at an appropriate time, and to gently place a beautiful and lovingly carved Spider-Man figure on to the casket. His eyes were misted with tears as he returned.

There isn't much I want to say about this.

*

His school wanted to mark T-Roy's passing, and invited us to attend a memorial section of their school assembly, which we did, and with Captain Anderson accompanying us in civvies, I was able to deliver a brief speech telling those assembled how much T-Roy had enjoyed school and their friendship, which was true, and they must have known it as well as I did.

I had dreaded that they might sing the `Joseph and his Amazing Technicolor Dreamcoat' song, `One More Angel in Heaven' which I had heard Roman singing, and he said it was a song he had learned at school. That would have been difficult for me to bear, and I would assume the same for Debbie, a beautiful song, don't get me wrong, but not for

grieving parents and not with the irony of the person grieved for in the song emerging alive and well to save the day. But I probably need to accept, that other people can be sensitive.

Supervised by their singing teacher, who belted out the tune on the old piano in the school hall, the assembled children sang two songs; `bad hair day' and `wiggly tooth' which the singing teacher confided to us had been T-Roy's favourite songs. They were doing their best, and I didn't doubt that they would mourn T-Roy as well. We did not have a monopoly on our loss.

I kept my silence as I knew that in his last weeks, and connected with his bike which was his main eighth birthday present, he had loved the Queen song `Bicycle' which he and I would sing together, me having been careful which verses to teach him, but I left the phrase `fat bottomed girls' in, which delighted him. We would take turns with the parts, while I jogged and he rode around me.

*

There was a memorial service at church to celebrate T-Roy's life, with a large photo of him which I felt was much more appropriate than a funeral urn, or having taken him there in his casket, even if the timescale had allowed.

This was attended by Captain Anderson, and Leon, of course, but my OC made time to attend as well, as well as my guardian from Ferndale Hall, who Captain Anderson had traced, and my house parents from Ferndale Hall, all in

civvies. That was from my side. A number of Debbie's colleagues, who I had met from annual Christmas dinners, and the occasional wedding attended, as did people we know from church, and Alvin and the others, who with the time that had passed, Roman seemed comfortable to chat with, and from a distance I exchanged glances with him to check that he was okay.

A children's choir had been formed specifically to perform; `I'll be a Sunbeam for Jesus', which was fine, and the Minister managed a suitably personalised sermon, and his present and most recent past Sunday school teachers had pleasant things to say about him, and touching little anecdotes, which I could believe, and I did not hold too strongly to the whitewashed version of my little boy, who was 100% a little boy, with his favourite specialist subject. If they didn't know, then well done to T-Roy for doing as we urged him, and putting the brakes on it when he wasn't with us. I suspect they were being discreet.

*

I was aware that wheels were turning behind-the-scenes, and I was grateful for what Captain Anderson was doing and he was compassionate – possibly he was well suited to his job. He alerted me that my Officer Commanding wished to have a discussion with me, not relating to the department. Normally I would attend his office, but `in view of the circumstances' he was willing to meet me on neutral ground – ` or at home,' Anderson ventured.

"He will be welcome here," I told Anderson. This was breaching all sorts of protocol, but we could re-establish this when life returned to normal – not that it ever would.

My OC arrived at the appointed time, seeming to soon be at ease in our living room, with Debbie making tea for him, and after he had been greeted and exchanged small talk with Roman and Colin. Captain Anderson took the boys away so that my OC could state the purpose of his visit.

"The powers that be have directed me to offer you the equivalent of a `Fallen Hero' ceremony." The ceremony offered was familiar to me, and I had attended and participated in such before; most significantly for Kevin. It consisted of a parachuting exercise where the members of the unit would all do a freefall parachute jump, with those closest to the Fallen Hero making a formation jump and before opening their parachutes, the cremated ashes of the Fallen Hero would be dispersed in the updraft.

I explained this to Debbie. "It is a great honour for T-Roy," I told her, but she understood this was a part of my world, even though she knew that at times I was cynical.

"I am not in charge of these things," he said appearing slightly uncomfortable, but I did not doubt he had instigated this. "It is also offered, that if they wish to, Mrs Maxwell" – he was being formal, and we all knew that in relaxed situations he had accepted her offer to call her Debbie. "– and Roman and Colin may participate as tandem jumpers." If I hadn't been flabbergasted by the organisation making

309

this offer for T-Roy, a civilian, I certainly was that this offer was extended to Debbie and the boys.

My OC could read my mind, and see my gratitude, but woman remained a mystery to him, especially strong woman like Debbie. "Do you want some time to think about it?" He asked, looking to Debbie.

"Do you want to?" Debbie asked me.

"Yes!"

"I don't want to jump," she was clear. "But I want it for you, and I want it for Roman and Colin. Obviously, if Karen agrees."

*

My OC smiled contentedly. Not quite chomping on a cigar and observing; `I love it when a plan comes together,' and he would not have understood the reference.

Captain Anderson was up to date with where the arrangements were. There was already a date which had been pencilled in for a significant single aircraft training jump at the major army and air force base in the region in several days time. The senior paratrooper NCO, who would choreograph the event, had been identified, and authorisation for all that would be involved had been agreed, including the inevitable budget, and the next steps would be put into place now that Family Maxwell had accepted.

I felt able enough now, after the several days that had passed, that I would be able to have a conversation about relatively neutral events, so I phoned Karen, assured her that all was well with Colin, as we did after his nightly calls home, where she insisted that he speak at least briefly to his stepfather, which we could see he really didn't want to do. I explained to her that my work had offered a commemoration ceremony for T-Roy, which Colin was invited to participate in, but we needed to make sure that she knew of and agreed to this. I very seldom talked about my military history to anyone outside the family, but my boys knew that I had been a paratrooper, which they were proud of, and certainly with T-Roy's complete inability to keep secrets, Colin might have been told, and if it was of any significance to him, he might have mentioned it to Karen. I had thought, as Captain Anderson had suggested, that if she was willing to consider this, we could arrange for him and me, my OC, the senior paratrooper NCO and the tandem jump master, that would be assigned to Colin, would attend, introduce themselves to Karen – and her partner if necessary – explain the procedure, show a child scale tandem parachute rig, explain the absolute safety of the procedure and the great experience of the tandem master – a sergeant who had served on the National military freefall team. Then, after having barraged her with all this information, amongst us we would be able to answer any questions.

She asked if I couldn't please give her a bit more information, rather than wait on a meeting with another

four men she didn't know, and I thought it was only fair to do so, knowing the dangers that an imagination could create in the absence of information. I explained to her about the parachute jump, about tandem parachuting, and the offer had been made for Roman and Colin to do tandem jumps.

I knew it was a lot for her to take in. "What does Debbie say?"

"She doesn't want to jump herself, in a tandem. She's happy for Roman to do it, although it's his choice. We haven't asked Colin yet. We wanted to know whether you would consider allowing Colin to do it as well before we put it to him."

I could tell by her silence she was thinking. Much to think about, with so much coming so out of the blue. "You are invited as well, either to watch from the aircraft or from the ground. And your partner – although there wouldn't be room in the aircraft for him, but he is welcome to watch from the ground."

I heard her intake of breath after a moment of reflection, and she said; "Max, if you think it's a good idea, and if Debbie will let Roman do it, then that's fine with me." Then another pause. "He is so grateful for everything you do for him. He loves you so much!" Pause. "I thank you so much that you still will have him now…" (Don't say it! For God sake, don't say it! I'm holding it together so well …)

"He is welcome in our family," I told her, possibly too hurriedly, to stop her finishing that sentence. "We love him!"

"Do you want to discuss it with your partner?" Her answer left me in no doubt that there were difficulties in that relationship. But, in summary, she was entirely willing to make that decision on her own.

"I would like you to meet the skydiver who Colin will be tandemed to," and for the man in charge of the... `Event'.... To be able to show you the equipment, so you'll know exactly what we have planned." She was okay with this, and we arranged a meeting at her house.

I am sure that the curtain twitches on her street would have had a field day, when the two cars drew up outside. Okay, they would have been used to mine, me fetching or returning Colin, until now with both my boys, but it would have been an order of magnitude for Debbie and me to arrive with Captain Anderson, Roman and Colin, followed by the car containing Sergeant Major Kemp, Sergeants Tate and Murray, in their ultra-smart paratrooper uniforms, and my OC, who, although dressed in civvies, they venerated. Karen had risen to the occasion, and although I had hardly ventured beyond the front door, the living room was immaculate, and she had paid attention to her own appearance, and had `scrubbed up' well!

Roman and Colin were to find out then what was on offer to them, suitably hyped by three paratroopers to whom

313

parachuting was next to godliness. They had been assigned in advance that Roman would be tandemned with Sergeant Murray, and Colin with Sergeant Tate. The boys wanted the familiar, and Colin, having first dibs, asked if he couldn't be `strapped' to me, and Roman, knowing that Leon would be taking part, wanted to be `strapped' to Leon. We explained that I didn't have the skills needed for this, and neither did Leon, but that the sergeants were very good, and that I would be immediately in front and Leon would be immediately behind them.

After the obligatory display of discomfort in mixing with civilians required of hard-core military men, the sergeants loosened up and spoke enthusiastically to the boys, hauling out the child size tandem rig they had brought along, putting the boys into it, and having brought along a videotape of some of their jumps, which we didn't watch there and then, but they allowed us to take home to watch later.

I noticed that there was no sign of Karen's partner, and Denzel tottered around happily with all the new faces to go up and beam up at. And he sported a fresh clean nappy.

Apart from the elephant in the room – or the blue whale in the room – or the whole of Mount Everest in the room, I was aware of other dramas and concerns ongoing. Colin had been concerned that with us all going to his mum's house, that it could be suggested that he remained there with her, but we discussed this with Karen in advance, citing our need for his company, and – let me give credit where credit is due – she didn't assert her rights as his mother, but said that,

314

while his home was with her, he was welcome to stay with us as long as he wanted to. I would happily have gone so far as to say 'needed to', but this wasn't required.

I noticed, and it is part of my profession to notice, that Karen could hardly keep her eyes off Sergeant Murray. Would she have preferred that her son, Colin, a repository of her DNA, was 'strapped to' Sergeant Murray, rather than Sergeant Tate? (Message to Sergeant Murray: 'Run, boy! Head for the hills! Run while you still can!')

I had alerted Karen in advance that it was best not to seed any suggestions in Colin's mind about him possibly having a fear of heights or anything like that. His experience, I could tell her from my own is that when parachuting, you feel that you are being held up, connected to the sky by two steel girders, and certainly in tandem they would be connected to strong and extremely experienced skydivers. Debbie and I agreed that we would work on the idea that the boys were enthusiastic about this, which they seemed to be, rather than put them in the situation for them to question whether or not they wished to do this. If they expressed any reluctance or reservation, we could have this discussion then.

Leon came for dinner, prepped that he was being given the opportunity to sell parachuting to them, and to bring along his photos and badges and anything else which would be of interest, and he rose to the occasion, having both boys spellbound on the carpet in the sitting room, while Debbie

315

and I watched – and I was glad that Debbie cuddled up to me, as we watched.

*

I remembered Sergeant Major Kemp from airborne school, during my foundation training. He remembered me; although doubtless he had done his research, and would have been able to place Leon, and Kevin and me and some of the others for whom becoming a qualified paratrooper was a requirement for our further roles, rather than an end in itself. He had let it be known that he could not comprehend how someone who could make the grade as a paratrooper could wish to move on into other branches of the military, with the traditional contempt for the intelligence branches.

It was obvious to me, though he would have wished to conceal it, that despite him knowing to express and to try to show suitable sympathetic remorse to a grieving family, he was delighted at the opportunity for an additional parachuting event, and one with added ceremony, which he would choreograph and essentially be the master of ceremonies of.

His disappointment was palpable when he found that I had not pursued my airborne registrations, let alone progressed to freefall parachuting, and formations, which was destiny from his perspective. There was a time window, which could not be extended long enough for me to train to the standard required for formation skydiving, and nor for Leon, who

316

although he had continued with parachuting four years after me, had also let his licence lapse. He might have sensed that there was a delicate balance to how far I was willing to go to collaborate with the ceremony as he envisaged it, as he was correct in his assumption that it had been a necessary qualification for me, and something that I looked back on with pride, but that would not play a significant role in my life.

Sergeant Major Kemp had to work with the idea that, with a couple of supervised refresher jumps, I would be willing and able to participate in a static line jump, which would serve the objective and take advantage of the opportunity that had been offered. It fell short of what he had hoped for, a wheel of six or more skydivers freefalling and holding hands, plummeting earthbound, when on the signal, the smoke flares on our ankles would be pulled, and the ashes opened and dispatched to the four winds. No, he wasn't going to get that.

What he did get was the authorisation and budget for refresher hanger training for up to 25 military personnel, three flights for refresher jumps, and then one flight for the actual ceremony. Admittedly the people whose refresher training he could supervise were from the intelligence branches, who were seldom the most martinet in the military, which included me, Leon, and the officer commanding as well as up to 3 of his people doing the tandem jumps with Debbie, Roman and Colin. If they chose to jump, that is!

317

Debbie observed the strangeness of the mindset of how it was necessary to do three practice jumps from an aeroplane in advance of doing an actual jump from an aeroplane, but having made her point, to me, she did not challenge the establishment.

There was a full complement of volunteers from my unit for the training and jump, all of whom would have encountered – I think he would have liked that word! – T-Roy at unit barbecues and so on, so it had some meaning for them.

This had to take place at the main regional base, where I had trained, but which Debbie and – I can't yet call them `the boys' because in my head that still very definitely includes T-Roy – Roman and Colin hadn't been to. In its inevitable way, the actual jump was scheduled for Saturday morning, and at that time of the year, suitable weather could be taken for granted. This gave Friday to Sergeant Major Kemp for the hanger training, and practice jumps, and although he didn't like the way this was compressed, he tried to conceal his annoyance, and accept the opportunity that had been offered to him.

There was much bargaining and organising going on behind the options that were offered to us, but we settled on what was now the four of us travelling out to the base – several hours drive – on the Thursday night, staying in accommodation at the base, me doing the refresher training on Friday with Debbie, Roman and Colin watching if they wished, with rides on the flights, or they were free to do as they wished, accepting that we were in a military base, but

318

we certainly wished to be together, so it was not an option that Debbie, Roman and Colin stayed at home and only joined us for the Saturday jump.

Debbie's mom was invited, with the option of remaining in the aircraft, with Debbie and my OC, or to watch from the ground. She decided that she would travel in the aircraft, which was a pleasant surprise for me. She did have something about her, and some bravery and sense of adventure. Traits which Debbie had inherited from her. Such a pity she had chosen the wrong man to spend the best of her adult years with – although she didn't know!

I gathered bits and pieces of information in the months that followed, but I gathered that the message had come down from authorities above my officer commanding, that `it is the Brigadier's wish that Family Maxwell be offered the best of hospitality that the unit can provide.' Captain Anderson remained our liaison officer, but there was no shortage of goodwill offered by hardened military personnel – who knew of my exalted position from `the Ferguson case', but also found themselves able to provide to enthusiastic and receptive ten and eight-year-old boys – as they were by this time – the most fun thing that were available to the military.

The paratroopers that would be the tandem jumpers with Roman and Colin did the necessary training with them, which the boys enjoyed, especially the zip wire part, and were excited about the next day. To build the relationship, they had been assigned as the minders for the boys, and to spent their time with them during the programme of

activities that Captain Anderson had organised. This was really good for the boys, as it distracted them from our loss, as they were taken for a ride in a helicopter, were taken for rides in tanks, and were taken to the shooting range where they were gently instructed and given the chance to shoot at targets with low calibre weapons. Debbie tagged along with them, with Captain Anderson in attendance. The assigned psychologists were present at the base, available should their presence be requested.

Meanwhile, back at the hanger, Sergeant Major Kemp and his staff put us through some PT and square bashing and the drills for exiting the aircraft, canopy safety, and landing drills, him having to calculate how far he could push us without risking any of us getting injuries which could prevent us from participating in the main event the next day.

"Nice new smock," I complemented Leon, seeing his smock was brand-new compared to his weathered combat trousers. "Was the old one getting a little tight?"

"Fuck off, Max!" I was glad that he had stopped the incredible niceness driven by sympathy.

From the corner of my eye, at the start of the day, I watched Roman and Colin with their paratrooper minders, watched over by Debbie during rehearsals of getting a presentation, with a sweet being put into their top right pocket, after a shaking of hands, after which the stand-in NCO would stand back and salute them. The boys were instructed to stand

still, while their paratrooper minders would return the salute from behind them.

I knew that it was being planned that they would be even honorary paratrooper wings at the closing ceremony after the jump tomorrow. Again, here was the contradiction of the monolithic State, the bureaucracy which we served to protect, and which would look after us, and the many people at different levels in the State who had thought of sweet little indulgences that the State could provide to its valued children, at a time such as this.

That evening there was a barbecue put on at a reserved area for our group, and many of our group were known to Roman and Colin from the barbeques, and despite the rigorous workout during the day – remember these men are younger than Leon and me – they were still willing to give the boy's shoulder rides, and joust with them as though on horseback. It was a different venue but a familiar social situation, and I kept almost expecting T-Roy to run out of the crowd for a brief rendezvous with me before scampering back in to play with whoever was his friend for the evening. Although there was a sombre overtone to the evening, in view of the next day being the memorial for T-Roy, I was glad to see Roman and Colin losing themselves in enjoyment.

My OC and Debbie's mother arrived that evening, and joined in the tail end of the party, my OC having arranged for her to be fetched in the car that brought him. When they saw them, Roman and Colin ran over to greet them, hugging them. Debbie's mom was used to this, but my OC was not.

"Can't you control your children, Maxwell?" he chuckled at me, while patting their shoulders.

It was going to be a big day – not to mention a bizarre day for us - the next day, despite all of the activity that we had been involved in this day. Debbie and I agreed that the time was right for us to head back to our accommodation. Captain Anderson had asked our requirements, and we had requested a room for Debbie and me, Roman and Colin together, with a separate room for her mother nearby. The boys were reluctant to be called away, having lost themselves in familiar enjoyment, and I could see the mood settle as we made our way to the accommodation block.

There were four separate single beds in our room, and Debbie suggested that we make a nest on the floor, with nobody mentioning it, but all of us knowing this was a tribute to T-Roy. We shifted the mattresses and bedding, and I was surprised that Debbie positioned Roman to the edge of the nest, so that she was sleeping next to me, with Colin on the outside. I don't think Debbie and I slept much that night, if at all, with the symbolism clouding over us, but Roman and Colin went out like lights.

*

Soon the next morning was upon us, and it was time to get dressed. Colin automatically prepared to come and shower with me, but Roman held back then – and afterwards Debbie told me that she hadn't said anything to influence him – he came along with me as well.

322

There was a timetable for us to fit in with; we had been given a time at which we would be fetched, have breakfast at the officers mess and then there would be some inevitable downtime before we would be taken to the hanger, where some senior officer would make a brief speech after which we would be kitted up and embark. I don't know how he did it, but Captain Anderson had sourced overalls in our official camouflage in the right sizes for Roman and Colin, which they were delighted with, and they were familiar with their tandem rigs from the previous day's training. Suitable sized helmets had been found for them, and camouflage cloth covers produced.

There was a speech from the Brigadier of the base, who outranked my OC, who stood beside and behind him on the mobile podium. The Brigadier had never met T-Roy but had been briefed and acknowledged that authorisation had been granted from 'on high' for a tribute jump for Troy Maxwell – okay, Captain Anderson hadn't emphasised everything to the Brigadier – who was 'considered to be a friend of the Directorate, and one of three mascots of the Directorate'.

We gathered for the official photo of the event, on the spectator stand outside the hanger, with the base Brigadier, my OC, Sergeant Major Kemp, me with Debbie next to me, Roman and Colin with their paratroopers standing behind them. Debbie's mother didn't want to be in the photo, which was accepted, and the official military photographer did what was required, but I noticed that he also focused in and took several photos specifically of our family group.

Sergeant Major Kemp approached me when he noticed the helmet I was about to wear. It was a standard issue helmet, but the cover was in the camouflage of the country that we were 'advising' fifteen years earlier. He didn't need to ask; he enquired with a glance. "It's candidate officer… Lieutenant Kevin Snowden's," I told him. The Sergeant Major knew exactly who Kevin was, who at the time of his death had been a paratrooper, and who on his death had been promoted to the rank that he was heading for. "Snowden is tasked with looking after my son!" I clenched my jaw in an attempt to hold back the tears as I said this. Sergeant Major Kemp saluted me, or the helmet, turned and strode away.

For the past days I had tried very much not to cry as much as I did, but I probably didn't need to have bothered. It was a matter of pride for me, but I was failing. It would be seen by my comrades, but I knew that they would not judge me badly. I had read their thoughts previously of how, after their lack of comprehension of my decision to marry and have a family, with its direct consequences to my career progression, as they got to spend time with Debbie, and with my delightful sons at the barbecues, I imagine many of them started to understand, and possibly contemplate whether they might, too, want what I had. But then this might have ended abruptly, when they witnessed and contemplated the horror of losing a beloved child.

It was so much worse for Debbie. This was my home ground, with my comrades, and traditions and drills. She knew it was a part of my life, but the horror was ever present for her,

hidden behind her dark sunglasses, which everyone was grateful that she wore.

In a small pouch attached onto the top of my reserve parachute in front of me, were the ashes, wrapped in a cloth to make them easier to spread, as opposed to an urn or box with a lid that needed to be removed. This was a tried and tested procedure; part of the tradition that sadly there was a need for.

*

We stood formed up, while the aircraft taxied up behind us, and lowered the ramp – all four propellers still turning. It was a well-worn drill, with those who were to jump last boarding first and making their way deep into the aircraft, with Sergeant Major Kemp officiating, me to be on point, sergeants Tate and Murray as the tandem masters for Roman and Colin, and the boys, and Leon who would be the fourth to exit the plane before the ordinary members jumped. Sergeant Major Kemp showed Debbie, her mum, and my OC to their seats where they would get a good view of us jumping. All of us boarded!

This was a full-size aircraft used for dropping paratroopers, as opposed to the smaller one we had used the previous day for the familiarisation jumps, as Sergeant Major Kemp was making the most of the opportunity for him to get jumps in for as many of his paratroopers as he could, over and above those of us from my unit. I was amused to notice that in military parachuting circles it was seen as unthinkable that

one would not step out of an aircraft in anything other than a standing forward step; it would have been cheaper to have hired a light aircraft and had us climbing out onto the wheels and hanging on to wing struts et cetera, but that was not the military way, and I knew that I preferred the military way.

We were travelling light, in that we were just wearing our main parachutes and our reserves. It was styled as a training jump, so we were not carrying weapons and supplies that we would if it was a combat jump. Once our parachutes had opened safely, we could drift down to make safe landings, without having to expect that we might be shot at before we landed, or face people trying to kill us when we did.

I was again aware of many sensations, which I remembered from my paratrooper days. The tightness of the parachute harness – and the joke from training about you 'want it to be tight! You don't want to be falling out of it midair!' – The bulk of the parachute behind me, and the smaller reserve in front. I hadn't had occasion to wear my paratrooper boots for years, but I had checked that they still fitted, though were somewhat stiff before we left home, but – although we had done training and jumps the previous day – I noticed the hard clump of the soles of my boots on the concrete of the runway, smell of the avgas coming back from the engines, and then the difference of sound and sensation of walking up onto the metal panels of the floor of the aircraft, and the different sounds made when one stepped on the rollers embedded in the floor in their two parallel rows.

Roman and Colin were wearing their rigs, but didn't need to be connected up to their tandem master's until just before preparations for the jump started, so, leaving the seat next to the door open for Sergeant Major Kemp, as he indicated, I sat, with Colin immediately on my left, Roman beyond him, and then the paratrooper sergeants. On the opposite side of the aircraft facing us were the non-jumpers. My OC, the perfect gentleman asked whether Debbie wanted to sit closest to the ramp, where she would get the best possible view of what little she would be able to see after we jumped off the ramp, which she accepted, and I was proud of her. I am always proud of her. Her mother opted to be further into the aircraft, such that Debbie was directly opposite me, to her right was my OC, and to his right was my mother-in-law, and next to her we started with the paratrooper qualified members of my department before the remaining seats were filled with unrelated paratroopers. It did not pass unnoticed that, after having been driven out to the base together the previous evening, my OC and Debbie's mom seem to find plenty to talk about.

*

The back ramp whined closed, leaving us in the cavern with the webbing seats, the tiny windows which didn't let much light in. The overhead lighting was adequate, but did not detract from the sense of being in a cavern. The pilot started the procedure of revving the engines individually, with them having been turning for about 20 minutes by now. Then the plane lurched forward and started its taxi towards the runway. I shared an excited smile with Colin and Roman

next to me, glad that they smiled back as excited, and I smiled over to Debbie and gave her a thumbs-up. I sort of knew from when it had been suggested, that like an actual `Fallen Hero' ceremony, all of their procedures, routines, sensations, leading up to the spike of adrenaline when one was freefalling for those few seconds did distract from the reason for this whole event, and it was a surprisingly useful way of nudging people through the initial stages of a bereavement, considering that this had been thought up by the military.

Sergeant Major Kemp was in his element. I knew that he wouldn't sit in the seat that was reserved for him, as he made his way around all of his charges, which should not have been necessary. He would have known that this was only happening because a much loved child had died, but as part of his personality that had led him to his proficiency in his profession, he treated that as a matter of fact. Despite the horror that still haunted me, and caused the upper surfaces of my abdominal cavity to burn with acid, I could see some humour. It would have been offered to him to officiate at what would be a Fallen Hero ceremony in all but name, and he would have leapt at it. Then he would have been told that a large number of the jumpers would be from the intelligence community, and that he would have a day to whip them into shape, called `refresher training', which would include three parachute jumps each which he would have liked. Then he would have been told the double caveat; `By the way there will be up to four civilians jumping in tandem rigs, and' – rubbing salt into the wound – `two of

them will be children, aged eight and ten.' He would stoically have hidden his disappointment and obligatory disdain for anything to do with civilians, let alone children. Then there would have been the sweetener; `two of the leads are people you trained; Maxwell and Leon Marlow. You probably don't know that it was they who closed `The Ferguson Case'! Sergeant Major Kemp would have been happy again, not least for the bragging rights this would give him.

I was always surprised at how long it seemed to take such aircraft to taxi up to the runway, and I remembered the joke from when I was younger about whether we were going to take off at all, or simply drive all the way to our destination. But then the aircraft, after several turns on the runways, came to a stop. The pilot revved all four engines, and then eased the plane forward, speeding up faster and faster until the increased noises coming into the plane from the wheels ended as the aircraft lifted up, leading to the strange sensation of brief weightlessness and of one's stomach going through one's chest. I looked over at the boys, who were both excited. Colin looked back at me, and Roman looked across to his mum who smiled reassuringly to him and made a thumbs-up sign. He made the gesture back.

I wasn't paying attention to what the pilot was doing with the aircraft as he gradually took it up to jump level. Roman suddenly decided that he wanted to go over to his mum, which I signalled to Sergeant Major Kemp, who came over and escorted Roman over. It wasn't a problem while the doors were sealed, but I was more concerned that his

confidence might be wobbling. I thought it would be good for him – as with Colin – to have the experience of such a parachute jump, the adrenaline surge, and the sense of achievement but he was cautious – more so than T-Roy had been. But it had to be right for him! If he decided not to jump, I would try to persuade him, but not enough to upset him, and every man on that plane would have understood. We all knew people who had done all of the training, but had refused to jump, leading to them dropping out of Airborne School, and closing the door on being paratroopers, or some career paths that followed. All of them knew that the two boys had lost their brother only days before.

From the distance I could see Debbie kiss him and cuddle him, through the awkwardness of his helmet and the tandem harness, and beside her my officer commanding patted his back. I turned to Colin, and above the engine noise shouted into his ear through his helmet; "I am so proud of you! I love you!" I beamed at him, conveying excitement, betrayed by my eyes. He was excited and positive – I don't want to say `happy'. I read his lips saying; "I love you, Uncle Max!" back to me.

*

We were approaching the drop zone, and the final preparations were made. Sergeant Major Kemp fetched and escorted Roman back from Debbie, and my fears did not materialise, as after a last kiss, and a pat on his bum as he turned around, Roman willingly came back over, and

330

Sergeant Major Kemp and Sergeant Murray connected him securely into the tandem rig, and Sergeant Tate connected up to Colin beside me with Sergeant Major Kemp supervising.

Sergeant Major Kemp was in his element now as the ringmaster, as the ramp groaned open, and light flooded in to the cavernous hold from the clear blue sky outside. Everyone on board turned to watch, as everybody always did. We flew over the drop zone once, with Sergeant Major Kemp wearing his headset, in communication with ground control and the pilots. He turned to face us, giving us the signal; `Stand up!'

"Hook up!"

Leon leaned forward, and patted Roman, beaming excitement and encouragement at him, and lent further forward to do the same to Colin. Both rufty-tufty paratrooper sergeants, Tate and Murray had hands reassuringly touching the boys' chests in between their rigs.

"On the ramp!" He said looking in my eyes. I advanced to the point on the ramp, standing beside him, aware as I looked out to the blue sky at my level, and below from the edge of the ramp, the countryside rolling away from us so distant below.

Very close behind me, I was aware of Colin/Tate, and knew that very close behind them would be Roman/Murray, so as to prevent them from having the wider view, which could be

scary. They were protected by their view being obscured by my parachute pack.

Sergeant Major Kemp reached out and rapped my helmet above my forehead with his knuckles. He stepped back, and snapped me his best salute. I understood! I saluted back.

"Go!"

Two rapid steps, and I jumped, boots together. Into space!

As always, I still had the thought; `This is not a good idea!' As always, my body was thrown around by the slipstream, and my brain signalled to me that I was upside down. Waves of adrenaline erupted through my bloodstream.

It was cold! The cool breeze on my face.

I jerked to a perceived stop, as my parachute deployed above me, the increased pressure on my groin and chest as the straps took my weight, opposite the parachute that slowed my descent.

T-Roy would have loved it!

The sudden silence was profound – in contrast to the roar of the engines which was gone, the echoes of the aircraft hold, the sounds of boots on aluminium and the rustle of clothing and straps. I knew the joke; `it is so quiet that you can hear the ants whispering on the ground below you.'

Automatically, I checked that my parachute had fully deployed, and then I looked to see – as if I had doubted it –

the combinations of Colin/Tate and Roman/Murray deployed safely, and beyond them, the stream of parachutes popping open behind the receding plane.

I did my drills. I looked at my boys. I waved at them, and they waved back. They were fine!

There was the task that I still had to do before planning my landing. I popped the smoke canister on my ankle, leading to a virile trail of red smoke following me, which would have looked better if released during freefall. I opened the pouch above my reserve, took out the cloth, and after a moment's contemplation, I opened it and shook it, and the ashes dispersed.

People would have thought that this was a profound moment. But it wasn't for me. I was doing it for others. I am the only one who knows the secret.

T-Roy was not there. I am not making some philosophical whimsy about the spirit no longer being present in the body or its remains. He was not there.

His ashes were safely in the bottom drawer of my filing cabinet in my office, and they are still there. I was nowhere near ready to separate from him, and I doubt that I ever will be. The ashes spread in the air that day were from some anonymous person not collected that the director at the crematorium had given me.

If Debbie or Roman ever ask, I will let them in on the secret, but as I still feel today I want him available and with me, so

in the fullness of time when I am cremated, I want his ashes placed in the casket with me. He will become the boy who was cremated twice.

THE END

Made in the USA
Middletown, DE
02 May 2020